Hello, I Love You

Hello, I Love You

A NOVEL

KATIE M. STOUT

THOMAS DUNNE BOOKS
ST. MARTIN'S GRIFFIN
NEW YORK

THOMAS DUNNE BOOKS.
An imprint of St. Martin's Press.

HELLO, I LOVE YOU. Copyright © 2015 by Katie M. Stout. All rights reserved. Printed in the United States of America. For information, address St. Martin's Press, 175 Fifth Avenue, New York, N.Y. 10010.

www.thomasdunnebooks.com
www.stmartins.com

Designed by Omar Chapa

The Library of Congress Cataloging-in-Publication Data is available upon request.

ISBN 978-1-250-05259-9 (hardcover)
ISBN 978-1-4668-5459-8 (e-book)

St. Martin's Griffin books may be purchased for educational, business, or promotional use. For information on bulk purchases, please contact the Macmillan Corporate and Premium Sales Department at 1-800-221-7945, extension 5442, or write to specialmarkets@macmillan.com.

First Edition: June 2015

10 9 8 7 6 5 4 3 2 1

For Macrae,
whose love for stories reminds me
why I started writing in the first place

Acknowledgments

Many heartfelt thanks and much love to . . .

The always lovely Emily Keyes, agent extraordinaire, who took the chance on me and my little book about KPOP.

My fabulous editor, Kat Brzozowski, and all the amazing people at Thomas Dunne. Y'all pushed me to write a better book, gave it a stunning cover, sold it to other countries, and gracefully dealt with all of my writer's angst. I'm incredibly blessed to have such an amazing team behind me.

Critique partner, friend, and soul sister, Kristin Rae, for the edits, squecs, and chats that got me through querying, marketing my debut, and everything in between. *Su su!*

The many writer and blogging friends who read early versions of the book, helped with my query, or just spread happy vibes about me and my book through the interwebs. I'm so grateful to know Kristi Chestnutt, Kim Franklin, Lori at *Pure Imagination,* Christina at *Reader of Fictions,* Jen at *Pop! Goes the Reader,* Katie at *Mundie Moms,* Steph at *Cuddlebuggery,* Gillian at *Writer of Wrongs,* and many more amazing people. Book blogging opened my eyes to the wonderful world of YA, and I'll always be thankful for that.

The best book club ever, who celebrated with me, even when there was an ocean separating us—especially Alli, Liz, Tiffani, Vania, and Sarah. I'm so glad I decided to read *Shadow and Bone* and check out my local book club!

Mom and Dad, who fostered my love of reading and never told me to stop dreaming about getting published one day; Brenna, for being the older sister who I looked up to and who inspired me to always be creative; and my entire family, who never thinks I'm weird for loving books as much as I do. There's no way I'd be here without each and every one of you.

My Lord and Savior, the Living Word, without whom I wouldn't have written words to share. Thank You, Jesus!

Hello, I Love You

Chapter One

Big Brother,

    I want you to know something: It wasn't your fault, not any of it. And I'm so sorry. Sorry for ditching the family and for shipping off to the other side of the world.

    But, mostly, I'm sorry I wasn't there for you when it mattered. I should have told someone before it got bad. It's just that you're my big brother; you've always been the strong one. And I miss that.

    You're probably laughing hysterically right now, imagining me—the foreign language–challenged child—bumbling my way through the airport, a lonesome little white girl with a Southern accent and too much hair spray. Just know that with every step I take farther from home, the more I miss you.

    Maybe this trip will give me time to figure things out. I certainly hope it does, anyway.

    I could end this letter with "from Korea, with love" like

*that James Bond movie in Russia, but the plane hasn't landed
yet, so I'll just leave you with . . .*

> *Almost in Korea, with love,*
> *Grace*

The subway doors open, and a flood of boarding passengers
sweeps me and my two giant suitcases onto the train. Elbows jab
into my sides, and the wheels on my bags run over toes as a
thousand of my closest Korean friends pack into the tiny metro
car. Half an hour inside the Republic of Korea, and I've already
been thrown into the life of a national.

All the seats are full, so I park my bags in front of an el-
derly woman, her eyes half-obscured by folds of wrinkled skin,
holding a plastic sack full of something gray and . . . slithering.
Octopus, maybe? I straddle one of my suitcases and sit, letting
myself sway with the rocking of the train and giving my jet-
lagged body a rest. Like I haven't just been sitting on a plane for
fourteen hours.

The man beside me plays the music on his MP3 player so loud
I can hear the singer wailing through the headphones, and he stares
at me like I'm an alien. I avert my gaze, letting it roam the rest of
the car. I'm one of two Westerners leaving the airport station, and
basically everyone besides me is on their phone. Except for that
couple a few feet away, who manage to canoodle in the microscopic-
size standing room, whispering to each other in Korean.

South Korea. It still hasn't registered yet—that I left everything, every*one* back in Nashville and set up camp in the "Far
East." I'm standing on a Korean train rattling through Korean tun-
nels toward my new Korean school.

I am insane.

For possibly the millionth time since my plane took off from
Atlanta, I ask myself what I'm doing. Sweat moistens my palms,

and I have to close my eyes, my breathing bordering on hyperventilation.

Hydrogen. Helium. Lithium. Beryllium. Boron. Carbon.

I go through the entire periodic table of elements three times, the repetition numbing my brain and slowing my pulse, emptying my mind of any anxiety. My AP chemistry teacher taught me the trick, told me it helped him calm down. I discovered this summer that it works for me, too.

The train stops at the next station, and we lose a few passengers but gain even more. The crowd shifts, pushing and pulling me against the tide of bodies, and I curse myself for not being willing to wait twenty minutes for the express train, which has assigned seating. Waiting longer would beat getting assaulted every time a new passenger boards the commuter train.

I glance down at the scrap of notebook paper I stashed inside the pocket of my jean shorts earlier, double-checking the name of my stop a dozen times.

The automated female voice announces the name of the next station, which thankfully sounds a lot like what I've written phonetically on my paper—*Gimpo*. The train lurches to a stop, and I grab the handles of my bags, forcing my way through a mass of humanity thicker than Momma's grits.

I stagger onto the platform just as the doors close, and, mustering as much gumption as I have, pancake any stray Koreans as I force my way through the crowd fighting to board the train. Once I climb the escalator and maneuver through the automated gate, I emerge into the surprisingly thick humidity of a Korean summer.

My grip on my suitcases tightens as I make my way to the line of taxis on the street. I ford through the throng of tourists with their own luggage.

The metro can't take me all the way to the Korean School of Foreign Studies from Incheon International Airport. Normally,

I could take the subway to this stop, then get on a public bus—as the representative from the school suggested to me via video chat last week—but when I planned this trip, I knew I wouldn't want to venture that with my luggage and zero knowledge of the area.

I stand by the curb and scan the line of taxis until I spot one of the drivers holding a sign that reads GRACE WILDE. I throw him a frantic wave, and he meets me halfway to the van. He helps me lift my bags into the back, and I collapse into a seat in the middle row.

He peers at me in the rearview mirror, obviously waiting for some kind of direction. I guess his superiors didn't inform him of our destination. Biting my lip, I flip through my Korean phrase book searching for the right words.

"Ahn nyeong ha se yo!" Hello. "Umm . . . " I stare at the Romanized translations, the multitude of consonants and letter combinations I've never seen—let alone pronounced—mixing inside my travel-weary brain like a blender on HIGH.

"Where you go?" the man asks.

"High school!" I sigh, thanking God this man speaks at least a little English. "Korean School of Foreign Studies. On Ganghwa Island."

"Oh, I know, I know." He shifts out of PARK, and we merge into traffic.

I sink lower and let my head rest on the seatback. The long hours of traveling are beginning to catch up with me. I was so hyped on adrenaline when we landed in Seattle and again in Incheon that I didn't think about the fact that I hadn't slept even a minute on either of my flights. But now a dull ache pounds just behind my eyebrows, and sleep seductively whispers to lull me out of consciousness.

Sunlight glares off the cars in front of us. We drive farther away from the city, away from Incheon—and away from Seoul,

South Korea's capital, which sits only about an hour by train from the airport. Fast food restaurants and digital billboards are quickly replaced by a long bridge that shoots us across the narrow channel of water separating the island from the mainland.

As the van bumps down off the bridge and onto island soil, I watch buildings pop up around us. Not a city, really, but a town. It reminds me of a beach town I visited with my family back in middle school, one of those with hole-in-the-wall restaurants on every corner serving local fishermen's latest catches, where the population doubles during tourist season and all the shops close at six in the evening. But instead of a diversity of people—white, black, Latino, Indian—I see only Asian. Dark hair. Dark eyes.

I finger my own blond curls, which flattened along the journey but still hang down to my elbows. Momma likes to call my hair my "crowning glory," a gift from her side of the family. I've always loved it; it matches perfectly with what my sister, Jane, calls my "hipster look," but I now realize it makes me stick out here like a goth at a country concert.

And trust me when I tell you, that's pretty obvious. I've been to my fair share of concerts, both country and otherwise. When your dad is one of the biggest record producers in the country music business and your brother has topped the country charts five years in a row, you start to learn your way around the Mecca of the music lover.

I'm tempted to reach into my purse and pull out my iPod. I can think of at least ten songs that would fit this moment perfectly, my own background music to this new life I've started. But I resist the urge, wanting to make sure the cab driver has my full attention in case we need to communicate in broken English again.

It only takes us a few minutes to pass through the entirety of the town, and then the cab's climbing up a hill into the mountains, which tower over the coastline. We drive up and up, until a thin layer of fog hovers over the road, and we emerge at the crest of the hill. To the right is an overlook of the town we just drove through, then the channel, and in the distance, Incheon, though I can't see it. On the left side of the street, though, is a giant arch that stretches across the entrance to a plaza-like area, gold Korean characters glittering in the fading sunlight.

My new home.

We stop just in front of the arch, and I step out of the cab. But once I've pulled in a breath of campus air, my stomach clenches. The cabbie lifts my suitcases out of the van, and I fumble with my wallet, examining each bill carefully before handing him the money.

The taxi pulls away, and I turn my back on the gorgeous coastal view to stare up at the white stone building directly across the plaza, its gigantic staircase leading up to what I assume are classrooms and offices.

I can't help but wonder how different life would be if I'd done what my parents wanted—stayed at the same elite prep school for senior year. I would have kept all the same friends, gone to all the same parties, been hit on by every aspiring musician trying to get to my dad, and watched my ex-boyfriend date every other girl in school like the douche he is.

But instead of a stuffy prep school in Nashville, I'm here. Completely alone in a foreign country, searching the grounds for the administration offices and the school rep who said he would help me get settled in.

Magnesium. Aluminum. Silicon.

Moving here was my idea.

Phosphorous. Sulfur.

I can do this.

Chlorine.

I can do this.
Argon.
I can.
Do.
This.

Chapter Two

"This is your room." The school rep, Mr. Wang, stops outside a door in the long hallway on the third floor of the girl's dorm. He takes my key and knocks, then unlocks the door.

We enter into a narrow, white-walled room with bunk beds that take up nearly all the floor space. Two desks are shoved against the opposite wall, and there's just enough room to walk between them and the beds without having to turn sideways.

A girl sits at one of the desks, her shoulder-length black hair bobbing as she shoots up to her feet, a massive smile brightening her face.

"You are okay now?" Mr. Wang asks in his thickly accented English, inclining his head toward my roommate and dropping the room key into my palm.

"Yes, thank you." I bow my head like I read is the custom and watch him leave, my pulse kicking into high gear when the door slams shut.

My roommate lets out a little squeal, throwing her arms

around me. I back up, both my suitcases clattering to the white tile floor. She bounces up and down with me still in her arms until I push her back with forced laughter.

"I'm so glad you're here!" She claps her hands in excitement. "And you're *American!*"

Her dark eyes are half-hidden behind thick, white-framed plastic glasses with lenses so big they look like they should be on a grandma's face, but I can still see them light up at the mention of the magic word, which I've already noticed makes you a celebrity around here. But this girl is different from the people I met in the administration building—her American accent is impeccable. She has a pale, narrow face, with eyes turned up at the edges and pink lipstick that every teen in the eighties would have coveted. And despite her ridiculous T-shirt, she's pretty in a tiny, impish way.

"My name's Sophie." She shoots out her hand and keeps it there until I hesitantly shake it. "Well, actually it's Sae Yi, but my English name is Sophie."

"I'm Grace."

"It's so nice to meet you." She's still beaming at me. "They didn't tell me you were American. Did they tell you anything about me?"

I reach down to pick up the handles of my suitcases, but she beats me to it. She hefts one onto the bottom bunk, which sports a bare mattress. I lift the other and place it beside the first.

"Umm . . . no," I say, searching the room for a closet or dresser or something. I spot two miniwardrobes, stacked on top of each other. Talk about space conservation.

"Well, I'm Sophie, and I'm a senior. I'm from here." She holds up a finger, as if to stop my train of thought. "'Here' being Korea, not Ganghwa. I live in Seoul, which is *way* better than this old place." She wrinkles her nose, then brightens an instant later. "But I grew up in the States. That's why my English is so good. And—and it's just so good to meet you!" Her cheeks redden. "But I already said that."

A chuckle falls from my lips unconsciously. This girl's crazy, but at least she's nice.

"It's just that it will be nice to speak English again with someone," she continues. "You wouldn't believe how tiring it is only speaking Korean when you grew up with English."

I unzip one of the bags and begin to unpack my clothes, shoes, and toiletries. My entire life inside two suitcases. It's sort of pitiful, in a way, that I fit it all into two such small spaces. Of course, I didn't need a suitcase for the emotional baggage I've dragged along with me from Nashville.

"So you're American, then?" I ask, though Sophie probably doesn't need my prompting to keep up her soliloquy.

"Well, technically, I'm a Korean citizen, since I was born here. But my twin brother, Jason, and I lived with my dad in New York from the time we were babies. We visited Korea every summer, but we didn't move here until we were fourteen to be with our mom in Seoul."

"And now you're here on the island?"

She scowls, the first negative emotion I've seen cross her face yet. "Unfortunately."

I laugh. "Why come if you didn't want to?"

She sighs, dropping down into her desk chair. "It's a long story, but it involves my brother running away from home and dragging me along with him, even though I was top of my class last year and a total shoo-in for top this year. I had to leave all my friends and everything."

With a grunt, I grab a pile of clothes and make to drop them in one of the wardrobes, but I realize once I'm standing in front of them that the doors are closed and my hands are currently occupied.

"Here, let me help!" Sophie opens the doors. "You're on bottom. Just like the beds. I thought it'd be better if that matched. You know, easier to remember."

I take in the excitement that's practically oozing out of her, and a fresh wave of exhaustion washes over me. Jeez, I need some sleep.

Sophie frowns. "Oh, you look tired. How long have you been traveling?"

"Over twenty-four hours, including layovers."

Her eyes bug. "Then you need to get into bed! I'll be quiet so you can go to sleep." She runs her fingers across her mouth like a zipper, and another laugh escapes my lips. I'm gonna like this girl.

I manage to unpack enough of my stuff to take a quick shower and brush my teeth and crawl into bed, after covering it with the school-provided sheets. True to her word, Sophie keeps silent at her desk, her knees pressed against her chest, poring over a magazine.

I pull out my phone for the first time since I landed in Korea and see three missed calls from Momma. I have no idea why she felt the need to call *again* after I told her I'd arrived. It's not like we talked much when I was home, so why start now? Maybe opting for the international phone plan wasn't such a good idea after all.

She left a voice mail:

"Hey, Grace. Are you at the school yet? Let me know. But don't call if it's too early here because you know I need my eight hours of sleep. Call soon. Bye."

It's nine o'clock and home is fourteen hours behind, so she's most likely about to wake up and get ready for her yoga class. Later, she'll probably be carting around my younger sister, Jane, and making plans for a lunch date with one of the wives of Dad's partners. I'm just surprised she took the time to call before going to bed last night. There's no message from Dad, though that's not surprising. I can't remember the last time he initiated a conversation with me.

I click over to the celebrity gossip site I frequent, reminding myself—as I do every time—that this is pointless. I scroll through the latest articles, but none of the headlines catch my attention. With a sigh, I toss my phone onto the bed and ignore the curious eyes of Sophie, who watches me like I'm some kind of museum exhibit.

After a few good punches to my pillow, I settle in deep beneath the blanket I insisted on bringing from home, the one my aunt quilted for my sixteenth birthday. I didn't appreciate it at the time, and I wish I had thanked her properly before she died last year. But now it's one of the few things that remind me of home. It still smells the same—like lilac fabric softener and my favorite perfume. I take in a deep breath and swallow the sob that catches in the back of my throat.

The heavy silence of the dorm room presses against my chest, and I blink back hot tears. What have I done? Why didn't I listen to Momma and Dad, and just stay in Nashville? I kept telling myself as I packed up my things, as I boarded the airplane, that this was the right thing. If I wanted to keep any sort of relationship with my mother, we needed to be separated for a while. I still have no idea why I decided we needed an entire ocean between us or why I even chose Korea—it was just the first place that popped up on Google when I typed in "international boarding schools," probably thanks to Jane's search history, since I'm not the only one who considered getting out of Tennessee.

My fingers curl tighter around the quilt and press it against my face in hopes of muffling my sniffles. I've got to hold it together. I didn't cry leaving the States. I didn't even cry over the "incident," as Dad liked to call Nathan's downward spiral. So why am I barely holding it together now?

I scramble for the first element in the periodic table, but my sleep-deprived brain is at capacity. Out of sheer frustration, I put my earbuds in and flip on the sleep playlist on my iPod, letting the soft melodies wash away all thoughts. I spend the next hour holding back tears and the crippling loneliness that echoes inside my head, competing for dominance with the music reverberating through my ears, until I finally slip into blissful sleep and escape.

My sleep is cut short, however, when sunlight blazes through the blinds and right onto my face. I fumble for my phone and see that it's only seven o'clock, but I'm completely awake. I lie in bed, tossing and turning, until I hear Sophie shift atop her mattress above me.

She climbs down from the top bunk, stands in the middle of the four-by-four-foot square floor space and stretches her arms above her head. Yawning, she waves at me.

"Did you sleep well?" she asks.

I murmur a yes, though my sore limbs and aching head protest.

Sophie and I throw on clothes, and once we've both deemed our hair and makeup good enough to be seen by the outside world, she says, "Do you want to go to breakfast with me? I told Jason I'd meet him at eight-thirty."

"Sure."

I stuff my feet into a pair of ankle boots and clap on a straw fedora I found at a consignment store in Nashville. After tossing my phone and Korean phrase book into my satchel, I follow her out the door.

Students pass us in the hall, and they all smile and bow their heads in greeting. Although most of the girls we see are Asian, I spot a few that look Filipino or maybe Pacific Islander and others with darker complexions and hijabs, maybe from India or somewhere in the Middle East.

When I researched the school, I was drawn to the fact that it boasted all classes taught in English and that it's apparently more relaxed than most Korean schools, which can be intense in both academics and discipline. Because it's targeted to foreign students who speak a myriad of native languages—mostly kids of foreign dignitaries, high-profile CEOs, or wealthy European expatriates—English serves as the common language for them all, a fact that still baffles me. I complained every day about the two years of Spanish I took—my sister, Jane, is the one with the ear for languages. But the people here have been taking English classes their entire lives. America is seriously behind the foreign language instruction curve.

But while English may be the common language, most students we pass stick with other kids who look like them and speak their own languages. A group of girls pass us, their black-haired heads bent close, giggling. One points at me, and heat climbs up my neck. But I force down the embarrassment; she probably wasn't even talking about me.

Sophie leads me out of the dorm and onto the plaza I saw when I first arrived. More students occupy it than last night, some boys playing with a soccer ball, another group just sitting and laughing.

A greenery-lined path leads around the plaza, which is circled by a ring of classroom and administrative buildings that stare down at me with condescension, like they're daring me to fail, like they know I can't handle this. A sidewalk leads a little farther up the mountain to more buildings, which Sophie tells me are the boys' dorms.

Despite the crowds of students milling around, the noise level across campus is hardly more than a hum. Coupled with the trees planted in front of and all around the buildings and the mountains towering over us, the quiet makes me feel more like I'm at one of those relaxed resorts than a school full of teenagers.

We climb the stairs up to a chrome building with red Korean characters, which Sophie tells me reads DINING HALL. The cafeteria has its own building? How big is this place? I mean, I know it's a school for rich kids, but still.

The dining hall is easily three times the size of my high school lunchroom, and anxiety pools in my stomach as I peer around the room—I'm in way over my head. Light filters in through the sloped glass ceiling, illuminating the myriad of long tables and benches filled with students, and providing a view of the mountains surrounding the grounds. I get in line behind Sophie, listening to the languages swirling around us. They buzz in my ears like white noise, none of them distinct from the others.

As we draw closer to the serving line, I sniff at a scent unlike anything I've smelled before. Sophie picks out some kind of soup with green leaves floating in it, but I steer clear of anything I don't recognize and opt instead for an omelette that I think has vegetables in it, maybe some kind of meat, I can't tell.

When we get to our table, I realize the only utensils available are silver chopsticks. Sophie fishes out the green bits from her soup with her chopsticks like a pro. How she's going to get the broth out of that bowl is something I'd like to see.

Hesitantly, I cradle the chopsticks with my thumb and middle finger. I pick up a piece of egg, which almost instantly slips back onto my plate. This process continues for a solid thirty seconds before I'm able to successfully transfer food into my mouth. I finally elect to hold the plate close to my lips and rake the salty omelette into my mouth. Other people are doing it, so it can't be bad manners.

Sophie checks her phone with a frown. "I don't know where he is," she mutters.

She scans the cafeteria, and I follow her gaze, searching faces for one that looks anything like hers. But I can't pick out anyone specifically in the sea of people I'm currently drowning in.

A wide smile breaks out on Sophie's face, and she waves her arm frantically above her head. I turn and spot a guy in a blue-and-white striped sweater left unbuttoned, with sleeves bunched at the elbows over a V-neck T-shirt. He strides toward us, hands stuffed into the pockets of his skinny jeans. He's taller than most of the other guys I've seen here, with inky black hair that sweeps across his forehead and full lips that look a lot like Sophie's.

He's the hottest boy I've ever seen.

And I've seen a lot of cute boys. I struggle to keep my mouth closed and eyes inside my head as he comes to our table.

And I'm not the only one staring. He leaves a wake of girls behind him who stare and point, and a few even snap pictures with their phones, their heads swiveling around, making sure nobody saw them.

Surprise zips through me. Maybe girls are just more open here about guys they think are cute. I'm pretty sure taking pictures of the guy and pointing at him behind his back in a crowded lunchroom wouldn't fly in the States.

But I'm pulled out of my cultural comparisons when he says something in Korean to Sophie, his voice clear and deep, and my heart sputters a little, which probably makes me just as bad as those other girls.

When was the last time my mouth went dry at the sight of a boy? Not since Isaac, my ex, when we met at that teen club where he was the DJ. When you grow up around cowboy hats and giant belt buckles worn by boys trying to get into your pants so your dad will give them a record deal, it's hard not to be attracted to slouchy hats, Converse, and flannel.

"Don't be rude, Jason," Sophie scolds playfully, tilting her head toward me. "This is Grace, *who speaks English.*"

I flash him my brightest smile, but he answers with a stony expression, his eyes running a quick scan across me. My enthusiasm flickers.

But I ford through the blow to my confidence. "It's nice to meet you."

He doesn't say anything, just keeps staring until my cheeks ache from holding my smile. I fight the instinct to glance down at my white lace blouse and black jean shorts to make sure neither sport a food spill.

"She's my roommate," Sophie says, coming to my rescue and diverting Jason's attention. "She's from America!" Her voice rises to a squeal on the last word. "Sit with us."

He sweeps the room with his gaze, a determinedly bored air about him and a glazed look in his eye, even though he has to see all the girls pointedly *not* looking at him. I'm starting to wonder if Sophie got all the people skills while they were incubating in the womb.

"I already ate," he says, thankfully in English—for my benefit? "I have to meet Tae Hwa in the music room. Are you going to The Vortex tonight?"

Her grin falls, and I'm irrationally tempted to punch Jason for causing it to disappear. "Of course," she says with forced levity.

He nods, then glances at me again, before turning and walking back through the cafeteria toward the exit. I stare after him, smarting at his obvious lack of both friendliness and regard for me as a human being.

"Is he always that cheerful?" I ask, unable to bite back my sarcasm.

Sophie waves away the question. "He's just quiet." But the disappointment that's swallowed her eyes says something different.

After breakfast, Sophie volunteers to show me around campus; she arrived a few days before me and already knows where everything is. The school is gigantic, the size of a small college rather than a high school—multiple classroom buildings and everything. She figures out where all my classes will be—all in the same room, like in elementary school—and points out the building, which is on the opposite side of campus as our dorm and on top of a hill so high it might as well be Everest.

Sweat beading on the small of my back, I ask Sophie if we can sit and rest for a minute. We settle on a bench beneath a gnarled tree inside a small pavilion between two buildings.

I wipe moisture off the back of my neck. It's not as hot here as in Tennessee, but the humidity sticks to my skin and sucks sweat out of my pores until I feel wrung dry.

"I'm going to have to walk this every day," I say, the horrible realization slamming into me like a Mack Truck.

"You should buy a bicycle," Sophie says. "It will help with getting around campus and the island."

A sigh escapes my lips. "I already miss my car."

She laughs. "Korean people don't drive as much as Americans. It's time for you to become Korean. Or, at least like someone living in Korea. Isn't that why you came here in the first place?"

No, it's not, and I could tell her exactly why I came, but I'm not ready to talk about it. Not to anyone.

South Korea is my escape, my RESTART button, where no one asks for my autograph when I go shopping or knows the rumored balance of my savings account. This is where I get to start over.

As we head to the dorms, I think back to meeting Sophie's brother this morning. He said something about a band room. Does that mean people play music here? I mean, normal music, like rock or hip-hop or folk. Or is it only traditional Korean stuff?

"Does your brother play an instrument?" I venture.

An ironic smile curls Sophie's lips, and she chuckles under her breath. "You could say that."

"What does he play?"

"Guitar."

So people do play Western music. "Is there a music program here at all?"

I didn't bother to check when I applied. Dad wants me to follow in his footsteps and take up the mantle of the company when he finally decides to retire, but business isn't my thing. Never has been. I may have music in my blood, but I have no head for the market—I wouldn't know which artists should be invested in. And I doubt he wants me to run his multimillion-dollar corporation into the ground.

So I'm thinking about studying chemistry in college—basically, the furthest thing from music you can get. Of course, it helps that balancing chemical equations and performing experiments that could potentially blow up the lab rings my bell.

"I think there's a symphony-esque band," Sophie says. "Like violins, cellos, that sort of thing."

"I take it he's not in that one."

Now she laughs for real. "Definitely not. He's in *a* band, but I don't think it's one the school would sponsor."

"What kind of music is it?"

Sophie stops in the middle of the walkway, and it takes me a good fifteen seconds before I realize she's no longer walking beside me. I backtrack until we're even again.

"You should probably know this now," she says, hesitance creeping into her voice. She stares at me carefully, as if gauging my reaction. "Jason is . . . famous."

"What?"

"He's a famous singer. Here in Korea."

My eyebrows shoot up, waiting for her to either cry, "*Just kidding!*" or, "*How crazy that we both have famous families!*" But she says nothing, just waits for my response, and I realize she must know nothing about *my* family.

This can't be a coincidence. Either fate or the director of residency—or maybe both—must have thought we'd have a lot in common.

And the way the girls in the cafeteria acted—it makes more sense now, explains why they took the pictures. All things considered, they were pretty calm about a celebrity in their midst. I might have expected a mob. Or at least a few asking for autographs.

"That's cool. What's the name of his band?" I ask, keeping my tone as blasé as possible.

Her entire body seems to sigh, like she's been holding on to this dark secret since we met. "Eden."

I snort. "Why—because they're perfect?"

"Exactly!"

Oh.

"They debuted at the end of last year, and they've sold a lot of albums. Have you heard of them?"

"Can't say I have."

She nods, picking up our walk again. "That makes sense. No one listens to KPOP in America."

My eyebrows rise. "KPOP?"

"Korean pop music."

"Right. KPOP."

Didn't Jane listen to that stuff in middle school? Or maybe it was Japanese pop music, which would be . . . JPOP? I can't remember. She went through an Asian obsession phase about two years ago, when she owned enough Hello Kitty paraphernalia to stock a toy store. Even when we tried to tell her there's more to Japan than Hello Kitty and sushi.

"The band is sort of taking a break right now," she says. "That's why they're here, to sort of get away from everything. But they're playing a small show at a club tonight, that lets in underage people, to try out a few new songs. It's called The Vortex. You should come! It will be fun."

I swore not to hang out at clubs anymore after Isaac, but it's not like I have anything better to do. And I highly doubt my ex-boyfriend would be a DJ at a KPOP concert. In Korea.

A snicker escapes my lips. KPOP. Heh.

"Sure," I say. "I'd like to hear them."

"Great!" She links her arm through mine and giggles.

My instincts scream for me to free my arm, but her enthusiasm is contagious and I find myself laughing along with her. Even though the familiar pain that's haunted me since the beginning of the summer still lingers in the back of my brain, I'm able to keep it quiet for now. I know it'll resurface—it always does—but right now, I let myself consider the possibility that maybe I really am getting a fresh start. And if I am, it's time for me to grab on to it with both hands.

Chapter Three

I peel the scarf off my neck and check my outfit for the millionth time. Really, the ensemble needs the scarf to be complete, but I think I'll suffocate in today's ultrahigh humidity if I have to walk outside for more than five minutes with it wrapped around my throat.

Sophie pokes her head into the bathroom, her black bangs pulled back with a headband and a mascara wand in her hand.

"Are you almost ready?" she asks. "The show starts in two hours, and it'll take a while to get off the island."

One more quick glance in the mirror: high-waisted jean shorts with a thin white button-up tucked in and a pair of wedges Jane bought me for my birthday last year. The scarf would have made it look so much better, but whatever. With a growl, I throw on a long beaded necklace instead.

"Ready," I announce.

Sophie combs her bangs back down on her forehead and slings a neon-colored purse onto her shoulder. "Then let's go!"

We climb down the two flights of stairs and head out into

the early evening air. It's cooled a few degrees, but the mugginess still threatens to crush my lungs.

Sophie leads me to the side of the building, where a long row of bicycles and Vespa-like motorbikes stand in a line. She fishes out a set of keys from her pocket and unlocks a baby-blue motorbike from the rest, taking out a helmet from a compartment under the seat. My pulse spikes as she backs it out of the line, the tires crunching stray bits of broken pavement.

"Umm . . . I hope you're just checking to make sure the tires aren't flat before we catch a bus or a taxi," I say, a nervous quiver in my voice.

She laughs and shoves up the kickstand with her heel. "Unfortunately not. It'll be faster if we just drive. We would be waiting at the bus stop for at least ten minutes, then it would make a zillion stops before we even get to the bridge. *Then* we'd get on the train to Incheon. I don't know about you, but I don't want to go through that kind of hassle."

"But I don't have a helmet."

"Don't worry. Nobody will say anything. And, if they do, just play up being a dumb foreigner." She winks.

I run my eyes over the metal frame. "Where am I supposed to sit?"

She pats the raised seat behind hers.

"I don't think that's a good idea . . . "

"Don't worry about it. We ride like this all the time." She sits on the bike and throws another wink back at me over her shoulder. "Just channel your inner Asian."

"Inner Asian. Sure."

I raise my leg to swing it over the side and slip on the black leather. The bike tilts in response, but Sophie keeps us upright.

"Put your feet on the silver pipes, there." She points. "Just don't let your skin touch them because they get hot."

Chewing on the inside of my cheek, I obey her instructions,

and she cranks the motor, then launches us into motion. I instinctively latch onto her as if my life depends on it. Which it probably does.

The death contraption wiggles, tipping to the side for a terrifying moment, before she rights it and propels us onto the street. We zip down the hill much faster than seems safe and rocket into town, where we speed past people walking; they don't even give us a second look. Like this isn't the first time they've seen a crazy American putting her life in the hands of the roommate she just met.

Wind stings my eyes, and every muscle in my body tenses as she weaves around pedestrians and dodges the cars that whiz past us. My dinner of sesame noodle soup threatens to come back up, and I close my eyes.

I always dreamed my first motorcycle ride would be behind a cute boy—preferably of the trendy, leather-wearing variety. Cozied up to my new roommate isn't exactly what I had in mind.

What seems like a lifetime later, after we pass through the mostly wooded and mountainous interior of the island, we zip by the beaches, which are probably crawling with tourists during peak season, then cut through a small beach town. Sophie turns us onto a bridge that stretches across the channel. A crisp breeze cuts through my thin layer of clothes, and I shiver as we drive onto the mainland and make our way toward Incheon.

My heart keeps sprinting inside my chest until I become somewhat numb to the fear. But by that point, we're entering the city. Sophie takes a sharp left down a side street, and we come to an abrupt halt in front of a line of shops and restaurants. She kills the motor and glances back at me with laughter in her eyes.

"You can let go now," she says. "I think we're safe."

My fingers release the fabric of her shirt stiffly, and I force my cramped legs to hold me up. I hop down, stumbling on shaky legs.

Sophie parks the bike next to a line of others, locks it, then stores her helmet. She takes my elbow, leading me inside a white-washed building with posters plastered across the front. We enter a dimly lit corridor with stairs that wind down probably two flights. We descend and meet a line of people that stretches into the room before us.

Shoving her way through the crowd, Sophie barks at everyone in Korean, and I stick close to her, following in her wake. We push to the front of the line, where a man is selling tickets behind a folding table. He gives Sophie a nod of recognition, then shoots me a suspicious glance.

Sophie places her hand on my shoulder and says something to the man. *"She's with me,"* probably. I've seen this a million times. Heck, I've *done* it—drag your friends along with you to places you're only allowed because of family connections.

The main room of the club looks a lot like the ones back home—dark, crowded, and full of people who smell like beer, though it's not as packed as I'd thought it would be, considering Eden is supposed to be a big-time band.

A bar stands in the corner, the bartender serving up drinks like it's Mardi Gras. The curtain on the stage is still closed. At least I didn't make us late with my motorbike panic attack.

Sophie weaves her way through the mass of people like she's done this before. Of course, I would bet she has. We camp out near the wall opposite the bar, in prime hovering position to snag chairs if any become available.

A pair of guys glance at us, one of them locking eyes with me. I flash a smile in hopes of him offering his seat, but he turns back to the stage. My game must be seriously off—spurned by two guys in one day.

The houselights dim, and the music pounding through the speakers fades into silence, replaced by applause and shouts. The curtain parts, and I see three figures onstage. Spotlights ignite, and the snare drum rumbles. A heavy guitar riff follows, splintering the damp, smoky air. Jason stands in front, a Fender Strat cradled in his hands. I have to give it to the guy—at least he has good taste. Jimi Hendrix played a Strat, though I've got to say I'm a Gibson girl myself—you just can't argue with Duane Allman's and Bob Dylan's guitar of choice.

Beside Jason is a guy on bass, his pants so tight they must be cutting off the circulation to important extremities. He bounces to the tempo on the balls of his feet. Behind both of them, the drummer taps out standard rhythms that are clean and precise but lacking any real flair.

Jason steps up to the microphone, and his clear voice cuts through the music. I have no idea what he's saying, but judging by the parent-friendly chords and painfully pop vibe of the entire performance, I'd guess it's about first love or something equally nauseating.

They play well, I'll give them that. The melody is clear and catchy, and the drummer harmonizes like an angel. But where's the emotion? Where's the rawness that claws its way from the performer into your mind, shredding your thoughts until all you can do is replay the notes inside your head like a track on repeat?

I glance at Sophie, who's grinning and clapping offbeat. The girl has no rhythm. It's painful to watch.

I'm not sure what I expected—that they would be good? *Pop* is in the name of the genre. That never bodes well for the quality of the music. But I guess I'd hoped that since they're a big deal, they would be more than your average bubblegum band.

After ten songs, my brain is ready to explode. I can't handle more than two Top 40 songs in a row in English, let alone sung in a foreign language. Everyone in the crowd screams and dances, especially the girls. A few hold up signs with words written in glitter and surrounded by lopsided, Sharpie-drawn hearts. Maybe it's just dark in here, but it looks like one girl near the front is crying.

I lean over to Sophie and shout, "So, why is the band playing such a small show?"

"The label wanted them to test a few new songs on smaller audiences," she yells back.

Memories of Dad giving his musicians similar advice surface in my brain, but he usually only said that if the band was having a rough time. My thoughts shift back to what Sophie said yesterday, about Jason running away from Seoul. I make a mental note to ask more questions about that later.

As the band continues to play, though, my brain wanders. The foreign words swirl around my head as meaningless background noise. I've never liked listening to music in a different language or watching movies with subtitles. Why would anyone listen to something they can't understand?

I'm reminded of Jane and her Japanese phase. She would love this concert. She would love being here, period. How is it that the sister uninterested in anything international got the acceptance letter to an international boarding school?

The set mercifully ends, and I let out a slow exhale. The silence rings in my ears until high-pitched screams replace the music as the band members exit the stage. You'd think those boys were the freaking Beatles or something.

Sophie grabs onto my arm and pulls me around the perimeter of the club. "Let's go backstage," she says.

I stifle a sigh. Exactly what I need—another awkward run-in with a sexy Korean who hates me for no good reason.

Two muscled men stand at the entrance to a door on the side of the stage. A throng of girls stands in front of them, craning their necks for any glimpse into the greenroom, where the guys of Eden are most likely coming off their performance high.

Sophie flashes the bouncers a bright smile and waves, and they let her through, with me trailing on her coattails. I glance behind us long enough to see a lot of angry fangirls throwing daggers at us with their eyes.

The back of the club could use a good scrubbing and maybe a few more lights, but it looks a lot like those I've seen before. Nathan and I like to joke about backstage being a "holding tank" for the musicians who, like fish, swim and puff themselves up before getting thrown out into the "shark tank" onstage.

The memory of laughing with my brother sends a sharp pang through my chest, but I shove those thoughts to the back of my mind where I can forget about them until I'm lying in bed tonight and unable to dwell on anything else.

A group of people congregates in the corner around a giant lighted mirror. I spot the bassist with the tight pants among them, running his hands through his dark, sweaty hair until it stands on end. He turns toward us as we approach, and a grin breaks out on his face.

"Sae Yi-yah!" he cries, breaking free from the group and rushing to her side.

They babble in Korean as I stand beside Sophie, pretending not to eavesdrop. Not that I would know what they're saying, anyway.

"Tae Hwa-oppa, this is my roommate, Grace." She motions her hand toward me. "Grace, Tae Hwa."

He bows his head, his eyes crinkling with his gigantic smile. "Is nice to meet you. Uhh . . . my English no good."

"No, no!" I can't help smiling back at this guy and the way he looks at you like he cares what you're saying—maybe I don't repel every Asian guy in a fifty-foot radius. "Your English is a lot better than my Korean."

He chuckles, though if it's to be polite or because I'm genuinely funny, I don't know. Either way, I've already decided I like him a lot better than Jason.

"Tae Hwa has been friends with me and my brother since we were little," Sophie explains. "Our fathers were friends, and he came to visit us in America a lot." She turns to Tae Hwa to, I assume, translate what she just said.

"Yes!" he exclaims. "I visit New York. Is very cool. You live there?"

"Oh, no. I'm from Nashville." I falter at the deep furrow of his eyebrows. "That's in the South."

"Ohhhh." He nods as if I've offered some sage advice on the state of the world. "I from South Korea, so I Southern also."

He grins, and we laugh together.

"Yoon Jae-yah!" Sophie motions for someone else to come over.

I look up to see the drummer heading toward us, a slight swagger in the way his long legs stretch. His hair is spiked, almost fluffy looking, and bleached white-blond. He's bulkier than both Tae Hwa and Jason, with broad shoulders and long arms, but he's got a total baby face, like his features never matured past the age of fourteen—totally adorable. Jane would love him. I'll need to email her straightaway with his name so she can Google him.

"Yoon Jae, this is my roommate, Grace." Sophie makes the introductions again.

He gives a half wave. "Hello."

"Hi." I attempt a bow like I read is customary, though I probably screw it up somehow.

"Where's Jason?" Sophie asks.

"He's talking to the owner," Yoon Jae says, only a trace of an accent coloring his speech. "He had a question about our next show."

What is with all these people speaking flawless English? I'm starting to feel uneducated.

"So why did you come to Korea?" Yoon Jae asks me as Sophie and Tae Hwa break off into a conversation in Korean.

"Just to go to school and, you know, get a new cultural experience."

A knowing smile tilts up the edges of his lips, and I'm positive I need to get Jane to Google him—he really is adorable.

"There are many schools in America," he says.

I shrug one shoulder. "I guess. But Ganghwa Island sounded like a lot more fun."

He laughs, pulling at the hem of his gray T-shirt. "Well, I'm glad someone is happy to be in Ganghwa."

"You sound like you're not."

A shadowed expression passes over his face, but it vanishes a moment later, like I imagined it. "Wherever Jason goes, we all follow."

"Why? It's not like the island is that far from Seoul. You could have stayed without him."

He shakes his head. "Our manager told us to stay together."

"Then you should have told Jason he wasn't allowed to go away to school!"

Yoon Jae chuckles but shrugs. "He is the leader, and if we wanted the band to stay together, we needed to go with him. He said he wouldn't stay in Seoul any longer."

Another mark against Mr. Jerk-Sexy-Pants Jason: selfishness. How is it that someone like Sophie can have such an unfortunate sibling?

Speak of the devil. Jason emerges from the posse of people I can only imagine are makeup girls, handlers, and security, and I'm struck again by just how attractive he is. What a waste. Why is it the cute ones are always lacking in the character department, like you can't have both?

He comes up to me and Yoon Jae, and says something to his band member in Korean. Which is just mean-spirited. We all speak

English, but I'm conspicuously the only one who doesn't speak Korean.

Yoon Jae looks to me, flashing a genuinely warm smile that might make my insides melt just a little. "It was good to meet you, Grace."

He inclines his head in respect before turning to leave me and Jason alone. My stomach twists, and I scavenge for any sort of conversation starter, not that he deserves one. I half expect him to disappear without so much as a word or explanation for why he ran off the only person taking pity on the pathetic American who's more out of place than she's been in her entire life.

But, instead, he says, "What did you think of the show?"

I'm momentarily struck dumb at the sound of him addressing me, but I gather my wits in time to reply, "You sing well."

It's true, and though he may irritate me, I don't have the nerve to tell him his music is heartless, mass-produced fluff.

"Have you ever been to a concert before?" he asks, more than a hint of sarcasm coloring his voice.

The lack of emotion or expression in both his eyes and voice makes me bristle. "Yes, actually." I bite back the *probably more than you* that wants to scratch its way out of my mouth. "A lot."

"How did this one compare?"

"It was small," I blurt.

He blows out a deep sigh, a glimmer of condescension flickering in his eyes. "It wasn't advertised. It was supposed to be small. We're not actively working right now, like on a break."

When I don't respond, he prompts, "What did you think of the music?"

Is he fishing for a compliment, or what? "I . . . umm . . ."

"It's a simple question," he says, his tone now thick with the disdain I glimpsed earlier. "Did you like our music or not?"

And I snap.

"Well, if you really want to know, I think you guys have

talent, but it's wasted on empty songs. Your music is clean but conventional, nothing that can't be produced by any wannabe with a guitar and GarageBand. I'm guessing that if you guys are famous like Sophie said, it's mostly based on pretty faces instead of actual quality of music."

He stares at me, the aforementioned pretty face not registering surprise or anger or anything that would reveal him as a sentient being. Then, just as I'm wondering if my harshness spurred a complete mental break in his head, the right side of his mouth tips up in a half smile.

And then he leaves.

I'm left staring after him, my heart racing and feeling as offended as he probably should be. Did he just *smile* at my tirade?

I just called him crap.

I said he didn't deserve his fame.

And he *smiled*?

I blink into the bright morning sunlight as I tighten my grip on my backpack and head off to my first day of school. With each step, my muscles protest. Riding back to the dorms on the back of Sophie's motorbike put enough stress on them that I feel like I did a full-body workout.

Thankfully, she wasn't angry about what I said to Jason. I couldn't look her in the eyes with any sort of confidence without fessing up, but she just laughed it off.

"He probably deserved it," she said. "Might be good for him, too. He's not used to people doing anything except fall all over him."

That makes two of us.

But that was it, all she said. Of course, I might have left out the bit about saying his music was lousy . . .

I fall into step behind a group of girls I think are Chinese, listen to their chatting and laughing, and watch their colorful backpacks bounce up and down on their backs. Envy blooms inside my chest. Not only do they have people to walk to class with, but they also fit in here, despite being from a different country. What have I got? My memories from Sophie showing me around yesterday and a campus map with words so small I need a microscope to read them.

I pull out my iPod and shove the earbuds into my ears, letting the sounds of the Black Keys sweep over me, a massage for my tense nerves. The jazzy grooves fill me with enough confidence to not break down in the middle of the sidewalk and cry until someone puts me on a plane back to America.

Too bad I couldn't walk to class with Sophie, but her schedule is totally different than mine. We don't have a single period together.

My first class is homeroom. I manage to find the classroom and sink into a chair ten minutes early with a sigh of relief. The room looks a lot like those at my old school, though maybe a little smaller, and it slowly fills up with students speaking various languages, representing all parts of the globe. I don't see any other Americans, but I didn't have high hopes that I would. Mr. Wang told me my first day that there are no American students this year besides me, since the only other two graduated last year. Figures.

Our teacher arrives last, banging the door against the wall as he enters and shuffling to the podium, his gaze fused with his shoes. He drops his briefcase on the desk with a clatter and finally looks up, his dark eyes moving nervously over each of us.

"Good morning," he says with a slight British accent. "Welcome to homeroom. My name is Mr. Yun, and these students will be in your class for the rest of the year."

He then launches into an explanation about the structure of Korean schools and how we'll be in all the same classes together, and we'll all be competing to be top of the class. I'm sure Sophie's getting this exact same spiel in her homeroom and she's lapping it up, ready to beat out all the other students to be number one.

He also explains that the school's staff will not take part in any unnecessarily harsh discipline and that bullying will not be tolerated, unlike what we might have expected or heard. I make a mental note to ask Sophie later about how normal Korean schools are, because apparently, they're more hard-core than American ones. Mr. Yun goes on to explain in-depth classroom policies, blah, blah, blah. I half listen, already thinking forward to my next class, Korean. Maybe it'll be easier learning another language if I'm immersed in it.

I fight a snort. Nothing's going to make language acquisition easier. At least, not for me. On a scale of one to ten, I'm a ten to the negative twelfth power in learning languages.

I'm still stressing over my future failure when the bell rings, and the class erupts in chatter. Unlike American schools, where we change rooms for each class, we stay in the same one and our teachers rotate in and out.

I absently flip through my blank notebook, trying to look busy and avoiding any glances from my classmates. Every seat in the room is full except for two, side-by-side in the front row. And the one next to me. We're grouped in pairs at tables, and everyone else has a seatmate . . . except for me.

"Hey!" a voice calls, and my head shoots up.

A girl in front of me tilts her head and asks me something in a language I don't recognize.

I hold her gaze for a few terrifying seconds, heat blistering my face, before I find the courage to say, "I'm sorry, I don't understand."

"Oh, sorry, sorry." She bows her head, fighting a smile, but when she turns back around, she and her table partner giggle together, and they both sneak looks over their shoulders at me.

I will my cheeks to stop burning, and relief explodes inside me when our next teacher enters.

"Everyone, take your seats please," he says in a high-pitched and thickly accented voice, standing behind the podium.

The class quiets down, and I can finally take a deep breath. But a couple seconds later, the door squeaks open again, and everyone's heads swing around, including mine. A familiar form in black skinny jeans, a red T-shirt, and red sneakers stands in the doorway, and my stomach plummets.

Jason bows his head. "Forgive me, sir," he says, no trace of embarrassment in either his voice or posture. "I was sick this morning and couldn't come to homeroom."

Two girls in the front row put their heads together and whisper behind their hands, and an excited titter rises up from the rest of the class. The eyes of every female in the room—besides yours truly—glue to Jason like he's their dream incarnate. It triggers my gag reflex.

So he's famous. Get over it, people. If you talk to him for five minutes, you'll see how annoying he is.

The teacher dismisses Jason's apology with a wave.

A girl sneaks her cell phone out of her purse and snaps a shot, but our teacher's attention zeroes in on her. He frowns.

"Cell phones away, please," he snaps, and the girl shrinks in her seat. "I will remind everyone that it is against school policy to take any photos on school grounds, especially of our"—his eyes cut to Jason—"students who don't wish for any attention. Failure to obey school rules will result in being expelled."

My eyebrows shoot up, but the teacher doesn't say anything else, and I'm left wondering if Jason somehow bribed the entire staff to keep the other students from squealing to the public that he's hiding out here.

Jason shifts away from the door, and I realize then that he still hasn't sat down. He scans the classroom, and my pulse kicks up when I realize the only available seats are the two up front and the one to my left.

He steps past the front row, and I know exactly where he's headed.

This is *not happening.* The thing about telling someone off is that it feels great at the time, but regret inevitably follows. No matter how obnoxious he was to me, he didn't deserve my telling him his band sucks.

I stare at my notebook and pink pencil, trying to keep my hair as a barricade between my face and his eyes as he sits. He says nothing to me, makes no sign of recognition, and my irritation flares. He can't not know who I am, right? I'm, like, the only freaking American at this entire school, and I can guarantee I'm the only white hipster walking around.

No, he's just ignoring me.

I quickly learn that this teacher, whose name I discover is Mr. Seo, is even duller than Mr. Yun, and I have to pay close attention to what he says, since his accent's so thick.

"Turn your books to page five, please," he says. "First, we will talk about the speech levels in the Korean language."

I skim the page, then look ahead at later chapters, which are full of characters and symbols that look more like miniature pieces of art than letters. Even the English phonetics beside the Korean characters baffle my brain, letters squished together and broken up to form unintelligible sounds and syllables I can't even guess how to pronounce.

I am in way over my head, and it's only the first day.

"The first level is called *Hasoseo-che,*" he continues. "It was used when a person talked to a king or official, but we don't use this anymore except in the Bible. *Hapsyo-che* is next, and it is called 'formal polite.' "

He keeps talking, but he's already lost me. I peer out the window and let my mind drift.

"Perform the exercise on page six with the partner beside you," Mr. Seo says, cutting through my daydreams. "Read the scenario and decide which speech level you would use to speak to that person."

Shoot. I should have been listening. I cut my eyes over to Jason, who shares my two-person table, and cringe. We have to talk. I can't ignore him, can't pretend he's not ignoring me. Marvelous.

I swallow the guilt weighing heavily in my gut. "So . . . do you understand any of this?"

He stares down at the page and doesn't answer.

"Kind of a dumb question," I mutter. "You're Korean. Why are you in this class, anyway?"

Other students around us chat about the exercise, but I read back over the instructions again. What am I doing in this class? I'm definitely going to need a tutor. This does not bode well for my GPA.

"Why are there so many different levels of formality?" I ask Jason, praying he's feeling gracious. "I don't get it."

"It has to do with respect," he says, shocking me. "You want to give respect to people who have authority over you or are older."

"Okay, I get that, but *seven* levels?"

"It's just part of the culture. And it's not like we use all seven every day." He still studies the textbook like it will reveal the cure for cancer or how to achieve world peace. "You'll need to be more culturally intelligent if you want to live here."

Culturally intelligent. Why didn't he just say *You'll need to stop being an American elitist?* That's what he meant. I think.

"Why are you even in this class?" I ask again, fighting my instinct to call him on the insult. "Don't you already speak Korean?"

He doesn't deign to respond, and my irritation flares.

"I mean, if *I* were a famous rock star, I wouldn't be in school at all," I say, hoping my sarcasm is apparent. "I'm surprised you even have time for classes. I would have thought you'd be too busy answering fan letters. That's what you were really doing this morning, right? You weren't sick, you were checking online message boards, Googling yourself. Shouldn't you have a private tutor that gives you all the right answers or something?"

He finally tears his gaze away from the book and looks at me. I mean, really looks at me, probably for the first time since we've met. I stare back at his dark eyes, jitters starting in my hands and spreading throughout the rest of my body.

"I came here because I wanted to go to a real school," he says. "If I didn't, I would have stayed in Seoul—with a tutor that 'gives me all the right answers.' "

"Or America."

"What?"

"You could have stayed in America, too. Then you wouldn't be taking a class for a language you already know."

His jaw tightens. "Maybe."

"Sophie told me you were running away from something when you came here. What was it?" A small voice inside my brain screams for me to shut up. I'm crossing a million social boundaries right now. But I can't seem to keep my trap shut.

"I wasn't running," he asserts, though his expression remains impassive. "I wanted to go to school."

I've got him on the defensive. I keep pushing: "And there aren't schools in Seoul?"

"None that I wanted to go to."

I squeeze fake sympathy into my voice. "Because you couldn't handle all the screaming fans? Yes, I'm sure that gets *so* tiring—being famous."

Actually, it does. I grew up with both Dad and Nathan complaining about it. That's why we didn't live in L.A. or New York—there are more paparazzi and tourists, and you get hounded a lot more. I also read online the other day that some KPOP fans can be kind of insane—like, stalker insane—way more intense than what Western musicians experience.

But I choose to keep my understanding to myself. I've had my fill of musicians and their fan complexes. You see your boyfriend with his tongue down another girl's throat after his show and the way the music industry destroyed your family, and you can't take another egotistical guitar boy.

"You know, you're pretty bitter for only being in high school," he observes.

My mouth literally falls open, and I gape at him. "You— you—" I sputter.

He tilts his head, a slight smirk curling his lips. "You've finally run out of things to say."

"And you've found your voice," I grind out between clenched teeth.

A chuckle rumbles in the back of his throat, and if I wasn't so pissed, it might strike me as cute. As it is, though, I just want to slap him. I've never met such an arrogant, provoking boy in my entire life.

"Class is over," Mr. Seo pronounces just before the bell, cutting into my glaring at Jason.

Jason gathers his things and stands as the rest of the students disperse for a scheduled break between classes, throwing over his shoulder in a voice thick with sarcasm, "See you around, sunshine."

My fingers clench around the edge of the table until my knuckles turn white, and I watch him disappear through the doorway. I don't care if Sophie is my roommate. I hate him. No, seriously. I'm about to get on his band's Facebook page and say all the slanderous things I can think of, then Google translate those insults and post them *again*—but in Korean.

It's going to be a long year.

Chapter Four

Thursday brings more classes, but they aren't as eventful as my first day.

Sophie and I meet up for dinner in the dining hall at five thirty, and I'm unpleasantly surprised to find the three members of Eden sitting together at a table in the corner, away from the other students, who all stare at the band—while trying to look like they're *not* staring.

I drag my feet behind Sophie as she rushes over to the boys and plants herself as close to Tae Hwa as is socially acceptable. Which leaves the seat by Jason on the other side of the table or the tiny space between Yoon Jae and the end of the bench.

I choose the latter.

Yoon Jae graciously scoots over to give me some more room, and I flash him a grateful smile. He really is cute. And nice. Take that, Jason!

"What did you think about our math teacher, Sophie?" Yoon Jae asks between bites of some soupy tofu concoction. "You were worried he would be difficult, yes?"

Sophie nods. "Yeah, but I really liked him." She leans her head toward Tae Hwa and presumably translates for him.

"What about you?" Yoon Jae directs his attention to me. "Did you have a good day? Too bad we're not in the same class."

I drop the piece of lettuce between my chopsticks. "Yeah, it was good. I don't really like my Korean class, though."

A snort sounds from Jason's general direction, and I suppress the temptation to shoot him a spiteful glare. Bitter girl.

"Yeah, I'm sorry you're in that class," Sophie says. "They split up our year into two classes, and you're in the one that has to take a Korean course."

I cut my eyes to Jason, but he doesn't give any sort of explanation for why he's conspicuously the only Korean in our class.

"Grace and I were planning to go to the mall tomorrow night," Sophie says suddenly, and I perk. "Do you guys want to go?"

Yoon Jae glances at Jason, who's still tight-lipped. "That sounds fun. I don't have that much homework, so I can go."

"Yes, yes," Tae Hwa adds. "We go."

"What about you, brother?" Sophie sticks out her lip dramatically. "Please?"

"Sure," he mutters.

Sophie claps her hands. "Perfect! We'll see you guys at four thirty then."

We spend the rest of the meal in comfortable conversation, Yoon Jae telling me about his classes this year and his little sister living in Beijing who wants to be a gymnast. We head back to our dorms with me not sharing a single word with Jason.

The next morning in first period, I get to class early. As I watch my classmates trickle in, I steel myself for today's Jason encounter. But when he saunters through the door, he snags one of the free chairs in the front of the room. As far away from me as he can get.

I scoff, shooting daggers at the back of his head with my eyes, hoping he feels all the hateful thoughts I have for him. So what if he doesn't want to sit beside me? I don't want to sit beside him, either. And I show him that the rest of the day by refusing to even look in his direction.

Four thirty rolls around sooner than I expect, and I barely have time to get back to my dorm and change clothes. I decide on a knee-length dress I ordered online last summer. What does one wear to a Korean mall? I've noticed that the girls here dress differently than back home. More high heels, short shorts, and screen-printed tees. I've yet to see many girls in boot-cut jeans or anything like what we would deem punk or alternative, but maybe there's more of that in the big cities. I can't help feeling like I stick out even more with my clothing choices than my skin and hair.

We meet the boys outside our dorm. Sophie latches herself onto Tae Hwa immediately, and I've got to wonder if there's something between them. He seems a nice enough guy, from what I can tell—which isn't much, considering we can't really talk to each other and our conversations consist basically of awkward smiles.

I fall into step beside Yoon Jae, Jason walking on his other side. I try to keep my gaze from shifting to Sophie's brother, but I can't deny that he's looking particularly cute tonight in his signature skinny jeans and a plaid button-up left open over a white T-shirt. He has the plaid shirt rolled up to his elbows, revealing his forearms, and there's a lot of collarbone action going on with the V-neck.

Stop looking, Grace!

Praise God, we get on a bus instead of motorbikes. I fumble for the right coins, embarrassment heating my cheeks, and Yoon Jae has to pay for me before the passengers behind us throw pointy objects at my head.

"Don't be embarrassed," he assures me as we squish into the crowded aisle and grab onto handles hanging from the ceiling. "I went to America last year, and I could never figure out how the money worked." He wrinkles his nose. "All the bills are the same color and have old white men on them."

We ride for nearly two hours before we reach the Incheon city center, and I realize why Sophie wanted to drive her motorbike into town the other day. Once in Incheon, Sophie leads us to a stairwell down to the subway, and I swallow a groan. More traveling?

But once we descend into the belly of the underground metro, my mouth literally falls open. Instead of a train platform and turnstiles, the long tunnel is packed full of stalls overflowing with clothes, jewelry, trinkets, and anything else you could want to buy. We're not taking the subway to the mall—this *is* the mall.

Sophie takes the lead, and we pass a furniture store standing opposite a perfume shop and a nail salon beside a pharmacy. The white tiled floors and chrome ceiling still look like a subway station, but the crowds aren't rushing to make their trains.

"So, where do we want to eat?" Sophie asks. "Western or no?"

Everyone looks to me, and I hold both hands up in the universal sign of surrender. "Hey, I don't care. I can eat Western food every day at home, so you guys get whatever you want."

They decide on a restaurant off the main tunnel, which offers both Korean and Western food. The waitress comes to take our order, but she just stares, the wheels of her brain turning and reflecting on her face. Suddenly, her entire expression lights up, and she cries out something that makes Jason wince. He shakes his head, and Yoon Jae pitches in, waving his hands in front of his face, but the woman isn't dissuaded. She points at the three boys, then fishes out her phone, and before I can protest, Sophie's shoved me off the bench and the waitress has taken my seat and is getting a picture with Eden.

Heads are turning throughout the restaurant, phones pulled out of purses and pockets, an excited murmur buzzes in the air. The waitress bows her head and says, *"Gomapseumnida,"* which

I remember from class means *thank you*—but don't ask me what level of formality it is.

The waitress leaves, but she's soon replaced by more fans and, thirty seconds later, there's a swarm of people snapping pictures and pushing pens at the three boys. I lose Sophie in the crowd, getting shoved toward the back. I pull in a sharp breath when an elbow jabs into my side and, gritting my teeth, I swim back to the front.

"Sophie!" I shout.

"Grace!" She reaches through the crowd, over shoulders, until she grasps my hand and pulls me forward.

Yoon Jae and Tae Hwa sign autographs and throw up peace signs for pictures, but Jason stays behind them, staring at the ground and scowling whenever a flash goes off.

The mass of bodies pushes at my back and pins me against our table until it hurts, but no matter how many dirty looks I throw over my shoulder, the crowd doesn't let up. Before I can get completely run over, Sophie steps between the band and their admirers, and shouts something over the hum of voices. And with the skill of a manager or handler, she ushers the boys out of the restaurant and onto the main walkway.

But we're greeted by more camera phones and people eager for a celebrity spotting. Sophie grabs my wrist, and we lead the way through the now-packed tunnel. Fingers brush mine from behind, and I glance back to see Yoon Jae reaching for me. He snags my hand, and our entire group makes a train as we weave through the crowd.

I tilt my chin up to suck down a breath of cool air. With bodies pressing against us and cameras flashing from every side, my pulse climbs, sending adrenaline-laced blood through my veins. I've been with Nathan when fans spotted him, but I've never seen this kind of mob in the States.

We climb up a flight of stairs and emerge back onto the street, but Sophie doesn't stop—and no one lets go of hands. Jogging, she leads us down a darkened alley, then another and another, until no one's behind us anymore.

She stops beside a Dumpster, and I press my palm against the brick building beside us, trying to mask my panting breaths.

"That was . . . kind of crazy," I say.

Yoon Jae catches my eye, and we stare at each other for a couple seconds before we both crack up, and then everyone except for Jason is laughing.

"Maybe we should go back to school," Yoon Jae says.

"Seriously? And let the crazies get the best of us?" Sophie sniffs. "We should go eat dinner and have fun, just to prove we can."

Still laughing, we follow Sophie through the winding back alleys of Incheon until we find a restaurant so far off the main roads it doesn't even feel like we're in the same city. A fishy smell lingers outside the restaurant's door, and I wrinkle my nose as we go inside and squeeze onto two wooden benches. The customers are all over fifty, and no one gives the boys a second glance.

The others peruse the Korean menu, and Yoon Jae offers to read me the choices.

"Just order me whatever sounds good," I say.

He studies the list. "Do you like fish?"

"Umm . . . "

He smiles. "You don't."

"Well, if that's what they specialize in here, that's fine. I'll be brave. Make memories and whatnot."

I'm thinking confident thoughts until our plates arrive. The bits I get stare up at me in menace, their smell daring me to take a bite and not vomit. I glare right back.

"I thought you wanted to be brave," Yoon Jae says with a sly grin.

I shoot him a mock glare, then hold my breath as I take a bite and chew. No gagging. Swallow. I did it!

Yoon Jae slips his phone out of his pocket. "Pick up another piece."

I obey, and he snaps a picture, then twists the phone around so I can see the image. "Now you can show all your friends in America that you ate fish in Korea," he says.

"Yes!" I pump my fist in the air.

He chuckles, dipping his own food into a small bowl of soy sauce. "You're funny."

For some reason, this comment raises a flush to my cheeks and the tips of my ears. But when I look over and see Jason staring at me, the heat that was warming my face turns cold, and I focus my attention back on my food.

Chapter Five

We all exit the restaurant together. We make our way in the direction of the bus station, but we're on the complete opposite side of town and can't take back alleys all the way there, so we have to merge back into the more crowded streets. The boys keep their heads down, and Jason goes so far as to slide on a pair of sunglasses, despite the dark.

Sophie leads, as per usual, and Tae Hwa drifts to the front of the group to stand beside her, leaving Yoon Jae, me, and Jason to trail them in awkward silence. I take advantage of the silence to study the Incheon streets and the trendy young people filling them. The boys are all well dressed, with perfectly styled hair, and the girls look like they walked straight out of a fashion catalogue. Watching them pound their skinny butts down the sidewalk in sky-high heels makes me feel very American and very fat.

We try shopping in some of the less-crowded shops, but no one has the energy anymore after the fan mob, especially when other patrons start recognizing the band and pulling out cell phones. When Yoon Jae suggests we head back to the bus station, we all quickly agree.

The station is packed with people. Sophie gets in line at the counter to buy our tickets, and I stand with the boys in an out-of-the-way corner, where they try to keep from being noticed. But no matter where I position myself, I keep getting hit by people walking by, their travel backpacks slamming into my arm or their luggage rolling over my toes.

The crowded space reminds me of the last concert of Nathan's I attended, of being surrounded by thousands of screaming fans who had paid lots of money just to hear him sing. It was a huge show, and I wanted to experience it like a normal person, albeit front row.

My friend Marcy and I had staked out our spots up front hours before they opened the doors. When the crowds had arrived, we got pressed up against the metal rails for the entire show, but it was so much more fun than standing backstage. I was caught up in the excitement, the enthusiasm of everyone spilling over onto me.

Of course, excitement transformed into terror when Nathan passed out in the middle of the show. That was the first day I realized Nathan's drug habit could be dangerous, that it could ruin his career and his health.

I shake off the memory, shoving down any feelings it inspires. This isn't the place for those kinds of thoughts. I can't afford to dwell on them now, not with this many people around. Not when they could see me lose my grip on my emotions.

Especially since I haven't talked to Marcy in months. I haven't talked to *any* of my friends since the beginning of summer. At some point, their calls and texts and emails stopped—probably when they realized I was never going to answer them.

Sophie returns with our tickets, and we hurry to catch our bus. The only seats left are two together in the front and three along the last row. Sophie slides into the window seat, with Tae Hwa beside her, so Jason, Yoon Jae, and I make our way to the back. Somehow, I end up between them, and I realize too late that I now have to sit beside Jason for two hours.

But Yoon Jae keeps me entertained with stories told in hushed whispers about crazy fans at concerts and the grueling practices their record label put them through when they first signed, including the time Tae Hwa was hospitalized for exhaustion because of Eden's hard-core schedule. I'm about to ask Yoon Jae how the band formed, when his pocket vibrates, and he pulls out his phone. He checks the number, and his face pales. Throwing me an apologetic smile, he answers in Korean.

I shift my focus out the window, but that requires me to look past Jason, and he might think I'm looking *at* him, so I turn my head. And see the two girls beside Yoon Jae staring and taking pictures on their phones. They giggle behind their hands, but when I catch their gazes, their expressions harden.

Great. Not again.

I steel myself for another mob, but Jason leans over me and hisses at them in Korean. The girls' faces pale, but all I can focus on is Jason's arm leaning against mine and the smell of his cologne coming from his neck, which is embarrassingly close to my face.

The bus pulls over at the next stop, and the girls stand abruptly.

They both fall into bows and mutter, "*Jwe song ham ni da,*" in unison—I'm sorry—before rushing off the bus.

Yoon Jae's still jabbering into his phone, leaning away from me, tension thick in his voice, but as the bus turns back into traffic, I turn raised eyebrows on Jason. "What did you just say to them?"

He shrugs. "Just told them to stop staring. They got embarrassed."

"Uh-huh." Because politely asking someone to stop staring

always inspires them to run away from you at the first opportunity.

We fall into silence, but then he breaks it with, "They were making fun of your dress."

"My dress?" I glance down at the gauzy fabric I thought complimented my skin tone. "What's wrong with it?"

He shrugs. "They said it was too long."

I roll my eyes. "Just because I'm not willing to wear a hemline that's practically showing off all my goodies, doesn't make me a prude."

A half smile appears on his face, and he catches my eye. "They also didn't like that I was sitting beside an American girl."

Surprise steals my thoughts for a few seconds before I can ask, "Would they have preferred it if I was Korean?"

"Probably."

"Interesting." Not really, but it's the only adjective I can articulate, at least out loud. "You'd think they didn't know you lived there for more than half your life," I muse.

The semipleasant expression on his face fades, and I realize that we've just had a complete exchange that didn't involve a single insult.

Jason shuffles his foot across the dirty footrest. "It's been a few years since I was in America."

Confidence streaming through my veins at our newfound civility, I venture to ask, "Why did you guys move back to Korea?"

Coldness swallows his eyes and freezes any emotion in his face, so he looks again like the boy I met in the cafeteria. Like he's completely cut off all feelings. "You can talk to Sophie about that," he says.

A few minutes later, the bus crosses the bridge and we're back on Ganghwa Island. But instead of continuing on through town and up the mountain toward school, we pull into a bus station, and the driver turns off the engine.

Passengers stand, collecting their things, and file off the bus. I look to Jason in confusion, but his blank expression reveals nothing.

We stand and shuffle toward the exit, and when we pass Sophie and Tae Hwa, she says something to Jason in Korean.

"What's going on?" I ask, but the twins continue their conversation.

Right in front of me, Yoon Jae hangs up with a huff and stuffs the phone back into his pocket. He cranes his neck around.

"The bus doesn't run all the way to the school this late," he says to me.

"So how are we going to get back?"

He runs a hand through his hair, making it fluff up like a cockatoo. "We walk."

A million protestations build in my throat, but I don't let them out, afraid of being *that girl,* the whiny American who can't cope with a new place and new culture. But as we trek through town and my shoes rub blisters on the backs of my heels, I seriously consider firing off complaints anyway.

To distract myself from the sweat rolling down my back—and how we're not even at the base of the mountain yet—I turn to Yoon Jae, who walks beside me, and ask, "Who was that on the phone earlier?"

He scratches the back of his neck and smiles, but it doesn't have the same brightness as it usually does. "My father."

The hike up the mountain seems endless. We walk along the side of the road, but it might as well be a cliff face. I have to stare at my feet to keep from slipping over the loose gravel.

I think I'm safe when we turn off the road and pass beneath the arch at the entrance to the school campus, but the tip of my shoe catches on a rock, and I tip forward. But before my face can meet pavement, a hand shoots out and grabs my elbow.

Stumbling, I peer up at Yoon Jae.

"Are you all right?" he asks.

"Well, aren't you just my knight in shining armor," I say, exaggerating a Southern accent for dramatic effect.

Yoon Jae beams, but the sound of a snort travels from Jason's general direction.

We're almost back to the dorms when I spot a group of students congregating outside the dining hall, a dance song with a heavy bass riff sounding from the middle of the circle of bodies. As we get closer, I stand on my tiptoes and see two guys break dancing inside the circle, acrobatics and all. It's like watching a dance show on TV.

"Hold on," I toss over my shoulder, then push closer to see.

The boys inside the circle physically taunt each other, performing a dance move, then holding out their arms or getting in the other's face. One of them has better footwork, the other better ground work, spinning on his head like a top, then walking on his hands. The song ends, and the crowd bursts into applause.

A second song begins, and another figure emerges into the circle, his movements jerky and in time with the beat. I figure out he's dancing at the same time I realize his identity—Yoon Jae! He pops and locks like a pro, his body twisting and jerking into bizarre movements that he makes look effortless. The other two boys resume dancing, and the battle is on.

I sense Jason beside me, and I turn to him. "I didn't know Yoon Jae could dance. Can all three of you move like that?"

"Just Yoon Jae," he mumbles, his brow wrinkled in an uncharacteristic display of concern. "He wanted to be an idol."

"A what?"

He clenches his fist and releases it, like he's grasping for the right words. "A pop idol, uhh . . . a superstar."

"How is that different from what you guys are now?"

"He didn't want to be in a band. He wanted to be in a pop group that just sings and dances, doesn't write music or play instruments."

"Oh." It finally clicks in my head. "A boy band."

Jason shrugs one shoulder. "They make a lot of money here."

We break free of the crowd, stepping a few yards away, and I can't help marveling at the fact that he hasn't shut down our conversation yet.

"So how did he end up in your band?" I ask. "It started with just you and Tae Hwa, right?"

"The record company chose him for us." Jason's gaze follows Yoon Jae, a sort of wistfulness in his eyes, like he's . . . jealous? "Tae Hwa and I auditioned together, and the record label wanted another band member, so they assigned Yoon Jae to be our drummer."

That explains Yoon Jae's lack of passion in his performance the other night. Boy wants to be dancing up a storm, not keeping beats for a pop-rock band.

"He was mad we're not dancing for the new video," Jason mutters, and I almost don't catch his voice over the cheering of the crowd.

I glance back at the dancers and see Yoon Jae mid–Michael Jackson moonwalk. Always a crowd-pleaser.

"What do you mean?" I ask.

Jason doesn't answer for a long time, and I think our momentary truce has been severed. But then he surprises me by saying, "We have a music video shooting next month. He wanted to dance, but I said no."

"You're shooting a music video?"

My mind spirals back to watching from behind the camera crew as Nathan and his band shot their videos. I doubt Eden's video will have any big trucks, girls in cowboy hats, or beer kegs, however.

He jerks his chin down in a nod.

"Well, that will be fun!"

His lips twist into a smirk. "Says the girl who thinks we're just a group of pretty faces instead of musicians."

My cheeks burn, but I hold his gaze. I swallow the sarcastic retort that bubbles on my lips. Sophie would want me to be nice to him. Hold in the snark, Grace.

"I'm sorry about that," I say, the humility burning my throat like acid. "It was rude, and I shouldn't have said it."

He tilts his head back and peers up at the sky, the stars dimmed by the lights of the buildings below us. "No, you were right."

"What?" I gape at him.

"Our music," he clarifies, emotionless. "It's terrible."

Yoon Jae breaks through the crowd, bumping into me in his hurry. His cheeks pink and sweat trickling down his temples, he grins at us.

"Sorry," he says. "It looked like fun."

"No!" I try to shake off the stupor Jason's words threw me into and focus my attention on the cute boy who actually might enjoy my company. "You were great out there, and I'm sure all the fans loved it."

His face gets redder. "Thanks."

Jason takes off down the sidewalk without another word, over to where Sophie and Tae Hwa linger near their dorm. Yoon Jae and I hurry to catch up with him.

"We decided to watch a movie in Tae Hwa's room," Sophie says when we reach them. "Do you want to join us?"

I'm exhausted after that walk, but I don't have many friends here. Playing nice with the ones I do have is probably a good idea.

"Sure," I say.

Tae Hwa lets us into their building with his student ID, and we climb five flights of stairs—*five!*—to his room.

His room is just as small as mine and Sophie's, but he has a

TV, DVD player, and gaming system sitting on his desk. A guitar and a bass have taken residence in the only empty corner of the room, sitting up in their stands.

Sophie climbs onto the top bunk, but I hesitate. Tae Hwa isn't a childhood friend like he is for Sophie. Am I allowed to sit on his bed? Or would that be weird? I wouldn't even think twice about it at home, but I'm not sure of the customs here.

Yoon Jae checks his watch, then says, "I need to work on a paper that's due on Monday. I haven't started yet." His eyes search out mine, like he's apologizing to me personally for having to ditch out on the movie.

"See you tomorrow!" Sophie calls from above us.

He flashes her a smile, then catches my gaze again. Not sure what he's waiting for, I wave. He lingers a moment longer, then turns and leaves.

Tae Hwa pops a movie into the player, then launches himself onto the top bunk with Sophie. Okay, seriously, *what* is going on between them? Jason crawls onto the bottom bunk, but I'm not about to cozy up with him, so I take a seat on the desk chair of Tae Hwa's roommate.

The movie pops up on the screen, and I realize within thirty seconds that I'm not going to understand a word of it. The actors speak in some Asian language, and subtitles appear at the bottom of the screen in another Asian language.

"Is this a Chinese movie or something?" I ask.

"Japanese," Sophie calls down, then cries, "Oh! You don't understand anything! Do you want us to switch the subtitles to English?"

"No, it's fine. I'll just watch what's going on."

But after ten minutes of only guessing the plot, my attention wanders. Tae Hwa's roommate has books stacked on his desk— Algebra II, Biology, a dual-translation Bible. On the top shelf of his desk sits a long row of albums, some Korean and some English, most of the spines too dilapidated to read. But I recognize a few—the Beatles' *Rubber Soul, The Freewheelin' Bob Dylan,* the Grass Roots. Someone's got good music taste.

It's not until I spot the ashtray filled not with old cigarettes but guitar picks and the syllabus for my Korean class that it hits me—Tae Hwa's roommate is Jason. I'm sitting in Jason's room. Granted, with two other people. But still.

I sneak a glance at him, but he's texting. Yoon Jae? A girl? I haven't seen him talk to anyone besides the band boys and Sophie. Not that I follow him around all day or anything. And I'm sure he would have girls lining up to get texts sent from his phone.

You know, because he's famous. Not because he's cute or anything.

Jason glances up from his phone and catches me watching him. For a terrifying moment, we just stare at each other. I divert my gaze, my heart hammering. He thinks I was checking him out. He thinks I'm some sort of obsessed fan. He thinks I actually *like* him.

Panic. Flooding my entire body.

"Grace?"

I peer up at Sophie, glad for the shifting attention. "Yeah?"

"You're bored, right?" She hops back down off the bed. "I'm sorry. Do you want to watch something else, or do you want to go back to our dorm?"

"Whatever you want," I say with as much lightness as I can muster, my pulse pounding in my ears.

"I'm tired, anyway." She picks up her purse and slings it over her shoulder. "Come on, let's head back."

I numbly follow her to the doorway, but she pauses there, shouting something back to Tae Hwa. He responds, and I peer back through the space between Sophie and the half-closed door.

Jason still sits on the bed, the phone no longer in his hands. He stares at me.

When Sophie finally shuts the door, I'm freed from his gaze and from him, only to realize that knowing Sophie's social life, I'll probably see him again tomorrow. And the next day. And all the others after that.

And I'm not really sure how I feel about that.

Chapter Six

Big Brother,

It may seem hard to believe, but I'm actually sort of transitioning into life here in Korea, although I do miss sweet tea and Southern boys who hold doors open for you.

I haven't gotten up the courage to email or call Momma yet. Every time I think about her, I remember seeing the judgment in her eyes, and I know. I know she blames me for everything. And maybe that shouldn't bother me because I know you don't think that. But it hurts, anyway.

I go to bed remembering all three of us—me, you, and Jane—camping out in the backyard and listening to Brad Paisley and Garth Brooks, and you saying you wanted to be like them one day. Well, you did it. You made your dreams real. I guess that's how we justify it all in our heads, that your success was worth the price.

I miss you. More than anyone else in the family, I miss you the most. (Don't tell anybody I said that, especially Jane!)

You'd be proud of your little sis, making her way in the

*big, bad Real World. I don't have anything left to say except
this: I think about you every day, for better or worse. And I
don't think I'll ever forget what happened.*

But for now, I'll sign off with

From Korea, with love,
Grace

I inch my way down the food line, searching the vats before
me for something that resembles macaroni and cheese, mashed
potatoes, or pizza. It surprises me what foods I crave when all I get
is unfamiliar dishes. The Korean food I've tried has been good,
but it's not what I'm used to, and sometimes, I just want something familiar.

With a sigh, I opt for some sort of beef dish.

I scan the lunchroom and find an empty table in the corner.
Even after all these weeks, I've yet to find friends outside Sophie's
social circle. Call me antisocial, but in my defense, it's hard to
make friends with people who refuse to speak your language outside the classroom.

I feel again for the book I stashed in my purse. Normally, I
hide in the library with my latest snack from the 7-Eleven down
the street, but I couldn't wait until dinner for a real meal today.
Korean class took a lot out of me. Who knew forcibly holding on
to any shred of patience I have while Jason studiously ignores
me would take so much effort?

After wrestling with my chopsticks, I get into a rhythm and
manage to prop up my book and stuff rice into my mouth at the
same time. But I'm only sitting here a few minutes before another
plate clangs against the table in front of mine.

I look up with a start and see Yoon Jae sliding onto the bench
across from me.

"Hey!" I cry, and relief floods me.

He grins. "You looked lonely."

"Well, you know, it's hard to strike up a conversation with someone when everybody speaks a different language." I laugh, but my heart pricks all the same. "I didn't know you had lunch at this time."

Sophie doesn't—she added an extra study period—and both Jason and Tae Hwa work on their music. I assumed Yoon Jae was always with them.

"Usually, I eat outside. I've never seen you in here, either, or I would have sat with you." He points to my book. "What are you reading?"

I hold up the novel I brought from home. "My sister gave it to me before I left. Romance novel." I roll my eyes. "Stupid, right?"

"Why is it stupid if you like it?"

I have nothing to say to this.

He takes a bite of cabbage with red sauce. "What's your sister's name? Is she very much like you?"

"Her name's Jane and, no, we're not alike at all. She's two years younger than me. She's a lot sportier and better at foreign languages." Pain swells in my chest, thinking about her. "She would love you."

"Me?"

A laugh escapes my lips. "Yeah, you. She would think you're hot."

His forehead crinkles in confusion. "'Hot'?"

"It means good-looking."

"Oh." He laughs, but not in an arrogant way. Like he knows he's attractive but doesn't put too much stock in it. And I can't help finding that confidence kind of hot in its own way.

We eat in silence a moment before he says, "Do you want to go to the music room with me after classes are over? I'm working on a song Jason wrote, and I want someone else's opinion."

"You're working alone?"

"He already finished everything, but he wants me to practice my part. There's something wrong about the way I'm playing it, but I'm not sure what. It just doesn't sound right."

"And what do you want me to do?"

He shrugs. "Any suggestions would help."

We finish lunch, put away our dishes, then part ways outside to go to our classes. After school, we meet up in front of the dining hall, and he shows me to the music and performing arts building, which I haven't ventured into yet. I've kept a big distance from it because it reminds me too much of my past, too much of what I left behind.

But when we enter, a sense of rightness, of wholeness, washes over me, so strong that it nearly steals my breath. Snippets of music drift down the halls—a splice of a melody on the piano, a girl practicing vocal scales. A smile appears unbidden on my face, and I can't squelch it, no matter how hard I try. It's been a long time since I surrounded myself with creativity.

Yoon Jae takes me into a practice room with full band equipment already set up. This must be where Jason and Tae Hwa hang out during lunch. Their manager probably negotiated the private room—that's what Nathan's would have done.

"Can you read music?" Yoon Jae holds up a few pages of sheet music.

I take them from him, skimming the bars with a critical eye. It's a pretty traditional pop song, nothing special, except for the chord progression in the chorus. The sounds reverberate inside my head, and I've got to admit it's pretty outstanding.

"Jason wrote this?" I ask, and Yoon Jae nods.

Maybe Jason has some talent, after all.

"This is my part here." He points to his measures. "I don't know what it is, but this part sounds wrong."

He sits down at his drum set and taps out the rhythm. Like

at The Vortex, he plays with no emotion—clean, but without passion. It's not the notes that sound wrong—it's him.

I bite my lip, unsure how I should explain. He's the professional, after all. Everything I know, I learned through a couple years of piano lessons but mostly through osmosis, listening to Dad or sitting in on Nathan's recording sessions. No matter how many times Dad tried to force me to take lessons, I wasn't into it.

"Well, I don't think there's anything wrong with the music," I say. "And you're playing it well, but you're not portraying the right feeling."

He tilts his head to the side. "What do you mean?"

"Let me show you." I come up behind him, reach around his body, and take the drumsticks. "You're playing it like this." I mimic his beats. "But it should really sound like this." I tweak it a bit, reading more into the sheet music than Jason actually wrote. "See? It's just a little different, but it completely changes the sound. Plus, you're not emphasizing beats one and three enough."

He cranes his neck to peer at me over his shoulder, eyes wide. "That sounds so much better!"

I repeat the rhythms in my head, reworking a few sections. Glancing back at the complete sheet music again, I refine the drum section so that it matches the bass better, creating a clearer, more streamlined sound.

"Here, try this." I make the changes on the sheet music with a pencil from my purse, then hand him back the drumsticks. "See what you think."

He plays the new beats, and it sounds exactly like what I imagined. Perfect.

Yoon Jae smiles up at me. "You're amazing!"

I laugh, coming back around to the front of the drum set. "You just needed to change a few little things."

"How do you know so much about music? Do you play an instrument?"

"Not really—I just played around with them growing up. I didn't have the patience for real practice."

"Then where did you learn about music?"

I pause, not sure if I want to get into that story or not—I'll never forgive myself if the truth makes Yoon Jae and the others treat me differently. This is why I left the States.

"Umm . . . " I hedge. "My dad uhh . . . he works in the music industry."

"Is he in a band?"

I shake my head. Bite my lip. "No."

When I don't continue, Yoon Jae prompts, "What does he do?"

I sigh. "He's a record producer."

Yoon Jae's eyes get even wider. "What label?"

Might as well tell him now. "He owns Wilde Entertainment."

He gapes at me, and I squirm under his attention. "Your father is *Stephen Wilde*?"

"Yeah . . . "

A grin spreads across his face. "*Jinja?* Really? Wilde Entertainment is the most successful country music label there's ever been!"

He pulls his phone out lightning fast, and before I can protest, he's shoving the screen in my face. And showing me a picture of myself in the Atlanta Airport that he just found.

"This is you!" He stares at me with new admiration. "You're famous!"

A nervous chuckle claws its way up my esophagus. "No, I'm not. My dad is. That only makes me famous by association."

He wrinkles his nose at this but keeps scrolling through pictures until I cover the screen with my hand.

"That's enough," I say, laughing when he tries to pull the phone out of my fingers.

"I want to see a picture of you in America."

I make a grab for the phone, but he dances away. And then I'm chasing him around the practice room.

"Let me look—" His gaze diverts over my shoulder. *"Hyung!"*

I turn and see Jason in the doorway, his backpack slung over one shoulder. "What are you doing?" he asks, though I'm not sure to whom he's directing the question.

"Noona was helping me with the song," Yoon Jae answers, taking a few steps back from me.

"Noona?" I ask, in hopes of diverting the awkward tension that suddenly springs up in the room.

Jason shakes his head in dismissal. "He's being respectful. It means 'older sister.'"

"Korean thing?" I venture, but neither responds.

"Why did you need help with your part?" Jason asks, ignoring what might have been misconstrued between me and Yoon Jae. "I showed it to you yesterday."

"I know, but it didn't sound right. And she fixed it! Did you know her father is Stephen Wilde?"

Jason cuts his eyes to me, and I fight the instinct to shrink back from his scrutiny. Instead, I take the moment to look him up and down. He's got on another pair of brightly colored sneakers and jeans that hug his thin legs. Heat stretches up my neck, and I force my eyes up to his face, though my mind doesn't find solace there, either.

"I've met Stephen Wilde," he finally says, "and you don't look like him."

I scoff. What, he doesn't believe it? "You're right. I look like my mom," I say.

Praise God. Dad has a terribly unfortunate nose that poor Nathan inherited.

"Why didn't you say anything about this earlier?" he asks.

"Because it didn't come up. I'm not in the habit of talking about my parents wherever I go."

I've had enough hangers-on that I'm sick of the attention. Though I feel sure Jason would never stoop to using his connection to me to get ahead. That would require him to admit he needs me.

"Would you like a complete family tree?" I add.

I hope not. Neither of them has put it together that Nathan's my brother. Most people don't know Dad's best client is actually his son, since Nathan adopted his stage name from Momma's maiden name—Nathan Cross. Dad decided it wasn't good business for everyone to know he produced his own kid's music.

"She could help with the new song," Yoon Jae cuts in. "You said you were having a difficult time with it."

The edges of Jason's eyes tighten. "I don't need any help."

I hold up my hands in surrender. "Look, I didn't mean to cut into anything. If you don't want me here, I can leave."

Breezing past him, I catch a whiff of fresh-smelling cologne that sends my head reeling. I reach for the doorknob to make a quick exit before I have to face my conflicting emotions, when Jason stops me with, "Let me hear what you did to the drum section."

I point to the sheet music in Yoon Jae's hands. "I wrote it down."

He takes it from the drummer and studies the changes. "Do you play drums?"

"She doesn't play any instrument," Yoon Jae provides. "She just knows everything about music."

"That's not true," I say. But I can't help smiling at his blind confidence in me. "I only know a few things."

"Would you be interested in helping me with a new song?" Jason asks, a grudging calmness sharpening his voice, like it physically hurts him to ask for help. "I need it finished and sent to the producers to approve before November, so a little less than two months."

I shrug, but my pulse accelerates at the idea—piecing together music like I used to do with Nathan when Dad wasn't around. "Maybe."

"I would tutor you in Korean," he offers. "I don't take anything for free."

"*Hyung* knows a lot of Korean," Yoon Jae speaks up for him. "He just can't read it, which is why he's in the class."

Jason shoots the other boy a sharp look but quickly shifts his attention back to me. We face off, and I find myself seriously considering the offer. It could be fun, even though it would mean spending a lot of time with him. But maybe Yoon Jae and Tae Hwa would stop by to break the tension. Or, I would sit alone with him, maybe in his room.

My pulse spikes again.

I suppress a cringe. I really need to rethink my priorities. Being alone with Jason anywhere means bad news. We already argue, no matter if we've had a few civil conversations. We are *not* friends. Period.

Still . . .

"Fine," I say, "but only because I need a tutor."

Yoon Jae shoots me a thumbs-up behind Jason's back, and I smile. Maybe working with Eden will be fun after all.

Later in the week, I meet up with Jason in the practice room. As I'm pushing through the door with one hand, I use the other to scroll through celebrity blogs on my phone. The conversation with Yoon Jae about my dad reminded me I hadn't checked up on the family in a while and typically, it's easier to find info online than getting an actual email from one of my parents.

There's nothing of note, though I did get a weird email this morning from someone claiming to be a reporter asking about an interview. I deleted it without even reading the entire thing.

When I enter the practice room, I find Jason picking at a battered acoustic guitar.

"That sounds like Bob Dylan. 'Masters of War,' right?" I slump into a nearby chair, putting away my phone—and my connection to everything back home.

He grunts in assent.

"It sort of surprises me that you like him," I say.

His fingers pause over the strings, and he looks up at me over the guitar balanced on his knees. "Am I not supposed to like American music?"

"No, I just meant that your band isn't anything like him, and people usually play the kind of music they like to listen to. But, then again, I'm getting the impression you don't like your own music."

He scowls, and even though he's mentally impaling me with his eyes, it's nice to see some human emotion in them. He's usually so devoid of any outward feeling that I question if he's sentient.

"There are a lot of great Korean rock bands, but I grew up listening to English music because that's where I lived," he says.

"Fair enough. So, are you going to tell me what you meant the first week of school about not thinking your band is any good?" I ask, perfectly aware of the rigidness of his shoulders.

"I only meant that we have room to improve," he says, voice tight.

"No, I'm pretty sure you used the word 'terrible.' No one says their band is terrible unless they mean it. And since I'm about to spend a lot of time talking music with you, I'd like to at least understand your take on the status of your music."

"You want to understand me?" he asks skeptically.

I shrug. "You. Your music. However you want to look at it. I can't help if I don't know anything about your music philosophy—even if I have zero interest in your personal life."

He snorts. "Did your father teach you that technique?"

I bristle at his mention of Dad, and Jason notices. He smirks. "You don't have a good relationship with him? Maybe he's a little too tough on you? You know, it makes sense now, why you walk around like a princess—you are one. Your dad's music royalty."

Normally, *princess* is a positive word, but not coming out of Jason's mouth.

"We're not talking about me right now," I shoot back. "How I relate to my dad is none of your business. But if you must know, yes, he *did* teach me that to work with a client, you need to have a handle on who they are as an artist. I'm sorry for trying to be of help to you. And, you know, if you think I'm such a *princess,* maybe you'd rather not work with me." I get to my feet, ready to make a break for it.

"Wait," he calls, just as I'm about to open the door. "I— I'm . . . sorry."

I turn in time to see him grimace. Somebody's pride doesn't like him apologizing.

"For what?" I ask, just because I want him to suffer, to eat some humble pie.

"For offending you," he grinds out between clenched teeth. "It was—"

"Rude?" I interrupt.

"Yes."

"You're right. It was." I head back to my chair. "But you're forgiven."

For now, anyway.

"So what's the song you want to work on?"

He lets out an almost imperceptible sigh, like he's relieved we're back on good*ish* terms, and hands me a piece of sheet music that's been scribbled on and has lines totally crossed out and rewritten. It's a complete mess, but amidst the sloppy revisions, I can see a clear melody that takes me by surprise.

"This is . . . different," I say.

"Do you want me to play it for you?" he offers.

"No, I think I've got it."

"Without hearing it?"

"I hear it in my head."

He hesitates to agree with me but stays silent anyway.

I hum a few bars, tracing my finger along with each subsequent note. "What is this song for? It doesn't really go with all the other songs I've heard you guys play."

"It's for a TV show. They want me to write the theme song."

"What TV show?"

"A Korean one."

"Obviously."

His eyebrows shoot up, but he says nothing, just lets me think.

"Is this all you have?" I hand back the page.

"Right now. I've been trying to finish the chorus before I write any of the verses." He looks at me expectantly, a gleam of insecurity in his eyes that strikes me as not only out of character but also incredibly adorable. "What do you think?" he asks.

"It's not bad. I . . . kind of like it, actually." Surprise, surprise. "But it's still a little too clean-cut, you know? Everything is just so even. Where's the syncopation? Where's the jazz? It's like you're trying to write something a little more bluesy but you're stuck in a pop mind-set. You need to step out of the box. Right now, you're the Beatles, but you want to be the Rolling Stones. Does that make sense?"

I search my brain for the correct terminology, but without a background in classical music, I come up short. Why didn't I listen to Dad when he told me to take those music theory classes? Two years of piano in middle school gave me enough info to sight-read, but I have no idea how to explain what I'm hearing in my head.

"I don't really know how to describe it," I say, "but it's like you're trying to fit a rock 'n' roll song into the conventions of pop music, and you're coming up with this, which isn't really either."

"So you're saying it's bad?"

"No, that's not what I meant." A growl rumbles in the back of my throat, my irritation swelling, not at Jason but at my own inability to articulate what I want to say. "There just needs to be more blues influences. I'm telling you. It needs to be grungier, groovier, more down-home."

"You do realize that I'm not trying to write a country song, right?"

"Yes," I snap. "But you asked for my opinion, so I'm giving it. You also said that you think your music is bad. Maybe if you listened to my suggestions, you'd like it better."

I'm ready for him to throw back a quip, but he just stares down at the sheet music. He mutters something under his breath that I don't catch, but when I'm about to ask him to speak up—preferably, in English—he says, "I think that's enough for today. We can come back tomorrow."

The way he avoids my gaze, a pinprick of guilt shoots through me. Could he be insecure about his music, if he feels it's not as good as it should be?

"I didn't . . . hurt your feelings, did I?" I ask.

His back goes rigid. "What?"

"I just want to make sure I wasn't too harsh or anything."

He levels a condescending glare at me. "There's nothing you could say that would make me feel bad about myself, Grace."

And just like that, any feelings of companionship that had blossomed between us die. But I can't help noticing that this is the first time he's used my name. And coming from his lips, it sounds good.

Chapter Seven

I lie in bed on Saturday morning, staring up at Sophie's bunk as pale morning light filters through the cracks in the closed blinds. My phone's heavy in my hands, Jane's message reverberating inside my head. We've sent at least a dozen messages back and forth over the course of the almost five weeks I've been in Korea. But not until her last one did I feel the least bit guilty.

Mom's pissed at you, she wrote. *Why haven't you talked to her yet? EMAIL HER!*

I pull up email on my phone, skipping over another message from the same reporter, and begin a message to Momma. But my fingers freeze over the keypad. What should I write? I finally manage to type out:

Momma,
School's going well. I like my physics class a lot. My roommate is really nice, and I'm helping out her

brother with a song he's writing. I'm getting tired of
eating rice every day, and I miss you guys.
Grace

The last bit is an exaggeration—I do *not* miss everyone, her included. But I don't think saying so will help our relationship any. The letter should most likely be longer, but I can't think of anything else to say, so it'll have to do. And, if I let my thoughts linger on Momma and the rest of the family for much longer, memories will surface. And I can't face those. Not yet.

I also fire off a message to Dad, which is just as brief, but I know he won't answer.

Sophie shifts on top of her mattress and pokes her head down at my bunk. Sans glasses, she squints at me like I'm tiny print.

"What are your plans for tonight?" she asks.

"Well, considering I really have no other friends besides you, I would say doing whatever it is you're doing."

She beams. "Today's my birthday."

"What?" I sit up so quickly, I bump my head against the slats above me. "Ow!"

She only giggles. "Tae Hwa texted me and said to be ready at six. What do you think we're doing?"

I rub the sore spot on the crown of my head. "I don't know. A party, maybe?"

"I don't think so. Jason doesn't like being around a lot of people, and it's his birthday, too, so Tae Hwa and Yoon Jae would have taken that into consideration."

"Oh, right, you guys are twins."

Jason's birthday? My brain attempts to comprehend what this means, but I can't come up with any significance. We're hardly friends. I have no responsibility toward him, including getting him a birthday present or being a part of the planning committee for a party. I *should,* however, have been part of the planning for Sophie's sake. I'm the worst roommate ever.

I crawl out of bed and search my wardrobe for something clean to wear. "So if we're not leaving until six, what are you going to do until then?"

"Probably study. I have a test on Monday."

"Okay, well, I need to run a few errands before we leave." I snag a pair of cut-off jean shorts and a Twisted Sister T-shirt, which I pair with combat boots and the largest sunglasses I own, to hide the fact that I'm wearing no makeup.

"You need to go buy me a present?" Sophie guesses.

"What? No!"

She laughs. "I'm not offended. Just make sure you don't get lost. Maybe you should take one of the boys with you."

I tie on my boots and steal Yoon Jae's number from Sophie's phone. He picks up after the second ring, and we make plans to meet in front of the dining hall. After brushing my teeth and fluffing my hair as much as humanly possible, I head out.

Yoon Jae's leaning against the stair railing that leads up to the dining hall, and a grin brightens his face when he sees me.

"Where are we going?" he asks.

"Anywhere on this island that I can find a present for Sophie."

We end up in the town at the bottom of the mountain, at the Korean version of Walmart. Yoon Jae follows me around the store without complaint, but as I keep wandering, unable to find anything, I can see him mentally checking out.

At least we haven't been assaulted by fans. Yoon Jae told me the locals on Ganghwa Island are used to seeing famous people or kids of famous people who go to the school. Plus, most everyone we've seen in town has been over fifty, and I doubt any of them are big Eden fans.

Finally, I find a pale pink mini-dress with a tulle skirt and a lace bodice I think Sophie will like. Then I pick out a faux pearl necklace and I'm done.

On the way out, we pass a music section. I should walk by, but I find myself heading over and buying a pack of guitar picks with the American flag on them. Just because it would be hysterical to see Jason play with them. Also, I'm a nice person who buys birthday presents for people who irritate me.

When we get back on the bus to head to school, it's three thirty. Before Yoon Jae and I part ways back on campus, I ask, "What exactly is the plan for tonight?"

"I don't know. Tae Hwa planned everything. But you should wear something nice. Like what you bought Sophie."

I climb the steps to the dorm laughing, but my mind rifles through my wardrobe for potential outfits. When I get to our room, I find Sophie vamping herself up with lots of eyeliner.

"So, what did you buy me?" she asks with a grin.

I pull the dress and necklace out of the bag, and she squeals. A stream of Korean spills out of her mouth, and she bounces up and down with the dress pressed against her chest.

"Can I wear it tonight?" she asks.

"Of course!" I laugh. "Why else do you think I bought it?"

We spend the remaining time primping to our hearts' content. I settle on a thigh-length black dress with an empire waist and bell skirt, which I pair with neon yellow heels that make my legs look maybe half as skinny as Sophie's. Absently, I wonder what Jason will think of my dress. At least I know Yoon Jae will appreciate it.

By the time Tae Hwa calls Sophie to let her know they're waiting downstairs, my insides are squirming with excitement. We could be riding around on the subway for four hours straight and I think I would have fun—amazing, what some mascara and high heels will do for your outlook on life.

The boys congregate just outside the building. Tae Hwa's attention attaches to Sophie like a magnet, and my heart melts a little just seeing the way he looks at her. If they don't start dating tonight, I'm going to shake her until she snatches him up.

Yoon Jae greets me with, "You look great!"

But I find my gaze sliding to Jason. Despite the warmth in the air, he's dressed in black jeans, a white graphic tee, and a hoodie under a caramel-colored leather jacket, his tousled black hair almost hanging in his eyes. My chest constricts just looking at him.

Get a grip, Grace. This is Jason. Condescending. Arrogant. Snobby. Sexy.

And that sexiness is obnoxious.

As a group, we head down the sidewalk, our voices and laughter surrounding us like a protective bubble that nothing can penetrate to kill our buzz. Instead of catching a bus, Tae Hwa leads us to a shiny black limousine sitting in front of the entrance to the school.

Sophie squeals as we all pile in, but the leather seats and minibar only remind me of riding with Nathan to the Grammys a couple years ago. But Yoon Jae starts taking drink orders, and I refuse to think about home tonight.

We drive into Incheon, and the limo drops us off at a nightclub. We zip past the line outside, and when the guys at the door recognize the boys, we're let in immediately, without showing IDs or anything.

I'm expecting the typical bar, but instead of the usual hiphop music and cocktails, the club has a more indie vibe, with dark wood paneling and Korean rock wailing through the speakers. The bass buzzes up through the scuffed floor and into my body, and I wonder why Jason and Eden don't just play this kind of music, if it already exists in Korea.

We make our way around the crowded dance floor to the bar, where we snag two barstools. Immediately, a crowd of fans forms a crushing circle around us. Yoon Jae and Tae Hwa pose for pictures, and Jason even signs a few autographs. But Sophie shoos the people away a few minutes later.

"It's my birthday!" she cries in English, amidst giggles. "No more signing autographs!"

Yoon Jae orders our group a round of drinks, but I decline.

He leans close to me and says, "No one will say something if I buy you a drink. I'm famous, remember? I can do whatever I want."

He winks, but I shake my head, anxiety clutching at my gut. I force a smile. "No, I'm fine, really."

I've seen what alcohol can do to a person, and I'm not ready to get in line behind my brother. I order a soda instead.

Tae Hwa holds up his shot. "Happy birthday, Sophie, Jason!" he shouts.

The rest of us raise our drinks and shout in unison, "Happy birthday!"

Sophie and Tae Hwa head to the dance floor, and Sophie grabs onto my wrist, dragging me with them. Yoon Jae follows, but Jason stays rooted at the bar. I glance back over my shoulder to find him already nursing a beer. Alarm bells sound inside my head, but I quiet them. We're at a club—drinking is what people do here. I'm just being overly sensitive.

As we meld with the crowd, I get separated from Sophie. A flash of panic rips through me before I spot Yoon Jae pushing through the crowd toward me. He reaches me, and I let my body relax, giving in to the hypnotic power of the music, which zips through my muscles and orders them to move.

I attempt to match my rhythm with Yoon Jae's, but it's obvious his dancing skills far surpass mine. Just watching him brings a smile to my lips. He personifies abandon, completely free from inhibitions and insecurities, and I envy him the release. Girls all around us watch him, and I can't really blame them—everything about him, from his easy smile and bold hairstyle to the self-assured way he carries himself, oozes potential boyfriend material.

The crushing heat of bodies sends me seeking refuge at the bar, sucking in deep, smoke-filled breaths. We've lost the other stool, but Jason still sits on his. He doesn't offer it to me.

"I didn't know you could dance," he says as I gulp down my soda.

"I didn't know you couldn't." I laugh until I see his expression darken and realize it's true. "Oh, come on. Everyone can dance. You just need to try."

He winces. "I don't think so."

Maybe it's the hint of anonymity the dimness in the club provides. Or maybe it's my rocking outfit, coupled with the adrenaline rushing through me. But, with a surge of confidence I've never experienced before, I grab Jason's hand and pull him off the barstool.

"Come on," I say as I drag him to the mass of swaying and jumping bodies. "It's your birthday. Have fun."

I find a place for us to stand, but he doesn't dance. With a huff, I grab both his wrists and pump our arms above our heads to loosen him up, like what Nathan would do to cheer me up.

Nothing better to get rid of the blues than to laugh at yourself, he liked to say.

But Jason just stands there, chin down and staring at me through his black hair like I'm a child to be patiently placated. I drop his hands, sighing, ready to give up on him as hopeless, when he steps closer and places his hands on my hips.

I freeze, my eyebrows shooting up into my hairline. He presses his body close, and my heartbeat kicks into overdrive, the skin on my arms prickling. The music slows to a groovier, sexier song, and I wonder if your heart can race so fast it explodes.

"Yoon Jae shouldn't be the only one with your attention tonight," he mumbles into my ear as we begin to sway.

My nose pressed against his shoulder, I pick up on the reek of alcohol. He's drunk. Mortification washes over me, and I'm tempted to pull away. But his hand, pressed into my lower back, anchors me, and I can't breathe.

This isn't right. He would never do this sober. I extricate his hand from my back and step away. Desire and hurt swirl in his eyes, a heady mixture, and my throat tightens. It's not real. Doesn't mean anything. Not any of it. The alcohol in his system is making him someone he's not, just like with Nathan.

I flee the dance floor, ignoring the curious glances from people who were obviously watching us. The lit-up sign indicating the restrooms draws me through the crowd, and I burst through the door of the women's bathroom and close myself in an empty stall. The smells of vomit and urine mix in the air, and I swallow a gag.

Pressing my forehead against the cold stall door, I suck in deep breaths through my mouth. Heat still courses through me, and my body aches to feel Jason's arms wrapped around me again. What is *wrong* with me?

My trembling fingers fumble with the latch on the door, and I exit to find a line of girls scowling at me. The first in the line pushes past me and slams the stall door closed, the sound jarring all the way down my spine.

I check myself in the mirror and see my cheeks flamed with a deep blush. Too emotionally spent to care, I go back out to the main room. I find Sophie, Tae Hwa, and Yoon Jae congregating at the bar, and I make my way toward them.

"Where's Jason?" I ask, forcing my voice to remain level.

"He's not with you?" Sophie asks. "I thought I saw you guys dancing. I'm proud of you for getting him out of his comfort zone."

"I don't think I succeeded. He's not one to let loose, if you know what I mean." I add a trite little laugh in the hopes that they can't see my face burning even hotter.

The others agree, then drop the subject, although Jason is the only topic filling my head. They go dance again, but I can't muster the energy or motivation to join them. I search the room for Jason, now a little worried that he's passed out somewhere. Maybe he's puking his guts out in the bathroom, though I didn't think he was *that* drunk. Yet. Also, I feel sure there'd be camera flashes tipping us off if something that exciting happened.

I pull out my phone and check to see if Momma responded to my email. Nope. But I have one from Jane:

> gracie: i looked up the sexy korean you told me about and OMG I WANT! please bring him home in your suitcase. or else. but the singer is cute, too! have you met him? you can have that one, but I call dibs on the drummer.
>
> love, your stuck-in-america little sis.
>
> p.s. you better write me! that one measly email with the james bond, "from south korea, love you" or whatever thing at the end (how lame is that, btw)? not enough. send me deets about the smokin' hot koreans ASAP!
>
> p.p.s. did you see that new article on e? totes lame.

I laugh so hard, I snort. So like Jane. I can hear her voice in my head, reading the words in that matter-of-fact tone she always uses. If I don't bring Yoon Jae back to her, she might disown me. She'll threaten to, anyway.

But when I click on the link she added at the bottom of her message, my stomach clenches. My face in JPEG form stares back at me, beneath the headline, "Where is Grace Wilde, and why isn't she with family during this hard time?"

I don't bother reading the article. I don't have to. I know what it says, what it's saying I did—abandon my family when they need me the most.

Sophie and the others party on, but I've lost the energy to dance or do anything besides linger at the bar and sip my soda, surfing the Internet on my phone, Googling my name and letting each new article about Dad or Nathan slam into me like a bus.

No one asks me to dance, and I can't decide if I'm more relieved or irritated to finally be just a girl instead of Nathan Cross's sister or Stephen Wilde's daughter. I left home to get away from people recognizing my face, away from reporters like the ones talking about me online, but now that I've finally got that anonymity, I don't know what to think of it.

Ten o'clock, and I still haven't seen Jason since I abandoned him on the dance floor. Anxiety grows inside my chest, but I push it back down. He's fine. And who am I to be worried, anyway?

Around ten thirty, Sophie drapes her arm around my shoulders and says through pants, "Are you ready to go? Tae Hwa said he has a surprise for us back at the dorms."

I'm not sure how many more surprises I can handle after my interaction with Jason, but I force a smile and a nod.

Sophie's gaze sweeps the bar. "Where's Jason?"

"I haven't seen him in over an hour," I answer.

Her face pales, then she says something to Tae Hwa, who disappears into the crowd. Sophie pulls out her phone and presses it to her ear like she'll be able to hear anything in here. She groans, still searching the room, and calls again.

"Shouldn't have left him alone," she says. "So stupid."

"What's wrong?" I ask.

She throws her phone back into her purse with unnecessary force. "I'm an idiot, that's what's wrong."

I open my mouth to ask her to clarify, but I spot Tae Hwa making his way through the crowd, half carrying someone at his side. My stomach drops when I recognize Jason, arm tossed across his friend's shoulders and head slumped forward.

Sophie rushes to him, taking her brother's face in her hands and letting out a stream of frantic Korean at him. He peers up at her with glazed-over eyes, and she frets over him even more.

"We need to get him back," she says, throwing bills onto the bar to pay for our drinks. "Come on."

She leads us out back where no one will see us, Tae Hwa hauling Jason a few steps behind us. When we step out onto the sidewalk, I can hear Jason muttering under his breath, though I'm not sure if it's Korean or just unintelligible English. He stumbles over a crack in the pavement, nearly sending both him and Tae Hwa to the ground.

Yoon Jae makes to support his inebriated bandmate on the other side, but Jason shoves him away.

"Get off me!" He staggers free of Tae Hwa, running a hand through his hair and swaying like he might lose his balance.

He looks at me and, for a moment, stands completely still. His eyes clear enough to reveal a rawness that lurks beneath the surface of his coldness, a pain that runs deep. Shock ripples through me at seeing my own buried grief mirrored in the eyes of someone else.

He takes a step toward me but lurches and almost hits the pavement before Tae Hwa catches him. We manage to call the limo driver and get Jason into the car. He sits between me and Tae Hwa, but he throws off his friend's restraining hand and leans his forehead against my shoulder. Heat radiates from that shoulder all the way to the tips of my fingers and up to my hairline, and my heart sputters when his palm falls on my bare knee.

"Oh, Grace, I'm sorry!" Sophie leans over and tries to move her brother, but he swats away her hands.

"No, it's fine." Only a slight tremble to my voice. "He's not himself right now."

A soft laugh rumbles deep in Jason's chest, vibrating into me. I feel his lips pull up into a smile against my shoulder, and he mumbles something I don't catch, his breath warm against my skin. I focus on my own breathing to keep it from verging into hyperventilation.

When the limo mercifully stops in front of the entrance to the school, we make the trek to our dorms, which has never seemed so long before tonight. Sophie and I follow the boys into their dorm. Yoon Jae heads up to his room, but I go with the others into Tae Hwa and Jason's room.

Sophie pulls off her brother's shoes and peels both jackets off his back. As she yanks the hoodie off his arms, his T-shirt hikes up and I have to look away from the strip of skin above the waistband of his jeans.

She gets him onto the bed, and he sprawls across the comforter, face smashed into the pillow and one leg half hanging off the side. Chewing on her bottom lip, Sophie wipes her index finger below both eyes, and I realize she's crying. I get that she's worried, but there's something more going on here than Jason getting drunk on his birthday. I resolve to ask her later.

"*Komawo*," she whispers to Tae Hwa, and he places a comforting hand on her shoulder.

They slip out into the hallway, probably for a private moment, leaving me alone with Jason. I stare down at his slack jaw and the steady rise and fall of his back, and my thoughts drift back to another boy passed out on another bed.

I had never seen Nathan drunk before that night. So when I'd wandered into the bedroom of the trailer he used on tour and saw the empty whiskey bottles on the floor and him snoring atop the bed with a half-clothed blond girl, I hadn't known what to think. I thought about saying something to Momma, but then Dad told me not to, said he would handle Nathan. We didn't know then that Nathan not only had a problem with Jack Daniels but also with tequila, vodka, and prescription drugs.

Tears pricking the backs of my eyes, less for this boy and more for the one I left back home, I fish out the guitar picks I bought for Jason's birthday and set them down on his nightstand, the Post-it note that reads, *Happy B'day, Korean tutor!* sitting on top.

I lean down close to the bed and whisper, "Don't do this to Sophie. Whatever your reasons, it's not worth the pain you'll cause her."

What I don't add, but am thinking, is: *Trust me. I know from experience.*

Chapter Eight

"Class is over," the teacher says right before the bell.

I slip my books into my tote bag, keeping an eye on Jason. I've got to know what happened Saturday night. When I asked Sophie why she freaked out, she wouldn't talk about it.

"I was just overreacting," she said. "Don't worry about it."

But I can't help worrying about it. Worrying about her.

Jason slips out of the classroom first, and I push my way through the other students to follow him. Nobody stares at him anymore or asks for autographs when none of the teachers are looking. I guess everyone's gotten used to having a celebrity in their midst.

I catch up with him at the end of the hall, where he heads down the stairs.

"Hey," I call out.

He turns, stopping in the middle of the stairwell. Other students walk around us, their bags banging against me as I struggle not to get swept up in the tide of bodies.

"We need to talk," I say.

"About what?" Boredom permeates his voice, like he's still sitting in class.

I take the high road and ignore his attitude. "About what happened on Saturday."

He glances up the stairs, like he expects someone with a video camera to record our conversation. Then again, maybe he should be worried about that—if the press found out about his escapades, they'd exploit it. Like they always do. I also wouldn't put it past the other students. They might not still giggle every time he walks by, but they watch him like vultures, like they're waiting for him to do something gossip worthy.

Jason continues down the stairs, leaving me standing in his wake, staring after him. He did *not* just ditch me. I run after him.

"Hey," I cry. "Hey!"

He disappears beneath the staircase, and I keep close on his heels. When he turns abruptly, I almost slam into him.

"I'd prefer it if you didn't talk about my private life in the middle of the hallway," he says through clenched teeth.

"Because you're *so* interesting." I roll my eyes. "No one cares." A lie, but I'd argue with anything he said right now.

He cocks his head to the side. "Coming from the girl with the famous family."

My heart jolts into overdrive, sweat moistening my palms, until I realize he's talking about Dad. He doesn't know about Nathan. He would have said something if he'd realized it.

"So, what did you want to ask me?" he says, yanking my thoughts back to the present with his tone, which reeks of forced patience.

"Sophie freaked the other night when you got totally trashed. I want to know why." I blow out a slow breath, exhaling the sharpness in my voice. "If there's something going on, you can tell me."

His gaze remains even. "I don't know what you mean, so I guess there's nothing to talk about."

I huff. "Don't give me that."

"Maybe you should ask her, since she's the one you said was upset."

"She won't tell me."

He shrugs one shoulder, obnoxiously calm. And that's his answer. Or lack thereof.

I step closer to him, further into the shadows. The bustle of students behind me dims, probably a result of everyone rushing to the dining hall. I suck in a slow breath, mustering as much courage as I have in my five-foot-six self.

Ignoring the way my face heats at being close enough to touch him, I point an accusing finger at his chest. "I get that you're going for the arrogant tool thing, and that's fine. But you're not intimidating me with all your sarcasm and aloofness. Because that's all you are—a jerk—and you don't scare me."

A smirk twists his lips. "Maybe I should try harder."

"I'm serious. Whatever happened, it freaked Sophie out. And she's probably the nicest person I've ever met, so I'm not going to let you hurt her, even if she is your sister."

His confident smile fades, and the coldness in his eyes melts to reveal a normal guy underneath, not the conceited prick of a few seconds ago. His gaze drops to his shoes, his bangs shrouding his eyes from my view.

"You don't have to worry about anything," he says, voice flat. "She's fine. We're both fine."

"You sure about that?" I ask skeptically. "She practically hyperventilated at the club when we couldn't find you. Doesn't sound fine to me. Maybe you should check into just how *fine* she is."

Frustration souring my stomach, I turn, ready to head to lunch. I'll probably make it just before the bell if I leave now. But before I can take a single step, a hand clamps around my wrist and whirls me around.

"I'm serious," he says.

And I pause, because his tone is dangerously close to honest. He glances down at his fingers curled around my arm, then meets my gaze. A silent plea flashes in his eyes, and I falter. But before either of us can speak, the bell shrills overhead, and classroom doors slam shut as the last students leave them.

Jason's hand releases its grip, and I take a step back. I consider throwing him another warning, but the words die in my throat. I think back to sitting in the limo, his head resting against my shoulder and the pain that hid in his eyes. And all the fight inside me dissipates.

I escape to the dining hall, my thoughts spinning. Even when I hop in the lunch line and search the cafeteria for Yoon Jae, I'm still thinking about Jason.

And what could have created the grief I see inside him.

At dinner, Sophie's quiet. She absently pushes the rice around in her bowl, and I realize this is the longest I've seen her go without talking. When she drizzles fish sauce onto her apple, I can't stay silent any longer.

"Sophie, is something wrong?"

She looks up. "Huh?"

I point to her fruit, and she blinks the glazed look out of her eyes. She laughs, laying her chopsticks across the top of her bowl.

"Guess I'm done," she says.

"Are you still thinking about what happened on Saturday?" I venture. Maybe I'll finally get to the bottom of whatever's going on.

She shifts uncomfortably on the bench. "No."

I wait for her to continue.

"I talked to Jason earlier. He told me about the conversation you two had. After Korean class. I let it go the first time, when you guys argued after the concert. So I guess it just sorta bothered me that you did it again." She picks at her napkin, ripping off pieces. "I don't want you to get the wrong impression of him. He's not a bad guy. Really."

I fight the urge to snort. Could have fooled me.

"He just . . . has some problems, you know? He's been really stressed since Eden debuted, and their label puts a lot of pressure on them. I mean, he's always been a perfectionist, but he's gotten more so since the album released." She chews on her bottom lip. "He's my brother, so sometimes I get upset with him. But I don't want you to think that he's . . . you know . . . a bad person."

A blush blooms in my cheeks from what feels dangerously like shame.

Sophie straightens her spine and levels an even gaze at me, her eyes hardening behind her giant glasses. "I would really appreciate it if you would try to be nicer to him. And umm . . . Jason and I can take care of our own issues."

My embarrassment soars, now twisting in my stomach and threatening to bring my supper back up. I push my bowl farther away from me, the smell close to triggering my gag reflex.

I'm ready to hold up a white flag, but she keeps going: "Yoon Jae told me about your dad, about you growing up with someone famous for a parent. I'm sure you had to deal with a lot of people being nice to you just because of him, and I know that gets old." She hesitates, her speech slowing like she's walking on dangerous ground. "Maybe you're not used to people being rude sometimes, but that's life, you know? Nobody's perfect. And I think it's sort of refreshing not to have people placating you all the time."

My eyes widen. She thinks I'm spoiled, that I've never had anybody stand up to me before. Although half of me wonders if she may be right, it doesn't lessen the sting.

"And honestly, you're going through culture shock right now. I recognize the signs. You've been sorta harsh about . . . everything. I know it's hard to adjust to Korea right now, but just realize that you're in transition." She winces, leaning back from the table, almost cowering. "You're not mad at me, are you?" she whispers.

I struggle to unravel my conflicting thoughts, vigorously shaking my head. "No! Definitely not."

I force a smile, and she sighs in relief, her entire body relaxing.

"Okay, good." She grins. "I was afraid you wouldn't want to be my friend anymore."

"Sophie, you're my only friend. I'm pretty sure I would be screwed without you."

"Right." She giggles. "I guess that gives me the power, huh?"

I guess it does. And after growing up as the one everyone wanted to hang out with, as the girl with the cool family who called the shots, I'm not sure how I feel about the role reversal.

Chapter Nine

Sophie doesn't bring up the come-to-Jesus moment again, and neither do I, even though it's all I can think about when I see Jason in class on Tuesday. He ignores me like always, but that night, I get a text from a number I don't recognize that reads: *This is Jason. Meet me in the library tomorrow night at 6 o'clock to study for the Korean test.*

Three thoughts rush through my head simultaneously—one, that he somehow dug up my number; two, that he must not be mad at me anymore; and three, that he is one of those annoying people who text with correct grammar and punctuation.

Wednesday evening, I scarf down an early dinner, then make the long trek across campus to the library. As I enter the gigantic, glass-faced building, I pull out my phone and send him a message: *Where are you?*

My phone buzzes a minute later. *Third floor. Walk all the way to the back left.*

I climb the stairs, cursing him with each step my already weary legs have to trudge up, then follow his directions. Although

I find a number of empty tables around the book-filled stacks, he occupies one in the back corner that feels completely isolated from the rest of the library.

My conversation with Sophie plays back through my head. Maybe she was right—maybe I'm being a diva about Jason not liking me. I squelch any negative feelings, channeling only Zen thoughts in hopes of being at least civil with him.

Friendships are so messy. Too bad they're not as easy to figure out as a math problem or balancing a chemical equation. If they were, maybe I wouldn't have such a hard time dealing with Jason.

Still huffing from the walk over here and the climb up the stairs, I slump into the chair opposite him and dump my book bag onto the floor with a thud. He glances up with raised eyebrows.

"You just had to camp out on the third floor, huh?" I ask, pulling out my Korean textbook and notebook and inwardly cringing at my snippiness—can't I be at least a little nice?

I force a smile and add, "I'm really glad you texted me. I'm freaking out about this test. I don't feel like I understand anything."

It's then that I see what's open on the table in front of him—not our textbook but a notebook of paper with musical bars printed on them and his penciled-in notes dotting the lines.

"Have you worked more on the song?" I ask, relieved to find something we can at least talk about without blowing up.

He nods. "I fixed something in the chorus, and I finished all the verses."

"Wow! Can I see?"

He slaps the cover of the notebook closed, and I startle. "Studying first," he says.

I straighten my back and salute. "Sir, yes, sir!"

His eyebrows meet in the middle of his forehead and he studies me a second before shaking his head and pulling out his textbook. Judging by his lack of response to my sarcasm, I'd bet Sophie had a talk with him, too. And for some reason, this puts me in a much better mood.

We delve into the composition of Korean grammar and how to string sentences together, and I follow along pretty well. I even manage to write the few characters we need to have memorized, which includes our names, written phonetically. A grin stretches across my face at seeing my name drawn out in *Hangul*, the Korean writing system.

"You know, this kind of writing is a lot more artistic than English writing," I say. "It looks more like a picture than a word."

"They're just different," Jason answers. "The symbols represent the pronunciation of one syllable, symbols built from multiple *Hangul* characters in the alphabet, so they're sort of compounding on each other." He brushes bangs out of his eyes. "Different kinds of writing systems."

I stare down at the characters on my paper again, comparing the ones I wrote to his examples. Although he has messy boy handwriting, his lines are clearer, the spaces between them more distinct. I focus on making mine look more like his.

"You know, you sound a little bit like a smarty-pants when you talk about language," I say, keeping my gaze focused on my paper.

He snorts, his voice thick with sarcasm, when he says, "Anyone would sound smart to you. You don't know anything about languages besides English."

I shoot him a glare. "Look, I get it, I should have studied harder in my foreign language classes. But I didn't know I was going to move to the other side of the world. And I'm pretty sure my *Español* is still a lot better than yours, so why don't we cut the attitude?"

He holds my sharp gaze with his reserved one for a few moments before asking, "Are you done yelling now?"

"If you're done insulting me." I huff. "Can we take a break? Let me see the song."

Hesitantly, he pulls the notebook out of his backpack and

hands it to me. As it transitions from his palm to mine, our fingers brush for the briefest moment, and my mind catapults back to Saturday night and his hands resting on my hips. Heat builds in my chest and threatens to spread, so I tilt my face down and try to hide it with my hair as I study the sheet music.

"I recorded the guitar part on my computer." He pauses. "Do you want to hear it?"

I yank my attention from the papers. "Of course!"

He hands me his iPod, and I place the gigantic headphones over my ears and press PLAY. Jason's guitar floods my thoughts, and I shut my eyes to better concentrate on each chord and how they all fit together, my head nodding to the steady beat. He *has* improved the chorus, though I can't help thinking it lacks personality. But it flows well with the verses, and the bridge at the end shows a lot of promise.

Admiration sparks in me. I look up and see him watching me, waiting for my response. Okay, I admit it—he's a lot more talented than I gave him credit for originally. Even if he does have an attitude problem.

I give him my assessment.

"I was inspired by Shin Joong Hyun, one of Korea's most famous rock stars. But you think I should make it more like your American music?" he asks.

"You say that like it's a bad thing."

He levels a skeptical gaze at me, which speaks more than his words could. And I'm struck with the realization that he has the most expressive eyes of anyone I've ever met. No wonder he doesn't talk much—he doesn't need to.

"Look, just hear me out." I flip through my notebook for an empty sheet of paper. "I'm sure these are some amazing Korean rockers; I just don't know them. You can get inspired by them, too, but I'm going to give you some songs to listen to. Take notes. Maybe you'll actually learn something."

He looks at me like I'm inflicting physical pain, but he takes the paper anyway. What we do for the sake of our art.

"If you're making me listen to your music, then you can listen to mine." He makes up a list of his own and gives it to me.

I stare at the scribbles. "Umm . . . you realize that I can't read almost every word on here, right? My Korean isn't that good yet."

"Sophie can read it for you. I'm sure she has all those songs. They're pop, but I have some Korean rock you can listen to later."

While the prospect of listening to a complete playlist of KPOP songs sounds worse than hours of Korean language homework, I keep my trap shut. No sense in creating any more tension between us. I'm officially on my best behavior.

We sit in silence a minute before he says, "Did you learn about music from being at your father's company?"

I shift in my seat, buying time and searching for the most diplomatic way of talking about Dad. "I've actually never had any formal musical training—I mean, besides basic piano—although my dad tried to get me to take classes all the time. I picked up a lot just being around the business, but I was never taught composition like my bro—" I stop myself before I slip up, a jolt of panic skipping through me.

If Jason notices me falter, he doesn't address it. "It surprises me that you can know so much without being taught."

"Was that . . . was that a *compliment*?"

He scoffs, but the edges of his lips curl up like they want to smile and he won't let them. "I just meant that you have a natural talent for music composition. But that's more of a compliment to your parents and their genes than to you."

"Well, what about you?" I lean back in my chair, crossing my arms. "How did the great Jason Bae become KPOP's newest rising star?"

He's quiet so long, I fear he won't answer. I take the time to notice the stiffness in his shoulders and how his hands clench and unclench.

"I started playing guitar when I was ten," he says, voice tight. "My father bought me my first as a Christmas present. Tae Hwa and I would play together when he visited, and when Sophie and I moved back to Korea, Tae Hwa and I decided to pursue a career in music."

"Just like that? You guys must have been pretty lucky to get picked up so fast."

"Tae Hwa's father knew someone who worked for the record company."

"Ahh, so you cashed in on connections."

Anger flashes in his eyes so fierce, I'm muted. Tension nestles between us, making the library seem even quieter than it did before.

"It was much more than that," he murmurs. "We worked hard for our debut."

I clear my throat. "I'm sure."

He stares a hole into the floor, muttering just loud enough for me to catch, "We worked a lot harder than Yoon Jae."

The easiness of our interaction having been shattered, I search for a way to regain any sort of politeness in the conversation. I flip to the next page in our Korean textbook, though I can't focus on the grammar lesson. This isn't the first time I've noticed strain in the relationship between Jason and his bandmate, but I can't imagine why, besides Jason resenting Yoon Jae's easier road to fame.

We finish our study session around eight and head out of the library together. He unlocks a bike from the rack as I make to head back to the dorms.

"I'll see you tomorrow," I say.

"Wait, are you walking back?"

"Well, I'm not sleeping at the library tonight."

He doesn't take the bait. "I'll give you a ride."

I imagine what it would feel like to sit behind him on the bike, my arms wrapped around his waist. That now-familiar heat radiates through my body again. How is it that Jason has turned me into the blushing type of girl?

"Don't worry about me." I wave my hand in dismissal. "I'll be fine."

He straddles the bike's frame. "I don't mind. Get on."

I hesitate a moment, but when I see that he isn't budging, I step up to the bike. "Uhh . . . how am I supposed to ride this thing?"

He pats the metal rack on the back of the bike, made for hauling inanimate objects.

"You've got to be kidding."

"I'm not going to kill you. Just trust me."

Trust. Such a small word. Which implies so much. I lost my trust in boys when Isaac cheated on me, then lied to my face about it.

Jason's gaze softens just a hair. "Come on, you'll be fine."

Biting my lip, I straddle the bike, stomping down any fear that threatens to grow in my chest.

Jason turns around to look at me. "Sit sideways, like riding a horse sidesaddle. More comfortable."

I follow his instructions, not sure how I'm going to balance myself. When I rode with Sophie, I was more afraid of falling and cracking my head open on the pavement, but with Jason, my fear lies more in my body's response to being so close to him.

Blowing out a slow breath to ease my nerves, I settle onto the metal rack behind his seat and pull up my feet. I knot trembling fingers in the fabric of his T-shirt, which hangs away from his body. But when he pushes the bike into motion, on instinct, I grab onto something more substantial. My eyes snap closed, and it takes me a good thirty seconds to realize my fingers are digging into his sides.

Though the wind that blows against us chills my skin, I'm so hot I feel I might spontaneously combust. Every time I attempt to let go of him, the bike teeters to the side.

"Hold on tighter," he says over his shoulder.

I spend the entire ride in my own personal Hades, torn between fear of falling and fear of Jason.

When he pulls up to my dorm, I jump off the bike so fast I stumble. He grabs my arm to steady me, and it takes an excruciating amount of effort not to rip myself away from his grasp. Memories of us dancing, of him leaning against me in the limo, flash through my brain, and a fresh stab of longing cuts through my chest. Seeing him sitting there, it seems like Saturday night wasn't even real.

"Grace?"

My heart sprints. "Yeah?"

He picks at one of the bike's handlebars in one of those rare instances of discomfort. "Do you want to go with us to the music video shoot next Friday?"

"What?"

"I'm sure Sophie would have asked you, anyway," he adds. "But I just thought you should go. So we can work on the song some more."

"The song. Right. Umm . . . sure." I wait for the fog to clear from inside my head, but it lingers. "I guess I'll see you tomorrow in class. For the test."

"If my legs can get me home. You were heavy to carry here."

I gape at him until I realize that was his idea of a joke. Jason just told a joke.

He gives an awkward wave. "Good night, Grace."

"Wait a second."

He pauses with his foot ready to peddle. "What?"

"Does this mean we're . . . friends now?"

"Friends?"

"Yeah. You tutoring me, and me helping with the song. Going to the shoot next week. Are we friends?"

Why does my breath hitch at the thought?

The scowl I've come to associate with him reappears on his face, and arrogance drips from his voice when he says, "I'll think about it."

But even in the dark, I can see his scowl has transformed into a smile.

Chapter Ten

I take another munch of my seaweed-flavored chips and desperately miss Tennessee—barbecue, biscuits, turnip greens cooked with ham. Sophie's right: I *am* in culture shock, but I don't know how to fix that. How do I stop being negative? Is there a twelve-step program for becoming a nicer person?

The boys left Ganghwa Island this morning to head off to the location of their music video after getting a pass from the principal to get out of Friday classes, but Sophie and I weren't so lucky, so we left campus right when we got out of class at four thirty.

I've never ridden a Greyhound bus in America, but I assume this is what that's like—a metal monstrosity with a bathroom built into the back, a TV playing a soap opera, and seats packed in tight, like on an airplane. We purchased our seats at the bus station, barely in time to snag two together.

We've been riding for over six hours, made one half-hour pit stop, and are now rumbling along the highway toward a fishing village whose name I can't pronounce. Why the band chose somewhere so far away, I have no idea, but I'm starting to wish I'd stayed back at school.

I bump Sophie's shoulder with mine. "Why didn't we go with the boys in their van again? At least we could have stopped and gotten out when we wanted to."

She sighs. "Maybe you don't care about skipping class, but I do. There's no way I'll make top of the class by the end of the year if I have any absences. Besides, this isn't so bad."

I point to the TV mounted on the ceiling. "Sophie, they're making us watch a soap opera."

She grins, her cheeks pushing up her gigantic glasses close to her hairline. "That's not a soap opera, it's a drama. Like, a prime-time show. This is a recording of an old one."

"So will the show Jason's writing the song for be like this one?"

"Probably. I'm curious to see how well he acts in it." She giggles.

"Wait. He's going to be on *TV*?"

Nathan got a lot of great opportunities after he won his first Grammy, but he couldn't act to save his life, so he never accepted any roles he was offered. I always wished he would have, though, so I could tag along.

"He didn't tell you that's what the song is for?" she asks.

"Well, he said it was the theme song, but I didn't know he'd be actually *in* the show."

She scoots down and props her knees on the seat in front of her, crossing her arms and leaning her head against the window.

"Well, the drama is about an aspiring musician," she says, "whose fiancée has amnesia. She was hit by a car on her way to the wedding, and he helps her remember her previous life with his music. Oh, and there's something about her dad being a crime boss or something, and Jason's character gets kidnapped by the dad. I can't remember."

"Sounds like a soap opera to me."

She laughs. "Yeah, I guess. But it should be good for his career. That's what their manager said, anyway."

"Are the other two guys going to be in it?"

"No, just Jason."

"That doesn't seem fair."

"He's the lead singer." She shoots me a wry smile. "Plus, if you haven't noticed, he's the cutest one. But I just like to think of that as a family thing."

I roll my eyes and force myself to laugh with her, hoping she doesn't notice the way my breathing has accelerated. I *have* noticed he's the cutest, though I would have guessed Sophie would think of someone else.

"What about Tae Hwa?" I ask. "He's cute."

"I guess," is all she says, but I spot the blush growing in her cheeks.

We spend the rest of the the ride trying to sleep. I shift a dozen times in my seat, but I can't drift off. So I stuff headphones into my ears and listen to the playlist Sophie made me of all the songs Jason suggested. The synthesized beats and squeaky-clean vocals grate my nerves at first, but I soon find myself tapping my foot and humming along. This KPOP stuff is catchy, I'll give it that. And at least they use English phrases a lot, mixed in with the Korean, so I understand some of it.

When our bus finally pulls into the station, the October night is chilly. Wrapping my arms around myself against the cold, I grab my backpack and shuffle out onto the pavement.

Tilting my head back, I peer up at the chorus of stars overhead, marveling at their brightness this far from the city.

"Grace, hurry up!" Sophie calls.

"I'm coming, I'm coming," I growl, slicking back my ponytail, which has totally frizzed after that long ride.

Sophie and I make our way through the bus station, which

is a lot smaller than the one we transferred through in Incheon. There are only two buses lined up at the stop, in contrast to the nearly fifteen there.

"Tae Hwa said the driver would meet us out front," Sophie says, her attention more on her phone than where she's going.

I grab her arm and maneuver her around pedestrians before she runs over anyone, and we camp out at the curb in front of the building. Lights dot the countryside before us, but mostly it's dark. Shadowy mountains stretch up to the sky, their round backs blotting out the stars. If I listen hard, I can hear seagulls, but we're too far from the water to hear any ocean waves.

A pair of headlights pulls up, and the driver stops right in front of us. A familiar face pokes out of the passenger side of a van.

"Get in," Yoon Jae calls.

Sophie and I climb into the van to find Tae Hwa behind the wheel, Yoon Jae riding shotgun, and Jason in the middle row. Sophie slides in beside her brother, and I sit in the back row.

"I thought the driver was going to come get us," Sophie says.

"Tae Hwa wanted to drive," Yoon Jae throws over his shoulder.

Sophie turns around and says to me with mock seriousness, "You had better put your seat belt on, Grace. Tae Hwa isn't known for his driving skills."

She laughs, but I search for a seat belt anyway, then realize nobody wears seat belts here unless they're on the highway. I can't find one anyway, so I shrug off any worries.

We rocket down the bumpy street, Tae Hwa weaving around bikes and motorcycles so close I fear we're going to run them off the road. I can't watch him almost squish pedestrians, so I peer out the window at the splattering of buildings we pass as we head into the town, which is built into the hillside that slopes down to the sea below.

We cross a bridge that stretches across the ocean, circle a roundabout, and turn off onto a side street that sports a myriad of tiny restaurants and tea shops closed for the night.

Tae Hwa pulls up to a weather-beaten white building, and we all pile out of the van. I look up at the three-story hotel with uncertainty. A breeze catches my hair and brings a scent of salt-water and old fish. A stray dog runs past us, yelping at the heels of a screeching cat, and a woman babbles in Korean at the top of her lungs in the restaurant still open next door. I glance in the alley beside the hotel. Are those . . . chickens?

I'm definitely not in Nashville anymore.

The boys already checked us in, so we follow them up the mountain that is the staircase. Yoon Jae takes the duffel from my hands and throws it over his shoulder, teetering under its weight.

Our room's on the third floor. Yoon Jae fishes in the pocket of his too-tight jeans and pulls out a key, which he uses to open the door for us. I find two twin-size beds.

I drop my backpack onto the bed nearest the door, then push open the sliding glass door and step out onto the stone terrace, which grants a view of the ocean below. Gorgeous during the day, I'm sure.

The balcony's larger than I would have expected. I then realize it's shared with the room next door.

Jason steps up beside me and rests his elbows on the railing. The wind tosses his dark hair, and my stomach somersaults.

"I hope that's y'all's room." I point to the other glass door.

He nods.

"Well, at least I don't have to worry about some strange man breaking into our room and kidnapping us." I infuse my voice with mock seriousness. "But those Koreans boys—I just don't trust 'em. Maybe I should sleep with some pepper spray or something."

He doesn't respond to the jab, though I didn't expect him to— this *is* Jason we're talking about. My brain buzzes with sudden jitters, a dozen small-talk starters falling flat even in my head. With his shoulder only a few inches from mine, I can't help but think back to the night of his birthday. I'm dying to know if he remembers, and if he does, what he thinks about it. I should have asked earlier, but I don't want to upset Sophie again. Still, I need to know.

Sophie's, Yoon Jae's, and Tae Hwa's voices drift to us through the open door, but they fade away and eventually cut off with a slam of the door. I glance over my shoulder and see that they've left me and Jason alone. I swallow, my mouth suddenly dry. The distance between our shoulders now seems much smaller.

He keeps silent, posture completely relaxed. Obviously, I'm the only one sweating bullets here, and I don't think it has anything to do with the heat. I clear my throat.

"I need to ask you a question," I start.

"Hmm?"

"It's about your birthday."

His shoulders tense. "What about it?"

"Do you . . . remember anything?"

He hesitates a long moment, staring down at his clasped hands on the balcony railing. "Why do you want to know?"

I clench my jaw. He's going to make me work for this. "Because I just do."

"I don't see how it has anything to do with you."

"You're my friend. I'm pretty sure it's my business whether or not you have any memory of being so wasted you passed out on my shoulder on the ride home from the bar."

He pulls in a sharp breath, so quiet I can hardly hear it. But he responds with, "Who says we're friends?"

I snort. "Don't pull that. You can say whatever you want, but I think we've known each other long enough to be past the acquaintance stage. Plus, I'm helping you out with your song, remember? And you're my Korean tutor. We're friends. We've been over this already."

He doesn't argue, and that speaks louder than his former protest.

"So are you going to tell me or not?" My stomach twists. "Do you remember what happened?"

Turning his head, he gazes at me with those dark, somber eyes. I search them for any emotion, but it's too dark to see more than the general outline of his irises. Still, my pulse kicks into high gear just being under his scrutiny.

"I—" His voice breaks off. "I don't remember anything."

I wait for the surge of relief, but it doesn't come. I should be happy he doesn't remember us dancing, our bodies rocking back and forth to the music, close enough that my mother would have raised her eyebrows at me. But, instead, I find myself a little disappointed.

"Oh," I mumble.

"Is that good or bad?" he asks.

I shrug. "Neither. I was just curious."

But I have to swallow the tightness in my throat.

"I wrote the words to the chorus of our song. Do you want to hear it?" He pushes away from the railing and doesn't wait for my answer before he goes into his room.

I blink back the stinging in my eyes, but I can't help smiling. He called it *our* song. And, you know, I guess that's what it is.

We wake up at the crack of dawn the next morning. Sophie tells me to wear comfortable clothes, so I opt for a pair of jeans, an Indian-inspired shirt that's beaded but lightweight, and tan saddle shoes I bought at a vintage shop in Nashville.

We meet the boys in front of the hotel. As soon as I step outside, I'm hit by a wave of salty air that churns my already queasy stomach. I went to bed with a stomachache and woke up to an even more unruly belly. I blame the seaweed chips.

The driver pulls up the van, and we all climb in. I slide in beside Jason, and Yoon Jae sits next to me, pushing me up close to Jason. Every time our knees bump each other, my heart hammers against the inside of my chest.

We zip through town, maneuvering around women carrying their vegetables to market on rickety bicycles and kids on their way to school *on a Saturday,* dressed in uniforms with backpacks sporting cartoon characters.

The driver takes us out of town and onto a bumpy dirt road that weaves its way through mountains that loom over the turquoise water. We pass long stretches of harbor housing rows and rows of boats, from modern ferries to one-person dinghies.

We drive past beaches left empty in the cool air. Water laps at the shore, backlit with rolling mountains in the distance. I watch the sandy beaches whiz past and transform into shrubbery-covered rocks and cliff faces that slope down into the sea.

The farther we drive, the more I feel like I've stepped back in time. Without any power lines or billboards, and with the mountains and sea surrounding us, I can imagine myself back before industrialization. I reach around Jason and open the window so the salty air blows against our faces. He scowls and pushes hair out of his face, but I flash him a huge grin and he keeps quiet.

Up ahead, a village appears, nestled close to the water, zero other signs of civilization within sight. The pavement ends, and we bump along on sandy gravel as we pass buildings so wind and salt weathered, they look like they might fall over in a strong wind.

The driver parks at the edge of a long row of docks that stretches into the calm water. A number of tents have been set up on the shoreline, with crew members rushing around them. A group of people congregates around a camera that's half assembled on the boardwalk.

I step out of the van and catch my breath, the beauty of the place really settling in. Spinning slowly, I take it all in, wishing I had a camera but knowing it could never capture everything— the wet scent on the air, the soft rustle of waves, and the emptiness of the village, whose inhabitants have mostly gone out to work on the boats that dot the harbor.

We don't have anything like this in Tennessee. You can drive out into the country and listen to the cicadas on a summer night or hike into the Smokey Mountains, but you can't find anywhere this untouched by modernity.

Sophie links her arm through mine, pulling me out of my thoughts. I realize that the boys have already disappeared, probably into a makeup or wardrobe tent. She leads me into the catering tent, but I decline the offer of dumplings and fruit that looks like it's been sitting out since yesterday.

"They won't be ready to shoot for at least an hour," Sophie says. "Do you want to explore the village?"

"Yes!" I rush after her out of the tent.

We wander up and down the streets of the fishing village, neither of us talking. Sophie and I drift apart as she continues down the street and I fall back, taking my time soaking in the scenery. I pull out my phone and stick one earbud in, finding the only song that can capture this moment—the Verve's "Bitter Sweet Symphony." The slicing violins lull me further into the surreal feeling, and all I want to do is dance. Or run. Or throw my arms out and spin until I can't see straight.

All the anxiety that's been brewing inside me since I arrived— since Nathan's incident, really—ebbs until I can no longer feel its presence in the back of my mind. For the first time since my brother called me that night, I can breathe. This feeling—this peace—will probably disappear as soon as I set foot back at school. But for now, I can relish not having to hold back emotions, to just be real.

As I walk through the village, a pack of children begins to

follow a few paces behind me, their big, dark eyes watching me with curiosity. One of them, a girl who's maybe seven, ventures closer. I pull the earbud out and wave.

"Ahn nyeong ha se yo," I say, not sure if they speak Korean or a local dialect.

She giggles, and I realize I probably should have said *hello* in a less formal way.

She steps up close to me, and I bend down. She fingers a lock of my hair, which has curled into a ringlet since I haven't washed it in two days.

"Yeppeun," she says, and I've picked up enough Korean to know she just said I'm pretty, and I wish I knew enough vocabulary to tell her she is too.

An older woman calls out to the kids, and they disperse with adorable squeals. Guess Grandma had stuff for them to do.

I peer at one of the homes, where a little boy peeks around the doorframe, and it hits me—this is what I've been searching for, here in this little village, so far from the school I never would have known it existed. Why I came to Korea in the first place.

This is what freedom feels like—totally lost, totally out of place. But in a good way.

In a *great* way.

Chapter Eleven

I wipe sweat off my forehead with the back of my hand, and a shudder zips down my back at the same time. Fighting a whimper, I set my palm against my stomach. My nausea has only gotten worse, and I haven't been able to eat or drink anything since I hauled myself out of bed.

The crew has set up the camera on a rickety raft that looks like it might capsize any second. Fishermen tie up their boats farther down the dock, hauling in their latest catch. Their fish fill the air with a murky smell that makes me want to look for the nearest bucket to hurl into.

Sophie's chatting up one of the camera guys, but I stand off a few paces to the side, not ready to whip out my Korean skills—or lack thereof. My one-word conversation with the kids will tide me over for at least a week.

A group of three fishermen head down the boardwalk toward us, wearing identical black pants that reach just below their knees and straw hats covering their faces. I wonder why their hands are empty until they get closer, and I recognize them. Laughter bursts from my mouth before I can bite it back, and Jason glares at me from underneath his wide-brim hat.

Sophie breaks off her conversation with the cameraman, and she joins in my laughter. "You three look ridiculous," she says through giggles.

Yoon Jae spins. "Really? I like it. I was thinking about wearing it at school."

Jason scowls, and when he catches my eye, I have to bite my lip to keep from grinning. The extra nausea is worth getting a good laugh at him.

The director arrives on set, and filming launches. The boys step into a boat barely large enough for all three of them. Yoon Jae is handed a pole to guide them through the water, and Jason and Tae Hwa each hold one side of a gigantic net.

Sophie and I stand to the left of the camera, snickering under our breaths. Again, I wish for my camera. Jason needs to see how ridiculously awkward and out of place he looks.

The boys launch into "fishing." I don't have any experience with the fishing industry, but I'm fairly certain they're not doing it right.

Yoon Jae manages to move them a few feet through the water, the muscles in his arms straining as he fights the tide. But Tae Hwa and Jason struggle to cast the net. They throw it, but it slaps the water only a few feet away from the boat.

Frustration visible in his scowl, Jason braces his foot against the rim of the boat and leans out to throw the net farther—

And pitches forward.

He hits the water face-first with a loud *clap*.

Jason's head bobs to the surface, and he sputters, hair plastered to his face. Once we ascertain he isn't going to drown, Sophie and I can't contain our intense amusement. I laugh so hard, I have to hold my stomach to keep myself from gagging.

Once his feet are firmly back on the dock, he rips the hat

from his head and stomps toward shore. When he passes me, he drips water on my shoes.

"Hey, watch it!" I cry with a snicker.

"Why don't *you* get in there and try it?" he snaps.

A flint of irritation sparks inside my chest at his snippy tone, and my hands gravitate to my hips. "I was just kidding. Loosen up."

He storms off, muttering in Korean.

I sigh. "Sophie, what is this song even about?"

She squints against the sun's glare off the water. "Unlikely love. The chorus talks about unexpectedly falling for someone who's different from you but trying to work it out. It's hard to translate into English."

I nod, but my pulse spikes at the mention of loving someone unexpected. The question of when Jason wrote the song springs to my lips, but I hold it back. The song probably appears on their album, one of the ones they played at the club where I watched them perform. Still, my mind clicks through every girl I've seen him talking to, trying to figure out who he might have written the song about.

Filming continues when Jason returns—freshly dried—with the guys performing various actions fishermen do every day. They grunt carrying giant nets full of fish across the boardwalk, and they get tangled in the rope as they try to tie the boat to the dock. The more I watch, the more respect I have for the people who do this type of work every day.

Around two, the boys disappear into wardrobe for about half an hour, then reappear dressed in their typical, fashionable ensembles. A pretty girl shows up in clothes similar to what the boys were wearing earlier, and she shoots a few scenes with Jason, mostly him following her around as she completes chores. It would be cute if I didn't feel like I were suffocating—both from the queasiness that keeps worsening and the irritation swelling inside my chest at watching him smile at her. I'll never be the recipient of that smile. We're barely even friends. And that shouldn't bother me as much as it does.

I turn to look away a little too fast, and a chill rushes all the way from my hairline to my toes, followed by a wave of light-headedness. Okay, weird. I sway, lights exploding and clouding my vision. I stumble into Sophie, who grabs my arm, and I shake my head to get rid of the dizziness.

"Are you okay?" Sophie asks.

"Fine," I mumble, though I'm starting to wonder if maybe I should get some water.

My legs quiver. I think the nausea is getting the best of me . . .

A breeze brushes against my sweaty skin, and I shiver. How long has it been since I drank anything? My knees buckle, and I slump against Sophie. She attempts to grab me, but I feel my body crashing onto the boardwalk as I black out.

"Grace?"

I blink my eyes until the blurry image in front of me clears into Jason's face, eyebrows pulled together and jaw tight. He leans so close, I can imagine his warm breath against my face.

"Grace, are you all right?" he asks.

"What?" I croak.

I push up on my hands and close my eyes against the swimminess in my head. Jason supports my back and passes me a bottle of water, his body shading me from the afternoon sun.

"Drink something," he says, our heads still bent close. "Do you feel okay?"

"I've been feeling sick to my stomach all day." I press my face into my palms.

"Is she okay?" Sophie shoves Jason out of the way to inspect me herself, eyes wide behind her glasses. "Grace, don't you *ever* do something like that again! You scared me!"

I chug half the bottle of water, my stomach flipping like it's on a roller coaster. "I'll try to keep that in mind."

"You should probably go sit for a while," she says. "If you're feeling sick."

I glance down and notice I'm still sprawled out on the boardwalk, the crew busy around us. Embarrassment heating my cheeks, I attempt to stand. But dizziness immobilizes me again, and I stumble. A hand grabs onto my elbow and steadies me, adding enough support to keep me on my feet.

"Be careful." Jason wraps his arm around me and hooks his hand on my waist, helping balance me as we slowly make our way toward the path to the village.

"Thanks," I mutter, all the blood that drained out of my head now zinging through me so fast it feels like I'm sprinting.

Heat flares where his body touches mine—our hips bumping each other, his fingers curled around my side—despite my already flushed skin. I peer over my shoulder to see most of the crew members, along with Sophie and the boys, watching us, and I'm struck with the desire for the ground to swallow me.

We inch our way down the dock. I search my thoughts for anything intelligible to say but come up with nothing. He doesn't say anything, either, and I have to wonder if his body is buzzing like mine. Does he catch his breath each time I stumble into him or my hair brushes his cheek? By the time we make it to the camp of tents, I'm near hyperventilation. My body screeched to a halt before I fainted, and now it's running on overdrive.

Jason deposits me in a plastic chair underneath one of the sideless tents and brings me another water bottle and a pack of cookies, along with the backpack he brought with him from the hotel this morning. And I'm struck with the realization that he's being . . . helpful.

Helpful Jason.

Huh.

"You should rest for a while," he says. "Are you sure you're fine?"

"Yeah." I wave away his concern. "I'm sure it's just a virus or something. It'll pass."

He hesitates a moment, his eyes searching out mine. "I'm serious—just take it easy for a little while, all right?"

I force a smile, but my stomach somersaults. "Will do."

He rifles through the backpack and pulls out his iPod. "Here, you can listen to this if you want to. I uploaded the songs you told me to research."

I take it from him, making sure our fingers don't touch. "Is any of your music on here?"

He frowns. "Yes."

"The song this video is for?"

He nods. "In English, the title is 'Love Story.'"

"Like the Taylor Swift song?"

One of his rare smiles cracks his reserved exterior, and I catch a glimpse of real emotion. Our gazes meet, and my chest tightens.

Jason backs out of the tent and turns back toward the docks. I watch him retreat, marveling at the amount of concern he showed me. Very un-Jason-like. *Or maybe it is Jason-like, and I just haven't seen this side of him before.*

Filming continues for another few hours. Sophie comes to sit with me, and we chat about school, the fishy smell that makes us wrinkle our noses, and how long it will take for the crew to finish. After a few crackers and some medicine from the crew's medic, my stomach's settling.

Shooting ends with Eden setting up their instruments in the middle of the village and playing the chorus a few times.

As we all head back to the van, Yoon Jae falls into step beside me. "Are you feeling better?" he asks.

"A little, yeah. Thanks."

"We were all worried."

I scratch the back of my neck. "Yeah, sorry. My blood sugar was really low, I think, and whatever I've got was making me light-headed. I didn't mean to interrupt."

"No, don't worry about it. I wasn't trying to make you feel guilty."

We drop into silence as he slides open the van door. Yoon Jae holds onto my elbow and helps me in while I crawl into the back row, and he sits beside me. Sophie and Tae Hwa follow us, sitting in the middle row. Jason enters last. He looks back at me and Yoon Jae, his expression darkening a moment, then slides in next to Sophie.

I reach into my bag and pull out Jason's iPod and offer it to him, my arm resting on the back of his seat. "Here. Thanks for letting me listen to it."

He glances at my outstretched hand, then away. "Keep it for now," he says, studiously not looking at me. "I don't need it."

"It's fine, really. I'd rather talk than listen to it in the car anyway."

His gaze slips to Yoon Jae for a moment, then snaps back forward again. "I think you already have someone to talk to."

I lean back, stung. "I . . . "

He folds his arms across his chest and slides lower in his seat, closing his eyes. Like he could sleep in here with Sophie jabbering on at so high a decibel. I stuff the iPod back into my bag with unnecessary force and throw myself back against my seat, staring out the window at the red sun setting behind the mountains. He helps me to the tent, he *smiles* at me, and now he insults me? What is he, bipolar? I should really reevaluate my friendship with this boy.

We head back into town and make our way to the hotel. By the time we arrive, it's dark, and I feel disgusting. Sand and dried sweat make up a thick film on my skin, and all I want is to take a shower and scrub it all off.

But Sophie pipes up with, "How long do we have before we need to leave?"

"We go eight thirty," the driver says through his rolled-down car window.

"Wait, what?" I say.

Sophie glances down at the phone that's permanently glued to her hand. "The band has a meeting with their manager tomorrow afternoon in Incheon, so we need to leave tonight."

I check my watch. If we're leaving at eight thirty, that gives me thirty minutes. Just enough time to throw my things together and take a quick shower. I sprint upstairs and into our room, peeling off filthy clothes before I even have the water in the shower running.

Fifteen minutes later, I'm pulling on a pair of leggings, an oversize T-shirt, and some sandals. Not my best look, but it'll have to do for an eight-hour road trip. I tie my hair into a loose bun and meet the others down in the lobby, where the boys are posing for pictures with the hotel staff.

After the band manages to gracefully escape their fans, we all get back into the van. But this time, I share the back row with Jason. As he settles into his seat after I'm already in, I notice I'm not the only one who showered—he sweeps wet hair out of his eyes with his fingers.

I take out his iPod again and replace his headphones with my earbuds, then stick them in my ears. After searching through a myriad of songs whose names I can't read, I find a playlist called *Grace's Music*. As I scroll through the list of bands that includes some of my favorites, all I can think about is the fact that my name is on his music player and how stupid I am for reading anything into that.

I sneak a sideways glance at him, but he's just staring out the window, shoulders rigid and jaw clenched. Sophie and the other two boys carry on a conversation in front of us, leaving Jason isolated. Because he thinks no one's looking, he's let down his guard, and in the pale light of the streetlamps we pass, I make out melancholy etched deep in his expression. And I'm reminded of my brother.

Again, I remember that there's something deeper here, something he doesn't want anyone to see. I suppress the jolt of dread that rockets through me, fear that he has some dark secret like Nathan. I don't know Jason well enough to leap to such conclusions. But I *can* surmise that his isolating himself and keeping his feelings away from everyone else isn't helping.

Shoving the memory of him snapping at me earlier to the back of my mind, I pull out one of the earbuds and reach across the darkness between us, offering it to him. He stares at it a second, then takes it from my fingers and places it in his ear. The cord pulls taut between our heads, and he has to scoot closer, our shoulders brushing. I smile and close my eyes, leaning my head back against the seat and getting lost in the relaxed melodies and soft, plucking guitar of Bon Iver.

Drowsiness settles on me as the subtle rocking of the van and the long day breaks down any fight in me to stay conscious. As I hover between sleep and wakefulness, I feel a soft touch on my fingers that rest on the seat between me and Jason.

"Grace?" Jason whispers.

But I don't answer, eyes heavy and lips parted in half sleep.

Another brush against my hand. A solid, warm pressure. My brain jolts awake when Jason threads his fingers through mine. I swallow hard, and my breathing accelerates.

I risk a quick peek at Jason, my eyes squinted so I can shut them again at a moment's notice. He peers out his window still, but instead of tension making the lines of his body sharp, he angles himself toward me, muscles relaxed. A soft smile plays at the edges of his lips, and his fingers twitch against mine, our palms pressed together.

Does he think I'm asleep? Should I tell him I'm awake? My mind races through possible motivations for him grabbing my hand, followed by what might happen if I revealed my not being asleep. He would probably say something mean, and we wouldn't talk for the rest of the trip. So I just keep my mouth shut and let him hold my hand.

And enjoy it entirely too much.

Chapter Twelve

Big Brother,

Do you remember that conversation we had before you left for the Grammys two years ago? I confronted you about how much you were drinking, and you told me that I should "just let it go." Well, I did. I even ignored all the "signs" of depression you exhibited that they write about in those little pamphlets they give away in the school counselor's office. You probably didn't even know I was paying that much attention to you.

But when you got back from Los Angeles, I thought we could talk about everything. I knew Dad wasn't going to help; he was in denial about the whole thing, the way he is about all our family issues. (Either that or he thought I couldn't handle knowing the truth.) But when I saw you, you seemed better. Happier. You wrote some new songs.

I realize now that you were faking it. That's what life was for you back then, faking—don't deny it! I get it now. I just wish I'd understood then.

Sometimes I think I was the one who was supposed to save

*you from it all. Momma sees what she wants to see, Dad
checked out of our lives ten years ago, and Jane is too busy with
her own life to notice something messed up in ours. So that left
me to help you, and let's be honest, I totally failed. I know that's
why Momma refused to look me in the eye after she discovered I
had known about the depression and did nothing. Maybe that's
why Dad pretends like it never happened, because he can't face
his oldest daughter and how she screwed up his family.*

*Maybe that's why I feel better here, in Korea. Because
nobody knows about my past. Nobody knows about our family.
I can pretend Momma doesn't hate me and that God isn't
trying to get back at me for being stupid. And I can just be me.
You understand that, right?*

*I still miss you, and I'd love more than anything to hear
back from you. I want to hear you tell me you don't think I
caused this. I want you to say it's not my fault.*

*From Korea, with love,
Grace*

October flies by with me studying like crazy for midsemester exams in November, which all seem to hit at the same time. Sophie and I don't go out on music video shenanigans with the boys anymore. We hole ourselves up in our room and hide away from the fact that we're going insane with all the homework and tests teachers like to give.

I thought senior year was supposed to be easy. Lies. The school doesn't have the same literature requirements as an American high school, so I don't have to read Tennyson or Walt Whitman or Fitzgerald, but instead I'm stuck with a multitude of essays on Buddhism, classical Korean poetry, and an entire unit on literature about the Japanese occupation of Korea. Talk about tough.

Sophie goes to tutoring after school, like a lot of the other students, so that leaves me a lot of alone time. I try distracting myself by hanging out with Yoon Jae, but I still worry about what I left back home.

Doesn't help that I'm getting *calls* from reporters now, wanting to know if I'm available for interview. The same one keeps leaving messages on my voice mail, really pitching a *"front page feature and maybe even a photo shoot."* He wants to hear *"your story, told in your words."*

Uh-huh.

More like he wants me to spill something juicy. I emailed Dad about it, hoping he could maybe pull some strings and get the reporter's editor to call the guy off, but in typical Dad fashion, he didn't answer.

And even though I'm beginning to wonder if school in Korea is harder than in America, I'm grateful not to still be in Tennessee. At home. With the press hovering and the awkwardness with Momma—and Dad ignoring us all the time. That reporter might have scrounged up my cell number, but at least he doesn't know what school I'm attending in South Korea.

Jason and I finish up his song for the TV drama right before the deadline, although he refuses to let me listen to the finished product.

"You can wait and hear it air on TV," he says when I pester him about it in class.

I give up asking him about it as November passes much like October did, but I can't shake the curiosity. And I'll be honest—I miss hanging out with him in the practice room, arguing over the sheet music. We still meet up in the library sometimes to study Korean, but that offers a lot less time for conversations about anything nonacademic. I'm a step away from failing that class, and he's taken it upon himself to get me through with a passing grade.

I wake up on Thursday to find a new email in my inbox. I

check it while brushing my teeth and almost drop the toothbrush in the sink out of shock. It's from my mother.

> *Grace,*
> *Your father and I want to know when your fall semes-*
> *ter is over so that we can buy your plane ticket home*
> *for Christmas. Please respond soon before ticket*
> *prices go up.*
> *Mom*

I snort but can't deny the stab of fear that shoots through my chest. Still, since when has a dollar ever held back my parents? When you've got more than $100 million sitting in your savings account, a first-class ticket from Seoul to Nashville doesn't even count as an expense—it's pocket change.

On my way to class, I can't stop thinking about Momma's email. Going home for Christmas. I hadn't even thought about it before now. I figured I would stay on Ganghwa Island. I can't go back to Nashville. I can't see my parents.

Are Sophie and Jason going home? I don't really know much about their family situation, whether or not they like hanging out with their parents—they don't seem to like talking much about their family. Their parents are divorced and their dad lives in New York, so I assume they'll visit their mom in Seoul instead.

During my math class, I fire a text to Jane: *Please tell me Momma isn't serious about me coming home for Christmas.*

She responds almost immediately: *r u crazy?! you HAVE to come home! im goin insane here w/out you!*

I glance up to see if my teacher has noticed me texting, but he's still writing equations on the board. I text back: *I can't face them. Momma hates me.*

My phone vibrates a minute later. *she doesnt HATE*

you . . . she just doesnt know what to say. PLEASE come see me! or buy me a ticket to come see you!!!!!

A smile pulls at my lips. I would love to show Jane around Incheon—or, better yet, Seoul: Introduce her to Sophie, take her to the famous shopping districts, watch her drool all over Yoon Jae. But Momma would kill me if I invited Jane and neither of her daughters was sitting at the Christmas dinner table this year.

Jane, I write, *you know that won't work. I'll figure something out. Do you want to video chat this weekend?*

Before I can even set my phone down, her text comes in: *YES!!!!!!!! AND BRING THE HOT KOREAN WITH YOU!*

I stifle a laugh, masking it as a violent cough, which makes my teacher shoot me a look of irritation. But at the end of class, I'm still chuckling over Jane's text. Gah, I miss her. I forgot how much we talked before I left, how much I depend on her humor. Sophie's a great friend, but she can't take the place of my sister.

When I get back to the dorm, Sophie's sitting at her desk, rifling through her notebook. She jumps to her feet when I enter and cries, "Where have you been? Didn't your class end half an hour ago?"

I drop my backpack onto the floor. "Yeah, but I had to run by the bookstore to pick up a few things. Why?"

"We're going out tonight."

"It's a Thursday."

"But it's an *important* Thursday."

"Sophie, what are you talking about?"

She rolls her eyes behind her glasses. "I can't believe you forgot. And you call yourself an American."

I watch her grab her purse and double-check her makeup in the mirror. "Okay, now I'm seriously curious," I say. "What are you on about?"

She shrugs. "I guess you'll just have to come with me and find out."

We head out of the dorm and hop on her motorbike. I close my eyes the entire way to Incheon. After she parks on a side street, she leads me into a part of town I instantly recognize. The neon lights, brick-laid courtyards packed with people, shops, and restaurants bubbling over with crowds. A soccer game plays on a huge screen attached to a building as we pass cosmetic and clothing stores blaring KPOP out their open front doors.

Sophie turns us down a side street onto a less busy sidewalk, and I'm beginning to wonder if we have some sort of meeting with Korean gangsters. What does this outing have to do with being American?

I'm just about to ask her what's going on when she turns aside to a building with *Hangul* lettering written on the glass storefront. I keep close on her heels, and when we walk inside, I'm accosted by a familiar smell. My heart leaps into my throat. This can't be. Surely not. It's impossible.

It smells like barbecue!

And I don't mean Korean barbecue, where you cook your own meat, which is good in its own right.

I'm talking *BBQ* barbecue.

Good ole Southern, slow-roasted pork in the most heavenly sauce ever invented. It smells like home.

I can't keep my mouth from pooling with saliva. When was the last time I ate American food? I've tried to keep my diet filled with rice and noodles, hoping it would help me transition into the Korean lifestyle. And although I'm really starting to like the food here, I've never missed my Momma's cooking so much in my life.

The host at the front of the restaurant offers us a little bow and lets us pass. Sophie makes a beeline to a back table, where I see two familiar faces. Tae Hwa and Jason both look up as we drop into seats facing them at a white tablecloth–covered table as far away from the window as possible.

"What's going on here?" I ask, after taking another deep breath of BBQ-flavored air. "Why are we eating American food?"

Jason shoots me a disbelieving look. "It's Thanksgiving. How could you forget that?"

"I thought we already had Thanksgiving last month. What's it called? *Chuseok*."

I only remember because we got out of school for three days. Sophie tried to explain that it's a huge holiday over here, which people spend with their families, respecting ancestors and eating lots of traditional food. A lot of students stayed at the school since most of us aren't actually Korean, but Sophie took me to a traditional Korean restaurant, so I still felt like I got to experience some culture—amazingly fun.

But Jason just stares at me with a bemused expression. "I mean *American* Thanksgiving."

"Wait." I freeze. "Are you serious?"

I whip out my phone and check the calendar. He's right. Today is Thanksgiving. In roughly fourteen hours, my family will be eating turkey and dressing, mashed potatoes, and pecan pie. Momma will make Jane eat yams before she can have a slice of pumpkin pie, and Dad will watch football all evening.

And I'm sitting at a barbecue place in South Korea. Talk about surreal.

"We thought you might be missing home today," Sophie says, skimming the menu with a wrinkled nose, "so we planned to take you out. An old American man owns this place. He stayed after the Korean War. Had we known you didn't even remember what day it is, we would have gone someplace better than this."

Jason leans across the table toward me and mock whispers, "Sophie doesn't like American food."

"That's not true!" She glares at him. "I just don't like *this* kind of American food. We should have gone out for pizza. Or burgers."

"We decided barbecue was better because Grace is Southern," Jason says.

"No, *you* decided barbecue because Grace is Southern," Sophie shoots back. "*I* thought she would appreciate a good Italian Thanksgiving."

Normally, I would laugh at the sibling bickering, but after texting with Jane this morning, hearing Jason and Sophie makes my chest ache. The backs of my eyes burn, and I stare down at the menu and blink furiously to hold back tears. Sophie launches into a conversation with Tae Hwa in Korean, and I attempt to shrink out of notice. But Jason catches my eye.

His brows pull together. "Are you okay?" he says in a quiet voice.

"What?" I force a tight smile. "Of course! It's so nice of y'all to do this for me. I really appreciate it."

He doesn't respond, but he doesn't look convinced, either. After a moment of awkward silence between us, he glances down at the menu, and I let out a deep sigh. With his attention diverted, I take the time to notice his blue button-down shirt with sleeves rolled up to the elbows and the silver cross necklace hanging between his collarbones. I'm not sure what it is, but he has the most attractive collarbones I've ever seen.

Heat climbs up my neck when I think back to the ride back to Ganghwa Island after the music video shoot. I haven't gotten up the courage to ask him about why he held my hand. Although he's been nice to me since then, he's never attempted any more physical contact. The only time I ever touch him is when he drives me to the dorms on the back of his bicycle, though I've mastered the art of balancing while holding on to as little of him as possible.

The server comes around, and Sophie orders all our drinks.

"And, Grace, don't you even think about paying," she says. "This is your day . . . Jason will pay for everybody."

She shoots a sly grin at her brother, who rolls his eyes but doesn't argue.

I order the biggest plate of pulled pork they have and chow down like I'm never going to eat again. A side of French fries doesn't compare to coleslaw and corn bread, but I'm just happy to be eating something other than rice for a change. The meat isn't as good as it is back home, but the sauce is Memphis style—sweet and spicy, with just the right amount of brown sugar and vinegar.

The owner even comes out to talk to me, and we reminisce about Tennessee and argue about which city's better, Nashville or his hometown of Chattanooga.

On our way out, a familiar song plays on the radio, and I point to the ceiling, where I assume the speakers are located.

"Hey, that's an Eden song!" I shoot Jason a grin.

Sophie beams, patting him on the back, but he just rolls his eyes. Still, he can't hide the blush that colors his cheeks.

Outside, Jason instantly slaps a pair of sunglasses over his eyes—like that's going to hide his identity—but I don't argue.

Sophie grabs Tae Hwa's arm. "Hey, we're going to run a few errands before we go back, and we'll take the motorbike. Jason, do you mind taking Grace back?" She glances at me. "Unless you want to come with us. I don't know how we'd all fit on my bike, though."

"No, it's okay! I need to get back and do some homework anyway," I say.

Really, I just don't want to cut into Sophie's alone time with Tae Hwa. Although she insists that they're not dating and that she only likes him as a family friend, I have my doubts. For one, she touches him whenever possible . . . like now.

I wrap my arms around her in a swift hug. "Thanks again for the surprise Thanksgiving."

"No problem," she says. "It was fun!"

She and Tae Hwa turn and head down the street, disappearing

into the crowd of other pedestrians and leaving me and Jason standing outside the restaurant. We make our way in the opposite direction from Sophie, his head down the entire way—whether because he doesn't want to be recognized or he's disappointed to be spending the rest of the evening with me, I don't know.

"Do you want to head back now or walk around a bit first?" he asks. "I need to let the driver know."

"Why does it not surprise me that you had someone drive you down here instead of taking the bus?"

He shrugs.

I peer up at the clear sky, where I know millions of tiny stars gleam down on us, even though I can't see them through the smog and city lights. "I've got a lot of homework waiting for me," I say.

His thumb hovers over the phone screen.

"That meant I don't especially want to go back," I add with a laugh.

"Oh." He flashes me a rare smile as he shoots off the text.

We wander down the street, just two people lost in the crowds we never see on Ganghwa Island. Traffic creeps down the clogged streets, even though it's already past seven o'clock and most work commuters have headed home.

A pair of girls brushes past us, then pauses, staring at me. One of them steps up to Jason, and I expect her to ask for an autograph. Or start screaming at the top of her lungs. Because that seems like a popular thing for Korean fangirls to do.

Though I really can't judge. I went through my own boy band phase in middle school.

But instead of throwing herself at Jason, the girl pulls out a phone and points it at *me*. She looks at Jason and says something in Korean, and he responds with a nod.

"She wants a picture with you," he says.

"*What?* Does she not know who you are?"

He chuckles. "I don't know, but she didn't ask for me to be in the picture."

The girl flashes me a smile. "Picture please."

"Umm . . . okay."

She and her friend giggle as they flank me. They throw up peace signs, so I jump in on that action. After Jason flashes the picture, the girls give me low bows.

"Thank you," they say, then scurry away, chattering to each other.

"What was that about?" I ask.

Jason laughs under his breath. "They recognized you from American tabloids. They said they like you because of your hair."

"Oh. Well, that's a new one."

The only people I'm used to being recognized by are aspiring musicians hoping to use me to get to Dad. Or, more recently, reporters looking for a new scoop on my family drama.

He shoves his hands into the front pockets of his jeans. "It's kind of nice. You being the one they recognize instead of me. Maybe I should hang out with you more often."

My stomach flips at the suggestion.

But then he says, "Not that I understand why they like you because of your hair."

I bristle, all fuzzy feelings now dead. "Well, maybe some people appreciate blond hair."

"I guess." He shrugs. "But it just looks fake to me. Almost everyone who's blond isn't *naturally* blond."

My temper flares, and I'm ready to inform him that I am, in fact, a natural blonde—until I see the wry smile on his lips. I roll my eyes. I almost liked him better before he discovered a sense of humor.

"Yeah, well, I can't really see why people like Korean boy bands, either," I say.

He chuckles. "So, did you like your Thanksgiving dinner?"

he asks as we pass a giant bank building with windows illuminated and people still sitting at desks.

"I did. I'm assuming it was Sophie's idea."

A smile plays at his lips. "Mine, actually."

I scoff, though I can't deny the spark of appreciation that ignites in my chest.

"I'm sure you miss being with your family," he says.

The warmth coursing through me at his thoughtfulness instantly freezes. "My family. Right. Well, actually, I'm sort of glad to not be there. It sounds terrible, but it's true."

He glances sideways at me. "Why don't you want to be with them?"

I blow out a long breath, scuffing my shoes against the sidewalk. "There's just a lot of tension at home these days. And I don't get along with my mother very well."

Saying it out loud, I feel a rush of relief. The anxiety piling up inside me since I received her email seeps out with each word.

My voice drops to a murmur. "She sort of hates me, honestly."

"I'm sure she doesn't hate you. She's your mom."

I bark a laugh, but it's filled more with pain than amusement. "You don't know my mother."

We're silent so long, I fear I've made him uncomfortable. I open my mouth to break the awkwardness, but he beats me to it. "My father and I haven't spoken in three years. Your relationship with your mother can't be as bad as that."

I deny the urge to gape at him, not because of his confession but because he said it at all. He's not exactly one to provide details about himself.

"What happened between you two?" I add quickly, "If you don't mind my asking."

His jaw tightens. "We disagree on a lot of stuff. He took Sophie and me away from our mother when he moved to America and wouldn't let us return to Korea until we were fourteen."

So he hasn't forgiven his father for separating him and Sophie from their mom. I can understand that, but it seems a bit harsh to not have spoken to him in three years. Not that I've been really chatty with Momma lately. If I could get away with not talking to *her* for three years, I'd probably do it.

"Why did your dad move to the States?"

He runs a hand through his hair, scratching at his scalp. "He and my mother divorced right after she got pregnant. My father . . . cheated on her," he says through clenched teeth, his tone thick with disdain. "And he went to America to live with his mistress. They just got married about three years ago."

"Was the woman American?" I should probably stop asking questions, prying into his past, but my curiosity outweighs any sense of social etiquette. Besides, he's still answering, isn't he?

He shakes his head. "She was Korean. His secretary."

Ouch. And talk about cliché.

"So she's your stepmom now?"

He slows to a halt in front of a crowded bar, staring out at the street with blank eyes. "Yeah. They live together in New York. With three kids."

The bitter sharpness in his expression melts into a wearied sorrow, like he's carried the weight of these emotions a long time without any sort of respite. The impulse to place my arm on his shoulder or take his hand to comfort him flashes through my brain, but I stomp it down, telling myself it would only complicate our friendship. He's finally decided he trusts me enough to open up; I'm not ruining that by crossing any boundaries.

"I'm sure your dad loves you," I say, more as a last resort because I can't think of anything better. "He obviously wanted you and Sophie to live with him."

Anger flashes in his eyes. "He wanted us to live with him because he wanted to ruin my mother's life, that's all. He never loved us."

I've no idea how to respond, so I keep quiet, hovering beside him, waiting for any cues as to how I should react. He stands there a moment longer before a light flashes, and I notice the gigantic camera suddenly in our faces.

The paparazzo guy shamelessly clicks away at Jason, gaining the attention of people passing by. Jason tenses, throwing his hand in front of the camera. He says something to the guy in Korean, probably, *Get out of my face, dude,* but the photographer doesn't budge.

With a huff, Jason turns his back on the camera, grabs my wrist, and pulls me away from the retina-burning flashes. We speed down the sidewalk at a half jog, and after a quick text to his driver, the car shows up and we disappear behind the protection of tinted windows.

The ride back to school is long and silent, and I can't help wondering if the run-in with the photographer ruined our evening, though it could be in my favor that Jason not think too hard about our conversation. I worry he'll regret telling me about his past, and I have no idea how to assure him that he can trust me.

The driver drops us off in front of the entrance to the school, and we walk back to our dorms, still not talking. My mind races for any words that might rewind our conversation to a place where we haven't lost any ground in our relationship. I'll kick myself if my prying questions have made him less keen on hanging out with me.

We pause outside my dorm, and he hesitates. "I'm sorry for . . . how crazy my life is sometimes," he says, not meeting my gaze.

"No!" I cry, with probably too much vigor. "It's fine. I umm . . . like hearing about you. And Sophie. Your family."

"What?" He tilts his head to the side and stares at me a second before his mouth forms an *O*. "No, I meant with the photographer."

"Oh! Well, that's fine, too." I breathe a self-conscious laugh. "I mean, I totally understand the crazy."

"Right." He gives an almost imperceptible nod, then mutters, "Also, uhh . . . thanks for listening. You know. About my dad."

"No worries. I mean, y'all planned the whole Thanksgiving thing. It means a lot to me that you guys—" My voice breaks off, and I bite down on my bottom lip. "That *you* would do that for me."

He jerks a nod, staring down at his foot, which scuffs the sidewalk. But even in the pale light from the streetlamps, I can see the smile curling his lips.

We fall quiet. I wait for him to leave, to interrupt our nice evening with an insensitive, inappropriate, or otherwise mean word. But he doesn't, and I feel the need to bridge the silence between us.

"I've got to figure out how to ditch my parents for Christmas." I force a laugh, though my throat feels like it might close up. "My mom emailed me today and said I needed to tell her when to buy my airplane ticket, but I definitely don't want to spend an entire month at home."

He catches my eye, a new, earnest spark in his. "Are you going to spend Christmas here, then?"

"No idea. But anything's better than Nashville. I just wish I could steal my little sister so we could be together."

"Well, Sophie and I are going home for the break, so you'll be in the dorm alone."

My heart sinks. The improbable hope that I'd held on to that they would choose to stay here at school withers. Looks like it'll either be a stressful or a lonely holiday for me.

"Oh," I manage. "Okay."

"We're going to spend Christmas with my mother," he continues. "And I have to start working on the drama."

"Oh yeah, your drama." I cut my eyes to him. "I'm sure you're excited to see your face on the small screen."

He scowls, but there's no effort in it. "I'm dreading it, actually. But what I was thinking was that, maybe you would like . . . if you have no interest in going home . . . I'm not sure if you would want to—don't feel you have to accept—"

"Jeez, Jason," I interrupt. "Out with it."

His cheeks redden, and my stomach flip-flops. I had no idea it could be sexy for a guy to blush.

"I thought you might like to spend the break with us," he finally says. "In Seoul."

I'm shocked silent. He wants *me* to spend Christmas with *him*? Or rather, his family? But he'll be there. Working, yeah, but still present. And hopefully in adorable scarves and gloves that match his colorful shoes.

Momma will kill me. No way will she let me go home with people she's never met. Especially not for a holiday.

Good thing she's not here to stop me.

Chapter Thirteen

After Thanksgiving, midterms arrive and throw me into one of the most stressful weeks of my life. I've officially decided high school in Korea—especially at a school for rich kids with parents who expect them to get into good colleges—is way harder than in America. Between long study sessions in the library and enough stress to keep perpetual purple circles beneath my eyes, I'm ready to quit school and buy a private island with my trust fund, where I can sit by the beach every day.

Also, cold weather has officially arrived. Venturing outside is practically like braving the Arctic tundra.

My first midterm is physics, my easiest class. The others are spread out throughout the week. After school, I head back to the dorm and find Sophie curled up on her bed with her laptop. When I slam the door shut, she shushes me.

"What are you watching?" I stand on the edge of my bed and peer up at her screen. "One of those Korean soap operas again?"

"It's not a soap opera!" She huffs, clutching the blanket over her mouth, her eyes so wide they might pop out of their sockets.

"Those shows can't be that interesting."

She tears her gaze away from the screen long enough to shoot me a death glare. "You don't even know."

I laugh, dropping back down to the floor. "Fine. What's it about?"

She pauses the video. "It's only the most romantic story ever!"

I yank off my shoes and collapse on my bed, a dull headache settling beneath my eyebrows. Physics problems float around my brain.

"You say that about all of them."

She sighs. "Be quiet and listen. It's about a guy who's trying to end political corruption, but he has to do it secretly."

"Like a superhero?"

"Exactly! But without the costume."

"And how is this romantic?"

"Because he can't be with the girl he loves!" She pounds her fist against the mattress with such vengeance I'm wondering if this show really *is* worth watching. "She doesn't know that he's actually the one outing all the bad guys, and she doesn't like him. But he's really a good person; she just doesn't know it."

"That sounds like Spider-Man. Or Batman. Or both rolled into one."

"It's wonderful." She bolts up in bed. "You should watch it. Now."

"I don't think so . . . "

"Come on! I've been trying to get you to watch a Korean drama for months. Give it a chance."

Sophie snatches up my laptop and searches for a website to view the show online with English subtitles, and I can't really say no when the alternative to watching the show is studying some more.

We spend the next *three hours* watching episodes from the beginning, and by dinnertime I'm starving but so addicted to the story that I have to know what happens. We run down to the cafeteria and eat as quickly as possible, then detox all the stress from midterms by watching four more episodes before crashing.

If the drama Jason's going to be in is this good, I might just have to watch it.

"You'll do fine, Grace," Jason whispers to me as we flip over our Korean exams. "Don't stress yourself out."

Don't stress myself out. Right. Calm. Focus. I can do this.

He flashes me a smile, and my insides squirm. How can I focus when he's freaking grinning at me? He smiles so little, I should fear the apocalypse.

I rip my attention away from him and focus on the paper.

I got this.

No problem.

Iron, cobalt, nickel, copper, zinc . . .

I move the pencil slowly across the paper, making my lines just like Jason showed me.

I move through the exam with a lot less difficulty than I expected. Each time I run across a translation I'm unsure about, I think back to our study sessions in the library, Jason's head bent over the textbook and his calm, even voice explaining vocabulary words and grammar.

An hour and a half later, I practically float through my next exam, knowing I did way better on the Korean test than I expected.

After our last class before winter break, Jason and I walk together toward the dorms. We tilt our chins down to hunker against the freezing wind blowing across campus.

"I can't believe I'm done with all my midterms," I say. "Done. Free."

Jason nods. "You have officially completed your first semester in Korea."

"You're right. Wow." I stop in the middle of the path. "That's insane."

He pauses and turns around to face me. "Why?"

"Because if I'd stayed home, I would still be at my old school, applying for colleges and stressing about the graduation test at the end of the year. I'm only seventeen, and I'm living in South Korea, going to graduate in six months with zero plans for college. My parents are terrible people for letting me do this."

Laughter explodes from his mouth, louder than I've ever heard from him, and a grin lights up his face. I resist the urge to clutch my chest as my heart threatens to stop, and not only from shock. I'll admit it—I'm incredibly turned on right now.

Breathe, Grace.

"But if they hadn't let you come here, you never would have met Sophie." His smile softens. "Or me."

If he keeps this up, I'm going to have a legitimate heart attack. I pray my face hasn't turned the bright red of his shirt. Just like a boy to send your head spinning and mean absolutely nothing by what he says. I prefer to think that Jason has no idea what he's implying instead of him buttering me up to get something.

I force my legs to resume walking, buying me time to think of a response. "Yeah, Korea is a lot more fun than Nashville. Promise."

And I mean it. It was an awkward transition at first, and I saw a lot of negatives for the first few months about basically everything. But now I feel like I actually belong, and I wouldn't give up rice and chopsticks for corn bread and grits.

He falls into step beside me. "I'd like to visit the South sometime. I met your father in New York, but he spoke highly of Tennessee."

"It's been sort of bugging me—where did you see him? No offense, but I'm not sure he recognizes any value in KPOP."

"My father owns a hotel chain that a lot of wealthy people

frequent. Your father stayed there while visiting New York, and my father introduced me to him."

"Well, I hope he wasn't too rude." I laugh, though I secretly pray he really wasn't—Dad's not exactly known for his social skills.

"He was polite."

"That's nice of you to say, but I'm sure—"

I'm interrupted by loud buzzing from my backpack. I fish out my phone, check the caller ID, and nearly drop it on the pavement.

"What's wrong?" Jason asks.

"It—it's my mom." My pulse kicks into overdrive.

This most likely has something to do with the email I sent her last week that read, *I'm actually spending Christmas with some friends from school. I'll email you later with more details.* Never did send that second email. Oops.

I take a steadying breath before I answer. "Hello?"

"Grace?" Momma screeches in my ear, like she thinks she has to talk extra loud because we're an ocean away. "Grace, is that you?"

"Yes." Who else would have my phone?

"I got your email." She falls silent, either waiting for me to respond or allowing a sufficient amount of guilt to build inside me before continuing.

"Okay," I finally say.

Another awkward silence.

Jason shoots me a curious glance, but I angle away from him, letting my hair fall to hide my face from his view.

"You can't be serious about not coming home," Momma says. "We haven't seen you in months."

"I know that, but I was invited and I said yes."

"Tell them you need to see your family." Her tone sharpens, revealing just how much family bonding time she's interested in—none. She's probably just concerned with what her friends will think if her oldest daughter doesn't show up for a holiday gathering.

"I already told you, I'm not going." I turn off the path and take shelter in the shadow of the stairs leading up to the dining hall, keeping my back to the people passing by. "Besides, Dad probably won't even be there. He'll be working, ignoring us like he always does." I huff. "We're not going to argue about this."

"You're right, we're not—because you're coming home!" She raises her voice. "This isn't up for discussion, Grace. You're visiting your family for Christmas. Period."

"*No,* I'm not." I lower my voice to a hiss. "You can't *make* me come home."

"We can yank you out of that school. And don't think I won't. I'm beginning to think you moving over there wasn't a good idea, after all. Do you know how much we've sacrificed for you? We—we need to see you."

Her voice cracks, and, for a moment, I think there might be actual emotion behind her words. But then she says, "And, really, what could you possibly be doing over there that's worthwhile, anyway?"

Tears prick the backs of my eyes, and I spit out through clenched teeth, "I want to spend some time with my friends."

And not with you, I want to say, but I bite back the words.

With my last bit of energy, I throw as much anger into my voice as possible. "I'm spending Christmas with my roommate, and if you don't like that, you can just get over it. I *hate* being at home. Why do you think I left in the first place? Maybe if you'd noticed that, we wouldn't be having this conversation." I swallow the sob that hangs in my throat. "We're done talking."

I hang up and let my arm fall to my side. My legs quiver, and I have to grab onto the side of the building to keep myself upright. Adrenaline courses through me, and my hands start trembling. I just hung up on my mother. I told her she could "just get over" my disobeying her, that I hated my home.

I press my palms against my face, the coolness of my hands meeting the heat of my cheeks. Tears seep through my closed eyelids and slide down into my mouth, but I hold in the heaving sobs that threaten to send me into hysterics in the middle of campus. I reach for the periodic table buried somewhere beneath the fear, the hurt, and the nerves. *Iron, cobalt, nickel, copper, zinc.* I fly through them until the flood of anxiety contracts enough for me to pull in a calming breath.

"Grace, are you okay?"

Jason's voice breaks through the terror and grief churning inside me. My head shoots up, and I swipe at lingering tears with the backs of my hands before turning to face him.

"Fine." I twist my lips into a smile, though it makes my cheeks ache with the effort.

"Was she upset about something?"

"What makes you say that?" I laugh, though it sounds fake even to my ears.

He frowns. "If you want to change your mind and go home, don't feel like you have to come with us. I thought—I mean, *we* thought you would like to come. But we understand if you can't."

"No! No, I want to go. And Momma can just deal with it if I don't go home." This time, my laugh is genuine, and it helps release some of the pressure built up inside my chest.

He still studies me, his gaze perusing my face, no doubt picking up on my splotchy, tear-stained cheeks and the red rims around my eyes. Gah, why can't I be one of those girls who's pretty when she cries?

"You're sure?" he says.

"Positive!" Either because my argument with Momma has left me off-kilter or I can't see how I could screw up any more relationships, I link my arm through Jason's and pull him back onto the main path. "I don't know about you, but I'm ready to celebrate my new independence from studying. Sophie got me obsessed with this Korean TV show. You want to go watch a couple episodes?"

He tenses at my touch but doesn't pull away. "Sure," he mutters.

We spend the rest of the evening holed up with Sophie in our dorm room, eating ramen and watching TV. Jason, Sophie, and I all huddle close on my bed, with me squished between them as we watch the main character in the show kick some major butt.

I catch Jason casting me frequent glances, and my chest tightens at his concern. He even lets me crack a few jokes about KPOP stars turned actors without defending himself, and I find myself calmed by his steadying presence.

And for a few hours, I'm able to forget about Momma and Christmas and how much it hurts to think about home. For a few hours, I can be New Grace—the one that finished her hardest midterm, held hands with a cute boy on a long car ride, and wrote a song with a famous Korean pop star because she kind of likes KPOP now.

I like New Grace. And maybe one day, Momma will, too.

Chapter Fourteen

gracie—

    i'm mad at you, p.s.

    you left me here ALONE with the 'rents, which is essentially the lowest circle of dante's inferno. not okay. i will never forgive you . . . unless you bring me back a cute boy, in which case we will be friends again.

    and i want to hear EVERYTHING about seoul. your little letters to me are pathetic, with your "from korea, with love" at the bottom that i feel sure has only one purpose—to make me insanely jealous. (shocker: it's working)

    how is it you are going to my dream destination right now?! (okay, so maybe tokyo is the dream, but seoul would be second.) you can't see me right now, but i'm glaring at you. i know you are anti-pictures,

but PLEASE take lots for me, okay? missssssssssss
youuuuuu!!!
from hell on earth, with jealousy,
jane

I stuff my phone into my pocket and throw my purse over my shoulder as we pass underneath the school's arch and officially leave campus for Christmas break. I follow Sophie's neon pink suitcase as she rolls it across the pavement toward the shiny black car waiting for us.

Jason trails behind me, a coat wrapped tight around his slim shoulders and collar popped, a pair of aviators perched on his nose—probably to look cool, as I'm not sure the glare from the sun reflecting off the thin layer of snow that fell last night necessitates sunglasses.

A sharp breeze blows in from the ocean, stealing my breath, and I shudder. Let's be clear: I'm a Southern girl; I don't *do* cold. And, unfortunately, it's been an unusually chilly December so far.

"Why is it so *cold* here?" I say through clenched teeth.

Sophie laughs, throwing her arms out to each side. "It's refreshing."

"For you, maybe," I mutter.

The driver exits the car, not the usual one who takes Jason to and from Incheon. This man has gray-streaked hair and a pressed black suit, and he wears a somber expression befitting a stern grandfather. Or a CIA agent.

Sophie squeals and runs around the front of the car to throw her arms around the man. A smile cracks his serious façade, and they greet each other in Korean.

Jason opens the trunk and fills it with all our bags before we pile into the car.

Sophie sits in the passenger seat, though judging by the driver's disapproving frown, she's not supposed to. But he pulls away from the curb, and we're speeding down the mountain, through town, and across the bridge.

Sophie turns around in her seat. "Grace, I want to introduce you to the wonderful Young Jo, our family's driver."

"Hello, Miss Grace." He meets my gaze in the rearview mirror and nods his head, stone-faced.

"Hi!" I wave at him and receive a tiny smile in response, which I take as a victory.

"We're going to have *so* much fun," Sophie gushes. "I'm so glad you came with us."

"Yeah, me, too."

But my chest tightens when I remember the last conversation I had with Momma on the phone. She called again yesterday, and we ended the conversation basically screaming at each other. I've never openly defied her, and I don't think either of us knows how to respond now. But it's done. Might as well enjoy myself.

Once through Incheon, Young Jo speeds us down the highway toward Seoul. Sophie babbles on about all the stuff she wants to do with me before we have to go back to school, but I only half listen, my nose plastered to the window.

A light snow begins to fall, and the industrial factories and long stretches of coastline transform into taillights and skyscrapers. I soak up the view with wide eyes, my pulse skipping through my veins.

My excitement grows bigger each second, seeing the crowded hubbub of activity, with people everywhere. Businessmen in suits. Kids heading home from school. Teenagers catching the bus. Coffee shops on every corner—literally.

People walk faster here than on Ganghwa Island. They wear sleeker clothes and hold briefcases. A pack of women hurry down the sidewalk in their sky-high heels, all wearing matching gray pencil skirts and blazers.

We drive over a bridge, and beneath is a long canal cutting through the heart of the city, wide sidewalks on either side of the water. We stop at a red light, and I peer down at the river walk, watching a couple stroll hand in hand.

Jason slips off his sunglasses. "So, what do you think?"

"It reminds me of New York City. It's huge. And . . . fashionable."

He nods. "Seoul is really Western, so I think you'll like it."

"Are you implying that I don't like non-Western places?"

He grins. "Well, you're not exactly known for your cultural sensitivity."

I laugh. "Okay, you got me there. I was totally crazy and judgmental. But I'm working on it!"

Young Jo takes us out of the downtown part of the city into a more secluded neighborhood with quieter streets and more residential buildings. We pull up to a two-story white house that's been built into the side of a hill and pass through a gate. Young Jo parks in front of a path that climbs up the hill to a porch which I suspect is the route to the front door. He helps us get all our luggage out and carts Sophie's and my suitcases up the path.

We climb the stairs onto the porch, and I follow behind Sophie as she pushes open the door.

"*Omma!*" she cries, kicking off her shoes in the entryway and sliding on a pair of slippers before rushing into the living room.

The plush room has a modern theme, with white walls and carpet, square wooden shelves that divide the room from the kitchen, and a black couch that looks too angular to be comfortable. Sophie sits beside a woman on the sofa, and a sudden batch of nerves twists in my stomach at the sight.

Sophie and Jason's mom sports a Chanel dress I saw online a few months ago that probably costs more than half my wardrobe.

But while all the women I have experience with who wear these kinds of dresses are anything but maternal, Ms. Bae oozes warmth.

The way a mother should.

She looks up when I enter with Jason, and a smile spreads across her face. Getting to her feet, she holds her arms out for her son and says, "Hyun Jun-ah."

He hugs her. "Hi, Mom."

"And this is Grace?" Ms. Bae directs her smile at me.

I drop in a bow. "Thank you so much for allowing me into your home."

"You're welcome," she says in perfect English.

"Mom, Grace is the best roommate ever," Sophie says. "I even think Jason likes her."

Jason's face wipes of all expression, though the slight reddening of his cheeks betrays him. Ms. Bae just laughs.

"She must be a wonderful girl, then." She waves me forward. "Come. Sit."

I drop down onto the couch and find it only slightly more comfortable than I originally thought.

"Sophie has told me this is your first trip to Seoul," Ms. Bae says. "What do you think?"

"It's great!" I respond, my nerves infusing a little too much excitement into my voice. "I mean, I've only been here for an hour or so, but everything seems awesome!"

Okay, since when does my voice sound like a chipmunk? Chill out, Grace. It's not like you're meeting your future mother-in-law, or something.

"I'm going to take her to the market later," Sophie says. "Maybe tomorrow."

Ms. Bae responds with proper enthusiasm, something my mother would never do. "That sounds like a lot of fun."

We spend the next hour talking with Sophie and Jason's mom, but it never veers into awkward territory. She asks about Tennessee and my college plans, and besides the polite questions about family, she doesn't pry—which I appreciate.

Before dinner, Sophie shows me to her room, where I'll be sleeping for the next month. With fuchsia-colored paint and giant posters of her favorite actors and cartoon characters plastered all over the walls, it's like stepping into the room of a preteen, but it somehow fits her. Her bed, covered in a fuzzy pink blanket over a silky comforter, is big enough for both of us, and I set my suitcase beside her dresser.

We migrate to the kitchen for supper, where I find Ms. Bae has cooked bibimbap, a traditional Korean dish of white rice with lots of sautéed vegetables and a fried egg, mixed with chili paste. Now that I've mastered chopsticks, I don't feel completely inept eating with their mom, but I can't hide my shock after the first bite, when my mouth feels like it's on fire.

I suck down a drink of water, and Sophie giggles.

"Spicy?" she asks.

I toss Ms. Bae a glance, not wanting to offend her. "No, it's great!"

My mouth still burning, I pick up a piece of cabbage with red paste rubbed all over it, a dish that's always served at school but that I've thus far avoided. But one bite and I realize it's even spicier than the bibimbap.

After draining my water glass, I ask, "What is that?"

Sophie points to the cabbage in question. "Kimchi. Good, no?"

"Uhh . . . yeah, but it's *really* spicy."

Note to self—bibimbap: good. Kimchi: a little too intense for me.

Beside me, Jason snorts a laugh when I swallow hard and discreetly pushes his drink toward me with the back of his hand. I'm caught between glaring at him for laughing and hugging him, but I settle with finishing off his glass, as well.

Once we've all finished eating, we turn in early. It feels like we've been traveling a long time, although the drive only lasted a few hours. But I couldn't sleep last night, the argument with my mother replaying over and over in my head. She's probably complaining to Dad about me right now, sending me evil vibes across the Pacific. I wouldn't put it past her.

My phone pings with a message, interrupting my depressing thoughts, and I open a picture message from Jane. She's standing behind Momma and pretending to hang herself. The text below reads, *kill me now. an entire month without school. alone, with our mother. you better be having fun.*

I suppress a laugh but allow Jane's words to sink in. I can't let myself worry about Momma's opinions of me or let them weigh me down. I'm in freaking Seoul for the Christmas holidays. It's time to have fun.

The next day, Sophie and I lounge around the house in our pajamas. Jason is conspicuously absent, and when I ask about him, Sophie says, "He had to go to the studio today to talk to his manager about the drama. They start shooting in a few days."

She flips through TV channels, stopping on a celebrity gossip show. Although I can't understand anything, I can decipher enough to know the candid shots of stars don't come with flattering commentaries.

A picture of Eden pops onto the screen, and I perk.

"Sophie, what are they talking about?"

She shrugs. "Nothing important."

The screen flashes to a video of Sophie, me, and the boys in Incheon, that night we went to the underground mall. There I am on Korean TV, my eyes a little panicked but my outfit looking pretty amazing, if I do say so myself.

"Are they trying to figure out what school Jason's at?" I ask.

"Yeah, but the press has been speculating since August. Seeing him in Incheon might help them narrow it down, though." She chews on a fingernail. "It's pretty incredible no one at school has leaked the information."

"Well, I think the school basically threatened their lives if they told. Nobody wants to get expelled if it's found out they told somebody."

"I guess," she says.

The screen flashes to Eden at one of their concerts, and Sophie scoffs.

"What?" I ask. "What are they saying?"

She rolls her eyes. "They're talking about how Yoon Jae went to China for the holidays, to stay with his dad in Beijing. They're trying to make a big deal about it, like the band is having trouble or something. Yoon Jae just wanted to be with his family."

Despite Sophie brushing off the issue, I have to wonder if the network has a point. I get the feeling there's some kind of tension among them. Or, at least, between Jason and Yoon Jae.

The front door opens, and Jason enters, bringing a brisk wind with him. I huddle below the pillows on the couch, drawing my knees up to my chest to protect myself from the cold.

He drops down onto the sofa beside me with a sigh and frowns when he notices the TV. "Why are you two watching this trash?" he says.

"Why do you care?" Sophie asks.

"Because all those shows do is lie and make money doing it." His face twists into a scowl. "You shouldn't waste your time."

"Well, if you don't like it, you can go somewhere else." Then she adds, "They were talking about you earlier, by the way. Said Eden is having some trouble. Apparently, you guys will be broken up by January."

She laughs, but the dark expression that passes over Jason's face keeps me from joining in her amusement. I catch his gaze, and he reassembles a blank look that reveals nothing. But it's too late because I've already seen his anxiety.

"What are your plans for tonight?" he asks, changing the subject. "It's Saturday night. Shouldn't you take Grace somewhere fun?"

"Don't you worry, flower boy," Sophie says.

I raise my eyebrows. "'Flower boy'?"

Jason sighs again, leaning his head back against the couch like he's exhausted, but Sophie shoots me a grin. "It's a pretty boy," she says. "Don't you think our little Jason is just the prettiest lead singer there is?"

He launches a pillow at Sophie's head, maintaining an expressionless face. She catches it before it slams into her nose, but she just laughs.

"Come on, Grace." She gets to her feet and stretches. "He's right. This time. Let's go get dressed."

After throwing on as many layers as I can and covering my hair with a pair of crocheted earmuffs Sophie has in her closet, I join her in the living room. Jason still sits on the couch, and he watches me enter. My eyes drop to my feet, a mixture of embarrassment and pleasure twisting inside my chest at his attention. We've had zero arguments since we arrived—Seoul sits well with him, apparently.

"Where are you going?" he says.

Sophie fluffs her hair in the mirror. "Gwangjang—I want her to try some good authentic food. We'll walk to the subway station."

"Are you going with us?" I ask Jason.

But Sophie answers for him. "He can't be seen in such a public place. Photographers would be following him around all night, and trust me when I tell you that's not fun."

My spirits sink, but I tell myself it's not a big deal. Why do I want to hang out with him, anyway? We'd just have to dodge paparazzi and insane fans—again—and he'd probably complain about how his fans hinder his life the whole time.

I brace myself for the cold as we step outside, but I still shiver at the snap on my fingers, which I stuff into a pair of mittens. Sophie only laughs at my inability to adapt to cold weather.

"You'll love this place," she says. "It's not the trendy hangout place, but it has the best street food in Seoul. And it's a lot more traditional than some of the newer markets, so you'll get more of a Korean feel, you know?"

I nod, though I can't listen. I can't help wondering what Jason will do while we're gone and whether or not he wishes he could hang out with us.

When a door slams behind us and feet pound on the wooden stairs, my heart soars in hope. I turn and see Jason trotting down the path toward us, half his face hidden behind a thick scarf, which wraps around his neck multiple times, and hands stuffed into the pockets of his leather jacket.

"It will be dark when you guys come home," he says. "You shouldn't walk back from the subway station at night. You need someone to drive you to Gwangjang. I'm coming with you."

Chapter Fifteen

Sophie doesn't protest Jason's announcement, though she shoots him a bemused look, then shifts her gaze to me and back to him. My heart skitters, but I keep a straight face instead of squealing like I want to. Which totally freaks me out. Since when do I get excited about hanging out with Jason?

I mean, he can be fun sometimes, and he's insanely hot—

Okay.

Maybe I have a tiny crush on him.

But it's not like I'm in love with the guy or anything.

Sophie and I climb into the backseat of the car Young Jo drove to pick us up from the airport, and Jason gets into the driver's seat. Sophie leans forward and turns on the radio, cranking the volume to an eardrum-shattering decibel. But I'm not complaining.

As Jason drives us down the narrow streets and Sophie belts KPOP at the top of her lungs, I'm swallowed by a surreal feeling, like I'm dreaming. I peer out the window, watching the blur of lights and people. I'm probably overthinking the situation, but I can't help feeling grateful—for Sophie, for Jason, for them welcoming me into their home. I know Momma would never allow me to bring a friend home, and Dad would tell jokes behind Sophie's and Jason's backs about Asian people. Because that's the kind of guy he is.

Sophie bumps my shoulder with hers. "Sing with me!"

I realize then that American pop music filters through the speakers. Laughing, I join her, throwing as much dramatic emotion into the lyrics as possible. By the time the song ends, we're gasping for breath and Jason has parked the car.

We all file out, and Jason pays the parking fee. He pulls his scarf up higher so all I can see are his eyes, and he pulls on a slouchy knit hat that covers his ears and most of his hair.

"You look like you're getting ready to shoot up the place or something," I say.

He narrows his eyes but says nothing, then falls into step beside me, close enough that our elbows bump every few steps.

This part of town is busier, the streets crowded with couples and groups of friends. Street vendors hawk food to those who pass by, and cars rumble down the street, beeping their horns at pedestrians who don't mind the crosswalks.

We turn off into a building with a foggy plastic or glass roof that, from the outside, reminds me of a train station. But when we enter, I realize it's some kind of bazaar. Open shops are built into the walls lining the long hall, and they show gorgeous displays of traditional Korean costumes and expensive fabrics. A musty smell hangs in the air, and voices echo off the metal walls. I linger in front of one of the stalls, running my fingers across a blue silk.

Jason comes to a stop beside me. "Do you like it?"

"It's gorgeous," I breathe. "All of them are."

"This market is famous for its textiles. Mostly silk."

The vendor, a middle-aged woman with frizzy hair and a thick black coat wrapped around her plump middle, approaches us with a polite smile. She inclines her head and says, "*Ahn nyeong ha se yo.*"

"Hi." I bow my head in response.

The woman holds up the fabric to me, and I shake my head. "No, thank you," I offer, then take in her uncomprehending expression. "*Aniyo* uhh . . . *kwenchanayo.*"

Jason takes over for me, saying something to the woman in Korean, and she nods. They launch into a conversation, with me listening to the flow of words rushing between them. She smiles at me again, then reaches under her makeshift counter, which is covered in a myriad of fabrics. She pulls out about half a yard of yellow silk embroidered with white flowers and holds it out to me.

"What? Oh, no! I don't want to buy anything." I try waving my hands in a gesture I pray translates into my declining the offer.

She says something in Korean and presses the cloth closer to me, her lips falling into a slight frown.

"Take it," Jason says. "She wants to give it to you."

Hesitantly, I take the silk from her, the fabric cool and smooth, like water in my hands. I bow again, and because I have no idea what else to say, toss her a quick "thank you."

I stare down at the fabric now resting in my palms. It's gorgeous, but what am I going to do with it?

"She said my American girlfriend is beautiful," Jason says. "*What?*"

His eyes crinkle, and I know he's smiling. "She wanted to know if I was marrying you for an American visa."

I sputter unintelligibly, my body unable to process coherent thoughts, let alone articulate sentences.

He shrugs, sarcasm dripping from his voice when he continues with, "I told her you were desperate for a Korean visa, so you were only dating me in hopes of getting one."

My brain recovers enough for me to slap his arm with the back of my hand. "You should have told her the truth."

"Maybe, but then you wouldn't have gotten the free fabric. She was adamant about us using it somewhere in the wedding— we're getting married in June, by the way."

My cheeks flame at this unexpected banter, and I turn away from him. Sophie's talking to a vendor farther down, and I make a beeline toward her, praying my face will resume its normal hue by the time I reach her.

"Ready to move on?" She glances down at the silk. "Wow! That's gorgeous. Did you buy it?"

I hear Jason chuckle behind me, but all I say is, "Umm . . . sort of."

The passage opens up to a long hall filled with more vendors, selling all kinds of food. The smells mix in the air to form a scent I've never experienced before. I recognize fish, garlic, onions, and mushrooms, but they mingle with spices and other ingredients I can't name. My mouth starts watering.

In the middle of the hall is a long line of picnic-style tables with benches that are almost all full. Naked bulbs hang above the tables, heavy with food, and the fires from the stalls make this part of the market warmer. Steam rises up from the sizzling pots, and a bustle of voices surrounds us.

We meander along the rows of cooks, who are mostly women. Some have long lines in front of their booths, while others call out to potential customers, holding up their products. I peer down at a table laden with different kinds of fish, lobster, and stillwrithing octopus. The next stall has different kinds of spices, the next, a selection of vegetables.

Sophie motions toward a nearby vendor who has a long line in front of her cart. The woman fries up thick yellow pancakes with meat and something that looks suspiciously like kimchi inside it.

"You have to try this," Sophie says as we step into the line. "It's called *bindaetteok*."

Sophie orders three servings, and we take our plates to one of the tables in the middle of the room. Jason sits across from us and pulls his scarf down from his face just long enough to pop a piece of the pancake into his mouth.

I pull the *bindaetteok* apart and hold a piece in front of my mouth, but after the kimchi incident when I thought my mouth would burst into flames, I decide to take a small bite first.

"What's in this?"

"It's made from mung beans, with onions and kimchi," Sophie says. "And I ordered pork to go inside. It's good. Dip it in the soy sauce."

It's chewy like a pancake, and the spicy kimchi ignites my mouth but not as bad as last night. The pork gives it a savory flavor, and the onions balance with some sweetness.

"This is good." I take another bite. "Seriously."

Sophie brightens. "You like it? Do you want to try something else?"

"Uhh . . ."

But she bolts up from the table and scurries over to another vendor, leaving half of her *bindaetteok* on her plate. I get a feeling I'm about to try everything this market has to offer that Sophie can shove down my throat.

"She likes showing you around the city," Jason says, his voice muffled behind the scarf. "It's nice of you to let her play tour guide."

I shrug one shoulder. "I don't mind. I like having somebody show me the ropes."

We take a few moments to enjoy our *bindaetteok,* but we're interrupted by two girls tapping Jason on the shoulder. They giggle, each trying to hide behind the other.

He waves them away, tilting his head down. They frown but don't move. He tells them something, and they back away, looks of disappointment and confusion on their faces.

"You're terrible with your fans," I say. "You probably just broke their hearts."

"I told them I'm not who they think I am." He keeps his gaze focused on his pancake, which he rips into tiny pieces. "You've seen how crazy they get when they recognize me."

"Maybe you should learn how to interact with them. It could help those rumors about you being surly and hard to work with."

His head jerks up. "What rumors?"

"That's what they said on that gossip show. Sophie told me all about it earlier—that Eden is supposedly breaking up because you are a prima donna and can't get along with Tae Hwa and Yoon Jae."

He snorts. "They don't know anything."

"Maybe. But it *does* seem like you and Yoon Jae aren't very close."

His eyes tighten. "I don't know what you're talking about."

I'm about to cite all the times I've suspected there's something brewing between them when Sophie claps a myriad of bowls and plates down onto the table. I gape at all the food.

"Are you trying to make me fat?" I ask.

She plops down onto the bench. "I just thought you'd want to try a little bit of everything." She points to each dish in turn. "That's *sundae,* and that's *mandu*—they're my favorites—and then *jokbal.*"

I pick up one of the *mandu,* which looks like a dumpling, and find it's even better than the *bindaetteok.* Spurred by the positive experience, I take a bite of the *jokbal,* some kind of meat served with a sauce that smells fishy.

"What kind of meat is this?" I ask between chews.

Jason watches me eat, his eyes lit with amusement. "Pig's feet."

I cough on the last bit of *jokbal* lingering in my mouth.

Sophie takes in my shocked expression. "What's wrong? *Jokbal* is good."

Jason unsuccessfully attempts to hide his laughter behind that obnoxious scarf, but I hear it and shoot him a glare. He only snickers louder.

"You're right, it's good. I'm just not sure I'm ready to eat pig's feet, knowing what it is, you know? I don't even like pork rinds in America."

But Sophie's face falls like I've disappointed her, so I stuff myself with more dumplings to placate her.

Jason stands. "I'll be right back."

He returns a moment later with a bottle of clear liquid and two shallow metal bowls. When he unscrews the top off the bottle, the distinct, sharp smell of alcohol wafts toward me. I wrinkle my nose, glancing over at Sophie. She frowns at the bottle, her chopsticks hovering over some *jokbal*.

"Is that vodka?" I ask, struggling to keep my voice emotionless as Jason fills the two bowls.

"No, it's *soju*." He hands Sophie one of the bowls and keeps one for himself. "I assumed you didn't want any since you didn't drink at the bar that night."

I don't say anything but watch him put the bowl to his mouth and drain it, like you would drink the leftover milk from your cereal bowl. But milk can't make you forget where you are or decide to drunk-call your ex-girlfriend.

Or think it's okay to take more pills than the bottle directs.

Sophie doesn't touch her bowl, just stares at her brother. Tension settles around us, but Jason doesn't seem to notice it. Or else he's ignoring it.

She abruptly gets to her feet, bumping the table and rattling the plates. Failing at hiding both her hurt and irritation, she says, "I'm—I'll be right back."

I watch her flee until she disappears into the crowd. Jason still doesn't address the awkwardness, so I take it upon myself to investigate.

"What's wrong with Sophie?"

He shrugs. "I don't know."

"I think it has something to do with the *soju*."

With my view of his face limited to his eyes, I search them for any recognition but find confusion instead.

"What do you mean?" he asks.

"She got upset when she saw you drinking." I hesitate, then venture to add, "Like the night of your birthday party when you were drunk."

"You're just being overly sensitive."

Irritation bubbles inside my chest, but I ignore it. "Am I? Ironic that the only times she's upset with you are when you drink."

He shoves the scarf down, and I get a better view of his face and see him blanch. He shoves the bottle farther away from him so roughly that it nearly topples over.

This is probably another one of those times when I should keep my mouth shut and let Jason open up when he wants to. But judging by how much I already know about him—namely, that you have to yank out any personal info like he's holding on to it with a death grip—I take the plunge. I'll worry about him getting annoyed later.

"Is there something I should know?" I ask.

I expect a sharp response, like I've gotten from my brother when I "annoy" him about his personal life. But Jason just sighs. He rubs a hand across his eyes, his shoulders slumping.

"She thinks I'm going to become an alcoholic," he says.

Shock rockets through me, but I keep my face composed. Of all the things he could have said, this isn't what I expected. Maybe she had a bad experience with a boyfriend who drank? She's opposed to it in general? But I never pegged Jason as an alcoholic, even if he did get drunk that one time—I've never seen him drink since, till tonight.

"Okay," I say, proud of myself for keeping my voice level. "Her concern can't be completely unwarranted. Do you . . . have a drinking problem?"

Now his eyes sharpen, and he snaps, "*No,* I don't."

Should his defensiveness be a warning signal?

"Did something happen that would make her think you do?"

He hesitates a second, then sighs. "Before school started, back in the summer, the paparazzi got a shot of me coming out of a club. I was—okay, I was really drunk, but it had been a bad week. Mostly, it was just bad publicity, but Sophie freaked out."

"I can see why she might," I mutter.

But he must not have heard me, because he keeps talking. "She thinks that just because our father is an alcoholic, I'm going to become one, too," he continues, frustration thick in his voice. "Like I can't control myself. Like I'm going to be just like him." He scowls, muttering, "I'm nothing like him. And, I mean, I'm nineteen. Only old people are alcoholics."

I consider arguing with him about the last bit but hold back. My mind searches for the best way to respond, knowing I'm on sensitive ground. Without Sophie here, I can dig a little deeper, but I fear Jason shutting me off if I prick too many nerves. But the hurt that's swallowed his eyes spurs me on.

"Why do you think Sophie's worried?"

"I have no idea! She's reading too much into it when there's actually nothing there."

I nod. "Maybe."

He rolls his eyes. "Everyone drinks occasionally."

"I don't."

We lapse into silence.

"You agree with Sophie," he says, eyes hard. "You think I have a problem."

"No." I shake my head. "I have no idea. But I'll be honest—I think you're hiding something. There's something else going on that you don't want to talk about. But, whatever it is, you need to get over it. Because your drinking really upsets your sister, and it's inconsiderate of you to do it when she's around."

Jason stares at me a long time. Until I squirm. But I hold his gaze, not willing to back down.

He looks away, and I give myself a mental high five.

"Maybe," he murmurs so I almost don't hear it.

We pick at the rest of the food, but most of it has gone cold. Jason throws away the rest of the bottle of *soju,* and the sound of the sloshing liquid hitting the trash can sends a shiver through me.

Sophie returns about ten minutes later, a shopping bag under her arm and her good mood returned. She clears away our leftovers, and we head back out of the market.

On our way back to the car, I slow my pace so I walk behind the twins, watching them. It's obvious they're close. And despite Jason's assertions that he's okay, I wonder if Sophie's fears are reasonable. I know he's reserved, but is it normal for someone to be that unemotional and detached most of the time?

I think back to Nathan before he got bad, and there are some similarities. But that could just be that creative type of brain and the moodiness which often accompanies it. Still, I determine to take more notice of his moods. I'm not going to watch another person close to me self-destruct.

As if he can feel me thinking about him, Jason slows and falls into step beside me, Sophie walking a few paces ahead of us. When we're in sight of the car, he grabs my wrist and stops me. We stand in the middle of the sidewalk, facing each other.

"I just wanted to say thank you," he says, peering at our shoes. "You—you were right about Sophie. It was stupid of me to think it wouldn't bother her. She . . . took getting a stepmom a lot harder than I did. I think Sophie always hoped our father would go back to our mom."

He looks at me, and I struggle for words. With him standing so close, his head bent down toward me, my articulation skills disappear, and all my attention diverts to the feel of his fingers wrapped around the skin between my glove and sleeve.

"You've been really good for Sophie." He swallows hard, shifting uncomfortably. "And me."

If my brain hadn't already melted, it would have now. His gaze bores into mine, like he's trying to communicate something he can't with words. But my brain's so fuzzy I can't figure out what.

I part my lips to respond with something—anything—but no sound comes out. All I can do is stare back at him, the heat in my cheeks increasing and the feel of his breath on my face sending shivers down my back.

His hand slides down my wrist to my hand, and our fingers do an awkward dance before they interlock, our palms pressed together and my pulse racing.

"I guess I'm just trying to say that I'm glad we met you," he says, voice falling to a murmur. "I'm glad *I* met you."

He squeezes my hand, but my focus zeroes in on the left side of his mouth, which tips up in a half smile. If this were a movie or one of those dramas Sophie got me hooked on, Jason and I would kiss now.

But it's not, and we don't.

He lets go of my hand and steps back, waiting for me to continue toward the car.

Sophie waits for us by the passenger door, tapping her index finger against the window and shooting Jason a look of irritation. He unlocks the doors, and we all climb in. Sophie doesn't turn on the music this time, just busies herself with her phone.

Silence reigns in the car, and I find myself unable to look at either of them. I peer out the window, my insides twisting. My brain flashes back to the conversation with Jason, with him holding my arm and my inability to say *anything*. I'm not the kind of girl who gets tongue-tied around boys, not even super hot boys like Jason. Maybe my feelings for him are more than a crush. But that's crazy. He's my best friend's brother, and he annoys me as often as he's sweet to me.

I glance at his reflection in the rearview mirror, regret growing inside my chest, and I'm unable to stop imagining Jason's lips touching mine.

Chapter Sixteen

The next morning, I accompany the Bae family to church. In Korean. It's mostly the same as back home, except I have no idea what the pastor's saying. And everybody says their own individual prayers out loud all at once in near shouts, which is sort of overwhelming. But I get to meet a few of Sophie's friends, who are all just as sweet as her.

I call Jane when we get back. After an hour-long conversation, in which she tells me all about how Momma's driving her insane, how her friends all have boyfriends and she doesn't, and how she wishes she were with me in Seoul, I'm left with tears pooling in my eyes as I hang up. I sit on Sophie's bed, staring at the silky pink comforter, a dull ache pounding in my chest. Jane's voice still echoes in my ears, and for the first time, I actually miss home. Maybe not the fights with Momma, or Dad's indifference, but Nashville, my friends who I've ignored for months, and American food.

But Monday brings the first day of shooting for Jason's drama, and I don't have time to feel homesick, because Sophie decides we're accompanying him.

"Na Na is in this show!" Sophie squeals as we file out of the car at the shooting site.

"Who's Na Na?" I glance around at the neighborhood, which looks like a part of history. Brick buildings line the narrow stone street, with houses behind wooden gates featuring heavy oak knockers. The roofs remind me of Japanese pagodas, and a thin layer of snow coats the tops of the walls separating yards from the road.

"She's only, like, the biggest new teen actress in Korea," Sophie says, like I keep up with actresses who speak a language I can't understand. "And I'm getting her autograph before this is over."

I laugh as we wander down the street toward the crew setting up in a courtyard. "But aren't you used to meeting famous people? Your brother is one."

She waves her hand in dismissal. "We were in the womb together. He doesn't count."

We kill time watching crew members set up the camera and lights and all the other equipment they'll need to start filming, when a girl arrives, her hair so long it almost skims her hips and high heels so tall they look like stilts. She has milky skin and perfectly pink cheeks, the kind of girl that makes your heart ache because you know you'll never be as beautiful as her. She beams at the crew, and they melt under her attention, basking in her radiance. This must be Na Na.

Sophie squeals next to me and fumbles through her purse as the girl gets closer to us. "I can't find a pen," she hisses. "Grace, I can't find a pen!"

"Is this the only day she'll be on set?" I ask.

Tilting her head to the side, Sophie shoots me a bemused look. "The only day? She's the main character. Na Na wouldn't take a smaller role."

"The main . . . " My voice trails off as this fact settles.

I glance at the girl again—her perfectly shaped mouth, the legs that go for miles. She's going to be playing alongside Jason for an entire TV show season? My heart constricts. What if they *kiss*?

Na Na passes us, and Sophie lets out a soft groan and allows her purse to fall back to her side. She must have resigned herself to getting the autograph another time.

"Sophie!" a voice calls from behind us.

I turn to see Jason heading toward us. My breath catches at the sight of him, dressed in faded jeans and a black leather jacket with scuffed, clunky boots to match. His hair's more tousled than normal, and he's wearing earrings.

"Did they pierce your ears?" she asks with a giggle.

He touches one of the studs. "No, they're fake. Apparently, they make me look more rock 'n' roll."

I join Sophie's laughter. "I don't know about that."

He doesn't respond.

"Are you nervous?" Sophie asks.

Jason scoffs, the arrogance he wore so often when I first met him now returning. He doesn't even look at me.

He lets out a long-suffering, self-righteous sigh. "Please don't embarrass me, Sophie."

"Hey, don't be a jerk," I cut in. "She was just trying to be nice."

His gaze flicks to me, then to the crew members carrying camera equipment who walk past us, a coldness swallowing his eyes. And I know he's shutting me out like he used to. The realization steals the rest of my words.

"I've got to be on set," he says. "I'll see you later, Sophie." He focuses on his sister. "Do *not* get in the way."

He turns, still not acknowledging me. I chafe at the slight, anger growing. Why is he acting like this?

Smirking, I wait until he's maybe a couple hundred feet down the road, then shout with fake sincerity, "Good luck, Jason! You'll do great!"

He whips around, shock clear on his face. Then he turns his head to each side, like he's gauging everyone else's reactions. But when they go about their business, he doesn't react, just turns back around and keeps walking. Except, even at this distance, I can see the new tension in his shoulders.

He joins the others, and I watch him talk to Na Na. Really, how can she wear such a short skirt in the winter? She's going to get frostbite.

My brain still grapples with Jason's personality shift. He was so nice before today. What's changed?

Then it hits me—before, we were always with his family. Nobody else was around. He didn't need to impress anyone. But here, there are people he works with, people who could either hurt or help his career. And for whatever reason, I'm in his way. I'm an embarrassment.

My cheeks flame at the thought, and I try to cover my swirling emotions with a heaping portion of anger. But the shame settles in my gut and crawls through me, pounding like a dull drumbeat in my chest.

I pull out my phone to text Jane, but my thumb hovers above the keypad. Why does his slight hurt so much? Why do I care? It shouldn't bother me this much.

But it does.

Because maybe—maybe!—I like him. More than as my best friend's brother. More than as a friend. More than a little crush.

I've only had one real boyfriend—Isaac. And that didn't turn out so well. But I've always had a thing for guys who sing, play an instrument, or, in Isaac's case, DJ.

Not that I need someone telling me musicians are fickle and high maintenance. Nathan's revolving door of girlfriends taught me that, and Jason wouldn't be any better, with all his drama.

Not that I want to date Jason. I *can't* like him, not more than just as an innocent little crush because he's cute and kinda fun to hang out with sometimes. I do *not* like Jason Bae.

Much.

"Where's Na Na?" Sophie cranes her neck around me, searching the faces of every person that passes us.

I sigh. "I don't know."

Sophie insisted we go with Jason to the photo shoot for the drama, even though I've been here for over a week now and haven't really seen any of Seoul besides the places the show is filming. Every morning, I ask Sophie what we're doing, and it's always the same: "Whatever Jason's doing." Not that he sees fit to tell us in advance what that may be.

And whenever he goes to a party, which might actually be fun, Sophie and I are conspicuously not invited. He and Na Na go together, like they're dating or something. And if he "forgets" to introduce me to someone again, I'm going to scream. You'd think he might be polite and try to keep me in the loop, but then again, this is Jason we're talking about—politeness isn't really his strength.

"You don't have to be so snippy," Sophie says.

"Sorry," I mutter.

She pouts, slumping into a chair along the far wall opposite the set. "I still don't have her autograph."

"And whose fault is that?" I tease, laughing. "We've seen her a million times, and you've never had the guts to ask her for it. Even *I've* said more words to her than you have."

She wrinkles her nose, slouching her shoulders even more. "That's not fair. Jason introduced you to her. He should have introduced *me*—I'm his sister."

"You weren't there."

"Because I was in the bathroom!"

What I don't tell Sophie is that Jason didn't introduce me—Na Na sought me out. I was lingering in the catering tent between takes a few days ago when she came up beside me and pretended to choose between a croissant and a banana.

"Your name is Grace," she said in Korean.

"Ye." I nodded.

She then spouted a flurry of Korean words at me so fast, all I could do was stare at her blankly, my brain failing to keep up with the translating. When she'd finished her monologue, she watched me with her nose scrunched and disdain in her eyes.

"You don't understand," she finally said in English, after an uncomfortable amount of silence. "You live in Korea, but you can't speak Korean."

"I'm learn—"

"You're so American," she interrupted, and my eyebrows shot up.

She glanced at the Danish on my plate, her lips curling in a mocking smile. "Maybe you should choose something with fewer calories. Jason needs to be seen with pretty girls around him."

She didn't need to say *like me,* because her tone implied it.

Even now, anger burns through me at the memory. Ever since that conversation, she's made a point of catching my eye while she's talking to Jason, casually touching his arm or leaning closer to him while holding eye contact with me. It's enough to make me want to throw a truckload of Danishes at her face.

A small crowd of people head in from an adjoining room, and I spot Jason and Na Na among them. Both have been styled to perfection, Na Na in a gorgeous silver sequined dress that shows off her thin legs and Jason with a pair of tattered hipster jeans and a T-shirt that hugs his shoulders. They look perfect together.

Sophie perks at Na Na's entrance but remains rooted in her seat, even when the other girl lingers by the snack table. I wait for Sophie to jump up and make her move, but she never does. I stifle a sigh. Am I going to have to get the autograph for her? If so, she better give me a gigantic Christmas present.

The shoot drags on and on. And on. Reality television makes photo shoots seem glamorous and fun. Maybe they are if you're the one being photographed. But once you've watched one, you've watched them all. And this one is even less entertaining, because I have to see Jason cuddled up to Na Na in a variety of poses. It's sort of nauseating.

When I think about our almost-moment at the market the Saturday after I arrived, I almost laugh. I thought Jason would be nicer now that we're on his home turf. False. He's turned into a bigger douche than he was at school.

Sophie's attention wavers and she retreats to her cell, but I can't tear my eyes off the couple in front of the camera. Na Na laughs and simpers, pouts and smiles, on the photographer's command. She's a natural, obviously. Beside her, Jason struggles to appear casual, but she has enough charisma for both of them.

"If you're not going to get your autograph, why don't we leave now?" I ask Sophie, forcing a lightness into my tone that I don't feel. "I'm sort of hungry. Let's go grab lunch."

"We rode with Jason," Sophie says. "We have to wait until he's done."

I swallow a groan. I rifle through my purse, searching for any *won* that I could use to pay for a cab or bus. If I have to sit here one second longer, I'm going to scream. Each snap of the camera shoots another jolt of irritation through me.

At the bottom of my bag, I find a few coins.

"We could take the bus." I hold up the *won*. "Why don't we go shopping or something?"

Sophie hesitates. "But I want to get my autograph . . . "

"We'll have tons of opportunities later," I say, pulling out my used-car-salesman voice. "We've been to practically every day of shooting thus far."

She shakes her head. "They're going to Busan tomorrow, about six or seven hours south, so we can't watch anymore."

Jason's going to Busan? I glance at him, but he's got his arms wrapped around Na Na from behind and rests his chin on her shoulder. He grins at the camera, and my stomach turns.

I confronted him a few days ago about being a jerk, but he denied everything. Like he can't see that he's using me and Sophie—wants us close by in case he needs something, in case we could be useful, but far enough away that we don't cramp his style. But every time I ask Sophie if we can do something on our own, she doesn't get it. She doesn't see the way he's ignoring us, like she's immune to his annoyingness. I guess if you share genes with someone, you get used to their idiosyncrasies.

It takes every ounce of self-restraint I have to swallow the sharp words threatening to explode from my mouth. Sophie hasn't done anything wrong, and I can't vent my frustration on her just because she's the closest to my blast radius. She's not the one who's hanging all over Na Na in front of an entire photography team. Or the one who's been basically ignoring me since the drama started filming.

So I rein in my inner diva and say as evenly as possible, "Well, I'll just go alone, then." I throw my purse over my shoulder. "I know you want to get that autograph. You just hang out here until you get it, then you can meet me somewhere."

Her eyes get wide. "But you don't know where you're going."

I wave off her concern. "I'll ask."

"You don't speak Korean."

I shrug. "Most everyone here speaks English. At least enough to give me directions."

She jumps to her feet and grabs my hand. "What if you get lost?"

Now I laugh. "Then I'll call you."

"Grace!"

The protective tone in her voice should make me feel good, but it just rubs my already sore nerves.

I force a smile, though with every snap of the camera's shutter, I can feel another shred of my control slipping. "Sophie, seriously, don't worry. I'll be fine. Just write down your home address in Korean, and I'll head there after I go see a movie or whatever."

Yes. Movie. The characters on the screen can't snub me in front of their industry friends or not tell me they're going to a different city with Korea's current favorite starlet.

Sophie chews on her bottom lip but eventually nods. "Okay, but call me if you get lost. Or bored. Or you run into any sketchy boys or mafia people." Her eyes get wide. "Grace, what if you get mugged? Or raped or—"

"Sophie," I interrupt, keeping my voice grave even though the panicked look on her face might be the most priceless thing I've ever seen. "I'll be fine. Everything will be fine. Okay?"

"Okay." She pulls me into a back-cracking hug. "Don't die. Promise?"

I chuckle, some of my frustration ebbing. "I promise."

I try to make my escape quietly, but a voice calls from behind me, "Grace!"

My heart constricting, I force myself not to cringe as I turn to face Jason. "What's up?"

He jogs over to me, the crew and Na Na all watching us. Heat blooms in my cheeks, and I force myself not to stare back at them and shout, *What are you looking at?* All the warm and fuzzy feelings I just had for Sophie have dissipated, leaving only irritation and hurt behind.

"Where are you going?" he asks.

"I don't know. Maybe to a movie?"

His eyebrows disappear beneath his hair. "By yourself?"

"Why not? I get around Ganghwa Island by myself just fine."

Concern seeps into his gaze, which only fuels my frustration. He doesn't have the right to worry about me. We're barely friends, and he didn't even tell me he was leaving Seoul tomorrow. He has hardly spoken to me in weeks. Does he expect me to check in with him all the time, but he doesn't have to?

Oh, heck no.

"Grace, I'm not comfortable with—"

"*You're* not comfortable?" I hiss. "What does it matter to you, anyway?"

His expression turns confused. "Grace, I—"

"No!" I bark. "Look, it's nice of you to worry and all, I guess, but I'm not an idiot. No reason for you to be concerned."

He rolls his eyes, now his turn to get angry. "Of course I have a reason. We're friends."

"Oh, we are? Because I thought friends told friends when they were going to Busan. Friends also tell friends when they're going to be practically making out with a girl for hours in front of thirty people." My voice takes on a harder edge. "And friends don't ignore friends when they want to impress other people."

His eyes open wide in astonishment. "*What* are you talking about?"

I wave my hands in front of my face in what I hope conveys dismissal. This conversation isn't getting us anywhere, and Na Na now watches me with a little more interest than I would like. She smirks, and I've never wanted to punch someone so much in my entire life. I catch Sophie shooting me a pitying look, and my throat tightens.

"Look, I think it's best I just leave." Before I embarrass myself any more than I already have. "I'm sure I'll be in bed before you get home tonight. I'll see you when you get back from Busan."

I storm out as dramatically as possible, but my epic exit is made much less impressive when Jason chases me into the stairwell. Doesn't he know how this works? He's supposed to stand in my wake, mouth hanging open, and realize how wonderful I am and how he's totally blown his chances with me.

"Grace, wait." He grabs my elbow, but I shake him off.

"Go back to the shoot. I'm sure Na Na is missing you."

He hurries ahead of me until we're face-to-face. "What is going on with you? This is really out of character."

"Maybe I'm just sick of getting the shaft from you."

His face screws up in confusion. "The shaft?"

"*You* were the one who invited me to Seoul, not Sophie. Usually when you have guests, you don't ditch them."

"But I've been working."

"Then maybe you shouldn't have invited me if you thought I'd get in your way."

He stares at me blankly. "Do you . . . feel like I don't want you here?" he guesses.

"Pretty much."

"But I don't feel that way at all," he hurries to say. "I'm glad you're here!"

"Then you have a weird way of showing it."

I can hear myself, my words cringeworthy, especially echoing through the empty stairwell. But I can't stop them. Watching him with *her* at the same time that he's been ignoring me spurred something nasty inside me, and all I want is to let him know just how he's made me feel.

"Then I'm sorry," he says. "I didn't mean to make you feel like that."

Normally, his apology would strike something inside me. I would remember how I've probably only heard him apologize twice the entire time I've known him; I would know that when he says he's sorry, he means it. But not this time.

"I don't really care what you meant," I say, now more tired than angry. "You're giving me seriously mixed signals here. You asked me to help you with your song, you take me back to my dorm after we study, and you planned a Thanksgiving meal for me. You freaking *held my hand* on the ride back to school after the music video shoot, and I don't care what you say—you *do* remember your birthday and dancing with me."

Somehow, he pales under all that makeup, but I push forward. "You asked me to stay with you guys in Seoul, so I came. But now you're ignoring me everywhere, like you're ashamed of me or something. In the time I've been here, we've hung out one time. Once. And you're all over Na Na like you're best buddies or her real boyfriend or something. So why don't you tell me what's going on?"

Jason's not a man of many words, but I've never seen him completely blank. At least his eyes normally give me a hint as to what's going on inside his head, but now—nothing. Like he has no cognitive function.

I'm ready to leave him standing there when he stutters, "I—" He stops. "I don't—"

I wave him off. "Whatever. I'm leaving."

"No."

He says it with such force, I pause. We lock eyes, and he deliberates. I steel myself for his verbal defense, but he surprises me instead by taking my face in his hands.

And then he kisses me.

Chapter Seventeen

Big Brother,
   You know how the older brother is supposed to take care of his younger sisters? And tell them what types of boys to avoid, which ones are bad news, so they can keep from getting played?
   Yeah, you've never been good at that.

   From Korea, not so much with love,
   Grace

For the first few seconds, I'm frozen in shock. One of Jason's hands slides from my cheek to the back of my neck and his fingers slip through my hair. My own hands involuntarily latch onto his waist, and I'm suddenly standing so close our thighs touch.

"Grace," he murmurs against my lips with such longing my heart twists.

But all thoughts empty from my head when he coaxes my mouth open, and I forget about Na Na, Jason going to Busan, and everything except how good it feels to have his lips on mine.

I pull away with a soft gasp, and all I can think to say is, "You don't kiss like other Korean boys."

His head jolts up, and his hands drop to his sides, leaving cold spaces on my skin. "*What?*" he says.

I fumble for an explanation, but all I can think about is grabbing that disheveled hair and yanking his mouth back toward mine. "In those dramas," I say, "the couples always sort of smash faces, and the girl keeps her eyes open, and it's awkward."

"And that wasn't awkward?"

No, it was glorious! "Umm . . . "

"You know those dramas aren't real, right?" he says slowly, as if I'm mentally deficient. "It's only for TV."

"Right." A thought jerks me out of my blissful haze. "You're not going to kiss Na Na like that for your drama, are you?"

He stares at me in confusion.

Another thought forms, this one louder than the others. "Wait. You just kissed me."

I gape at him.

"You just *kissed me*!"

He cringes, placing a hand on my arm. "You don't have to announce it to everyone."

My grin fades. "Are you embarrassed we kissed?"

"No, I just don't think everyone needs to know." He points back and forth between us. "About what just happened. Especially not the paparazzi, and if you keep screaming, I'm pretty sure everyone will hear you."

All the excitement inside me from when our lips touched dissipates completely, and irritation swells to take its place. "You don't want them to know because I'm not some famous Korean actress."

"No." He runs both hands through his hair, letting out a frustrated sigh. "That's not what I meant."

"Sure it is."

Heat wells up in my chest, but not the good kind. Anger. My eyes prick, and I realize I'm going to cry. Not okay. He's not going to see me fall to pieces over this. Over him.

I clear my throat to get rid of the sob that sticks there. "I don't know what that was all about, but I'm not interested in what you're selling here. Maybe you think it's funny to mess with me, but it's not."

I always complained about guys flattering me, but maybe this is worse. I'd rather be the trophy than the girl on the side.

His grip on my arm tightens, probably an attempt at comforting me, but it falls short. "I'm not trying to mess with you," he says. "I—I don't know what just happened, but it has nothing to do with you."

My eyebrows shoot up. "Nothing to do with me?"

He shakes his head. "That's not what I mean. Don't take it like that."

"Like what? That you just felt the need to kiss somebody and I happened to be close by?" I bark a mirthless laugh. "Wow. I never pegged you as *that* guy, but I guess everyone has their secrets. Glad I've seen the real you."

"Grace, stop." He places both hands on my shoulders. "I only meant that I'm confused right now. I don't know what's going on. I don't know where we stand." He pauses. "All I know is that I like you. A lot."

My heart soars, but I squelch any good feelings and tell myself I'll sort them out later. "You like me. But you're embarrassed by me, for some reason. Is it because I'm not Korean? Does it have something to do with my family?"

He takes a step back like I've struck him. "What? No! Why would you say that?"

"Because you're only ever nice to me when no one's around," I grind out through clenched teeth, my brain flashing back through every time he didn't introduce me to someone or didn't include me in a conversation, every time he was content with me hiding behind him or Sophie for the entire day, like I didn't exist at all.

Once I get going, it's like I can't stop. And I only gain momentum, my bottled-up emotions and confusion overflowing.

"You didn't want me helping you with the song with the other guys around," I continue. "And then you held my hand when no one was looking. Our only good conversations come when it's just the two of us, and now you kiss me but don't want anyone to know. What does that make me? Obviously not anything that important to you." My throat tightens, and I struggle to get the last words out. "I don't think my coming home with you guys was a good idea. Maybe I should've gone home for break, after all."

The thought sends a jolt of pain through me, not only because I would have missed out on meeting Jason and Sophie's mom and seeing their home and their city, but also at the thought of suffering through my mother's judgment and my father's indifference, and facing emotions I've managed to squeeze into the back of my mind since I left home. But right now, it almost seems better to have just gone to Nashville and avoided having Jason look at me like this—like I've betrayed him. When really, he's the one that hurt me.

I should have learned from Isaac. Boys that seem too good to be true usually are.

I actually consider going home for the holidays, but Momma's squash casserole on Christmas isn't worth the grief of looking her in the eyes. Though being around Jason is almost as bad.

Thankfully, he ships off to Busan for a week, and after Sophie takes me shopping and introduces me to a few of her friends who live in Seoul, she manages to convince me to stay for the rest of the break. But when Jason returns on Christmas Eve, the awkward factor leaps to a painful level.

I go with them to church again that night, then we head back to the house for another traditional Korean meal. I eat and talk and laugh along with everyone else, but my mind wanders to my house and my family, who will be eating our annual feast of honey-baked ham with crescent rolls, green beans, squash casserole, corn-bread muffins, and potato salad in about fourteen hours. I wonder if Dad will show up, or if he'll duck out, saying he needs to work—his typical excuse these days.

My fingers itch to find my phone and call Jane, but I know that if I hear her voice, I'll regret not going to see her. And I'll probably cry.

After dinner, Sophie wrangles us all into playing cards on the living room floor beside the Christmas tree we decorated yesterday. We play Spades, and the Bae family teaches me Go-Stop, a Korean gambling game. Jason seems distracted the entire time, forgetting his turn and checking the clock a million times.

As we all make our way to bed, Jason stops me in the hallway. My pulse spikes at being alone with him, but I force my nerves to chill. I need anger, to use it as a shield or whatever people say about protecting themselves. But I can't muster any. All I feel when I see him is exhaustion and regret.

"I need to talk to you," he says.

"What about?"

"About our conversation before I left for Busan. And about . . . the kiss."

I expect him to wince, but he keeps a straight face. An improvement, at least. Maybe he's over the embarrassment, though I doubt he'll ever mention it to anyone else.

He shifts uncomfortably. "You know I'm not good with words, and I feel like I offended you."

I snort. "That's awfully discerning of you."

He continues, either ignoring the gibe or not noticing it. "I need to explain myself. Explain what I meant."

"There's no need to explain."

"Yes, there is." Determination hardens his eyes. "What I said about being confused is true. There are a lot of things going on in my life, with my family and the band. I don't need any more distractions."

"And I'm a distraction?"

"Well . . . yes."

Ouch. Maybe I like being an embarrassment better.

"Sometimes, *good* things can be distractions, but they're still good," he says. "When I said I like you, I wasn't lying." He hesitates, like he's not sure if he should go on. "I don't think I've ever liked a girl as much as I like you."

My stomach somersaults.

Jason stuffs his hands into the pockets of his jeans. "But I think we should just be friends."

"Friends?"

Bewilderment swirls inside my head. When did I ever say that we should be anything more than that?

"Yes," he says. "I can't date right now."

"And you think I would ever date you?"

"I—" His cuts himself off. "What?"

I shrug, hoping for nonchalance when I actually feel like my insides are being squeezed. "Kind of egotistical on your part to think that just because you would want to date me, I'd be fine with it."

"But I—"

"Don't worry about the kiss," I interrupt. "It's already forgotten. And, you know, I don't really need any distractions, either. I need to focus on my studies right now. Besides, you're not really my type."

I consider throwing in a few other stereotypical rejection lines like, *It's not you, it's me,* but I couldn't say them in sincerity because it *is* him. And his gigantic ego.

"Merry Christmas, Jason."

I leave him standing there, just like girls do in movies. And for the first time, I feel like I could be one of them. My chest may be aching, but I comfort myself with the fact that I'm not letting him get under my skin again.

My feelings for him were nothing more than a silly crush. And now it's all over.

Chapter Eighteen

"But it's New Year's Eve!" Sophie pulls on my arm, trying to force me out of my chair.

I grab on to my desk to keep myself from getting yanked to my feet. "Actually, New Year's was weeks ago. This is the end of January and, you know, I think I'm still recovering from the travel back to school."

She rolls her eyes. "We left Seoul almost three weeks ago, and it's not like we traveled that far. And it's *Seollal,* the biggest holiday in Korea, and we were invited to the hottest party in Seoul!"

"I thought Korean New Year's was supposed to be a family thing."

She scrunches her nose. "Umm . . . it is. But my mom said it was okay for me to go to the party with Jason instead, so we're good." She gives me a serious look. "You can't ditch me."

"I have homework."

"Don't even start that. If *I'm* not worried about homework, you're not allowed to be."

She has a point. I do have homework, but the truth is I don't want to see Jason. I get twitchy when I think about another entire semester of sitting beside him in class every day.

Sophie digs through the pile of clothes I just washed that's resting on top of my bed and throws a black dress at my face. "You're wearing this. Let's go."

I groan, knowing I can't win. But I take my time getting ready, passive-aggressively hoping we'll be late. When I've finished curling my hair and touching up my makeup, Sophie's standing by the door with both our purses in hand.

We rush downstairs and meet up with all three boys of Eden. I try not to notice Jason wearing the black leather jacket I bought him for Christmas when it was on sale and I wasn't pissed at him, and instead wrap my arms around my middle and stare down at my fuchsia heels, shivering in the six inches of snow that fell last night.

We jump into the limo and begin the long trek to Seoul. The boys are booked for a big bash downtown that their agency wants them to be seen at; it's the kind with lots of star power and schmoozing. When Sophie heard her biggest celebrity crush was going to be in attendance, she weaseled her way into the party— dragging me along with her.

We reach downtown around seven thirty. Traffic's light, since most people are at home with their families, but when we reach the club, there are so many people standing outside I can't even see the front door.

The limo pulls up to the curb, and I crawl out behind Sophie, only to be met by a hurricane of flashing lights. A roar of screams fills my ears as Sophie links her arm through mine and we follow the boys down a short carpeted path to the front door, lined on either side by fans clamoring to get around the ropes separating them from their favorite stars. It's not a *red* carpet—it's white— but I feel like a celebrity all the same.

A bouncer hurries us down the line, and we slip inside the dark club. The cigarette smoke and heat in the air press against my face, which still smarts from the cold outside, and when someone offers to take my coat, I peel it off as fast as I can.

The club's decorated like a swanky lounge, with plush black chairs and sofas crowded with guys in flashy shirts and girls wearing lots of eyeliner. Arrangements of tall white candles litter the corners, and the bar sits inside a sunken seating area in the middle of the room.

An R&B song plays, giving the entire club a cool, relaxed vibe, but the crowds of well-dressed, beautiful Koreans send my anxiety levels rocketing through the ceiling. I scan the dimly lit room and find zero other Westerners. Or normal-looking people. It's like the club only lets in gorgeous people—and me. I take a reflexive step closer to Sophie.

Eden's manager pounces on us as soon as we're inside, and he shuffles the boys away from the entrance. Tae Hwa grabs Sophie's hand, and a surge of relief floods me as we follow them through the club.

Yoon Jae falls into step with me.

"Excited?" he asks.

I scratch the back of my neck, offering him a self-conscious laugh. "I don't really know what to be excited about."

He grins. "Maybe we can dance again, like we did on Jason and Sophie's birthday."

Embarrassment heats my cheeks, but Yoon Jae isn't the one filling my memories from that night. "You're a way better dancer than me. I'd just embarrass myself."

He bumps his shoulder against mine. "You're a good dancer."

"Not as good as you."

He laughs. "Maybe. But I've had more practice. My mom got me into lessons when I was seven."

My eyes bug. "You've been dancing that long?"

He nods, flashing me a wry smile. "But it was traditional dancing. From China. Because my mother was Chinese. She didn't let me do cool dancing until I was ten."

I laugh with him, and when he puts his hand on my shoulder to guide me around a pair of tipsy girls sloshing their drinks, warmth blossoms underneath my skin. My eyes shoot to Jason, but he's walking ahead of us, chatting with their manager.

"Sophie told me your dad lives in Beijing," I say, forcing my attention back to Yoon Jae. "Is that where your mom's from?"

His smile fades, and he diverts his gaze to the floor. "It is. That's also where I grew up. My father moved back there after my mother died two years ago."

"Oh, I'm—I'm so sorry!"

I place my hand on his shoulder, but I catch Jason peering back at us, and my hand slips back into place at my side. The stormy look in his eyes forms a knot in my stomach.

Eden's manager deposits us in a private room, and before we even have time to order, a round of drinks arrives.

I sit on the long leather couch between Yoon Jae and Sophie, but she and Tae Hwa disappear after only a few minutes. Although Yoon Jae continues to talk to me, the tension in the room rises until I can't believe he doesn't notice it. Jason sits in the corner, keeping silent. He stares daggers at Yoon Jae, which isn't unusual, but then I catch Yoon Jae scowling at Jason. Weird.

"Grace?"

I perk at the sound of my name.

Jason gets to his feet and holds a hand out to me. "Do you want to check out the rest of the club?"

"Uhh . . ."

He doesn't wait for me to respond and grabs my wrist before I can process our skin touching. He leads me back out to the main lounge, where the music has switched to a popular American hip-hop track. No one pays us any attention as we make our way through the crowd. They're all too cool to look starstruck, I guess. Either that or they're all famous, too, and I just don't recognize them.

I expect Jason to head straight to the bar, but instead he makes a direct line to a group of people congregating around a table deep in the shadows. He presses into the crowd, and they part with curious glances. I catch a few scowls directed my way from some of the girls but ignore the heat creeping its way up my neck.

At the round booth sit two guys and four girls, but it's clear who the important person is here. He's in his late twenties, with shaggy hair that plays across his eyebrows, cheekbones any model would covet, and a shirt halfway unbuttoned to reveal a lot of tan, muscled chest. Every woman within a twenty-foot radius has her eyes on him.

Jason says something to the guy in Korean, and he answers with an easy laugh. He then shifts his gaze to me, and I'm frozen under his attention.

"Jason tells me you go to his school," the guy says, in only lightly accented English. "Do you like Korea?"

"Yes!" I say, because it's the only word that comes to my embarrassingly dazzled brain.

He smiles, and it's like the entire club lights up.

"Good," he says, gesturing to Jason. "I hope you stay here. He needs a girl to make sure he acts like a good boy."

He shifts back to Korean—presumably, a translation—and the crowd around him twitters with laughter. With a nod, Jason and I are dismissed, and we meld back into the crowd.

Once we're away from the posse, I grab Jason's shirt sleeve and hiss in his ear, "Who was that?"

"His stage name is Storm. He's one of the most famous KPOP singers there is." He cocks an eyebrow. "Is there anyone else I should introduce you to?"

I stare at him in confusion, trying to process this friendlier side of him. I'm ready to question him about why he's now decided he wants to introduce me to everyone he knows, when a hand falls on his shoulder and turns him around before I can sputter a word.

Na Na.

She's wearing a black dress, like me, but the dramatically low neckline on hers makes the plain color seem bold. Her hair's slicked back into a tight ponytail that looks glamorous paired with her dramatic black eyeliner and cherry red lipstick. She pouts at him and says something in Korean, ignoring me altogether.

I tilt my head toward them in hopes of catching at least a few words I recognize, but the music's too loud and my nerves are too shot for me to focus on her simpering voice.

She lets her hand slide from his shoulder down his chest before lingering a second too long on his stomach. My eyes bug, and if she wasn't so gorgeous, I'd say she had to be drunk to feel him up like that in public. As it is, though, she's probably just used to every male specimen praying for even a look from her.

Na Na flicks her gaze past him to me, and it's like she focuses every evil thought she's ever had right at my face. My anger ignites, and choice words rip through my brain. But instead of letting the insults fly, I give her a tight-lipped smile and a mock bow, then turn smoothly and stomp my way back toward the private room.

My mind replays her hand running down Jason's chest, the way her fingers slipped across the fabric, closer to him than I've ever been. And my irritation swells.

"Grace! Wait!"

I keep walking, weaving my way through the crowds, ignoring the stares and outright glares sent my way. My eyes sting, and I blink hard, suddenly wishing to just be back in my bed.

"Grace!"

Jason jumps in front of me with an exasperated sigh. "I didn't know Na Na was coming tonight."

I cross my arms. "I don't care if she's here or not. I don't care what you do at all."

He shakes his head, his hands coming up like he might grab my shoulders, but they fall back to his sides. "I wanted you to meet people tonight," he says, "to be more a part of my life."

Something inside me softens, but I ignore it, focusing on the memory of Na Na's hands pressed against his shirt, the warmth of her palms seeping into his skin. My stomach knots.

"Just forget it," I say. "I don't want to meet any of your famous friends or get a better glimpse into your life. I know what fame is like, and I'm not into it." I steel my voice, preparing myself to hit him hard with it. "I don't want to be included in this part of your life. I don't want to be included in any of it."

His expression freezes, and I leave before he has time to pull his thoughts together. I swallow the burning in my throat, focusing on my steps so I don't stumble. I press a hand to my stomach, shuffle to the bathroom, and run my wrists underneath the cold water, then wet the back of my neck with it.

I stare at my reflection in the mirror, refusing to let myself replay the conversation, refusing to let myself consider how it could have gone differently. I did the right thing. This weird flirtation we have going on needed to come to an end.

I just wish I could believe that.

On my way back to the private room, my mind's so full of Jason that I almost run into the shadowed figures in the dim hall. A boy has his hands on either side of a girl, pinning her to the wall, which trembles with the bass echoing throughout the entire club. They're kissing like there's no tomorrow, and heat zips through my veins just seeing them.

I attempt to walk around them inconspicuously, but I bump into the guy and he looks up. A gasp escapes my lips before I can clap a hand over my mouth. Tae Hwa's eyes get big when he recognizes me, and he jumps away from Sophie, who adjusts the skirt of her dress. She should be more worried about her mussed hair and smudged lipstick.

"Sorry, sorry." Tae Hwa forces a strained smile, bowing his head, then disappears back into our room.

I stare at Sophie and wait for her to explain, my mouth twisting into a disbelieving grin, a momentary respite from my own drama.

She scowls. "Don't look so smug."

"I *knew* there was something going on between you two."

"There was nothing going on then. And there's nothing going on now."

"That didn't look like nothing."

She scoffs, but I spot the hurt in her eyes. I rest my hand on her shoulder.

"Hey, what's wrong?" I ask.

Her eyes well with tears, and I pull her into a hug.

"I like him so much," she says between sniffles, her face pressed into my shoulder. "But he said we should only be friends, that it wasn't a good idea for him to date his best friend's sister."

"Was this before or after you guys sucked face?"

I intended that to be a joke, but it only makes her cry harder. "I—I kind of—" She hiccups. "Kind of attacked him with the kiss."

I laugh. I can't help it. It's impossible for me to envision Sophie planting one on Tae Hwa, but I've got to give it to the girl. She took charge.

She pulls away, swiping underneath her eyes with her fingers. Good thing she went with the waterproof mascara.

"Why are boys so dumb?" she asks.

I sigh, unable to give her an answer. "No idea. I've been wondering the same thing myself."

Throwing my arm around her shoulders, I give her one more quick squeeze. We head back to the private room after Sophie has calmed down. But when I open the door, I freeze. Yoon Jae and Jason glower at each other across the knee-high table, both standing and leaning toward the other. His fists clenched at his sides, Jason watches the other boy with disdainful eyes. Yoon Jae barks at him in Korean, pointing at his bandmate with angry jabs.

They both shoot their gazes to the door when I enter. Yoon Jae rearranges his expression to a tight smile, but there's nothing friendly about the anger brooding in his eyes.

"Excuse me," he says, nodding at me and Sophie before pushing past us and rushing out.

I stare after him, then look to Jason. He watches Yoon Jae's exit, his shoulders still tense.

"What just happened?" I ask.

Tae Hwa attempts to blend into the sofa, and I don't know if it's because he's embarrassed that I stumbled upon him sticking his tongue down Sophie's throat or because of the argument I just interrupted. I glance back at Sophie, but all her attention's focused on Tae Hwa.

Jason picks up his jacket from the couch and shrugs into it. "I'm leaving," he announces.

But when he tries to brush past me, I grab his arm and stop him. "Hey, what's going on?"

He shrugs out of my grip, his gaze lingering on my hand a second too long. "Nothing you need to worry about. You don't want to be part of my life, remember?"

And with that, he leaves. I glance back and forth between Sophie and Tae Hwa, who studiously avoid each other's gazes, and I blow out a long sigh. I knew I didn't want to go out tonight.

Both Yoon Jae and Jason call cabs to pick them up, so Tae Hwa, Sophie, and I take the limo back to school. I watch the city lights blur past, unable to shake my thoughts about Jason and Yoon

Jae. There's always been tension there, but something has changed between them.

And I'm going to find out what.

The next morning, however, the entertainment news leaks the story and I don't have to do any digging—Eden is breaking up. After only a few weeks of the band working on their new album, their publicist announced they would no longer be working together and, apparently, the outing to the club was a last-ditch effort to try to fool the press.

Sophie seems just as shocked as I am.

She sinks into her desk chair, eyes glazed. "I just—I can't believe he would do this. Why would he break up the band?"

"Who?"

"Jason!" She hands me an entertainment gossip magazine, but it's in Korean, so all I can glean are pictures. "It says that Jason was the one who decided to break up," she continues. "I just don't understand why he would do that. Tae Hwa and Yoon Jae are his best friends."

I almost tell her Jason and Yoon Jae are, in fact, *not* best friends, but I decide to keep that to myself. Her face reddens, her hands ball into fists, and I'm afraid of contradicting anything she says at this point—she might punch me.

"How could he?" she whispers.

I shrug. "Maybe he just decided it was time for them to part ways."

She shakes her head. "No, that can't be it. He knows the band is everything to Tae Hwa. Jason can move on from this, still have a career. He's the front man, so there will always be options for him. But Tae Hwa? He's just a bassist. Without the band, he has no career."

I keep silent. She's right. I've seen it with some of the bands my dad produced—they'd break up, but the singer would get a future gig with another group or go solo. Sometimes, bands break up just because the lead singer wants to go solo, but I can't see Jason giving up his friendship with Tae Hwa for a new career direction, even if he didn't like working with Yoon Jae. There has to be another explanation.

"We don't know the whole story," I say. "Why don't you ask him?"

She scoffs, throwing a pencil across the room. "He doesn't deserve the opportunity to explain."

Slamming her school books closed and shoving her desk drawers shut, she mutters under her breath in rapid-fire Korean. I watch her throw on a jacket and wince when she yanks our dorm-room door closed behind her. Grabbing my room key and phone, I tail her.

As I expected, she heads to Jason and Tae Hwa's dorm. She pounds her fist against the door until Jason pulls it open. Dark semicircles beneath his eyes and hair sticking up like he either just rolled out of bed or had a rough night, he pokes his head out to see her.

"Get out of my way," she snaps. "I'm not here to see you."

He glances at me, and I shrug. With a sigh, he lets us into the messy room. Clothes are strewn all over the floor, furniture is pulled away from the wall, and books are stacked in piles across the room. I peek into the bathroom and spot toothpaste, hair gel, and other toiletries all sitting out on the counter. Tae Hwa stands at his desk, throwing books and pictures into a suitcase.

Sophie helps Tae Hwa, but I hang back, standing beside Jason. He won't look at either of them, just leans against the wall with his arms folded across his chest and eyes downcast.

"Sophie's pissed at you," I tell him.

"Noticed," he mumbles.

"Why did you do it?"

But he doesn't answer.

Sophie whirls around to face her brother, throwing angry Korean words at him. I have no idea what she's saying, but judging by her tone, it can't be pretty. Jason has the decency to at least look chagrined.

"Grace." Sophie turns to me. "I'm sorry you had to see this."

After a few more seconds of glaring at her brother, she takes Tae Hwa's hand and they exit, leaving me alone with Jason. We stand there in awkward silence a few moments before he begins to toss clothes into Tae Hwa's bag.

I bend down and help him pick some up, then fold them before placing them into the suitcase. Jason watches me with wary eyes, like he expects me to scream at him the way Sophie did.

"I'm not going to get mad at you, if that's what you're worried about," I say. "If I had to guess, I'd say Sophie already said enough."

He doesn't respond.

With all the clothes packed, I move to the stacks of books. "I'll be honest—I would like to know why you did it, too. But that's none of my business. This is between the members of the band, not anyone else."

He's quiet a long while, then murmurs, "I just couldn't do it anymore. I hated it. All of it."

"What? Being in Eden?"

He scrubs his face with both hands. "You don't understand. I never wanted to be a part of Eden. I wanted to make my kind of music. But then we signed the contract, and the producer made us change everything." His voice sharpens. "Then they added Yoon Jae."

"You really dislike him, don't you?"

He scowls but doesn't deny it.

"I just don't understand why you dislike him so much."

"He wasn't supposed to be in our band!" he cries, then slumps against the wall with a long exhale. "It's not fair. Tae Hwa and I worked hard for our debut, but he just waltzed in after one audition. I'd thought we could be friends, but we just—we just can't. He ruined the band."

I consider mentioning Jason's distaste for his music but change my mind with a sigh, standing. "Look, just let Sophie take some time. She'll get over it. I mean, you're her brother. She can't be mad at you forever."

I make to leave, but Jason stops me with, "Grace?"

"Yeah?"

His face melts into a half smile. "Thanks."

"For what?"

"For understanding. Or trying to, anyway."

Even though you said you didn't want to be a part of my life. It goes unsaid because he doesn't have to say it. We both know he's thinking it.

"I'm not letting you off the hook. I just don't think it's my business to judge you when I don't know the circumstances. Maybe you *are* a jerk, I don't know. But it's not my place to tell you that. You need to figure it out yourself."

And even though I want to tell him off, to yell at him about how he snubbed me and how introducing me to some famous guy doesn't erase him ignoring me all Christmas break, I leave. I shut the door and try to think of the way Momma talks to me, like I purposefully screw up everything I touch. No one deserves a guilt trip, especially when they're already hurting.

I know that from personal experience.

Chapter Nineteen

The gossip surrounding Eden's breakup doesn't die down, and by the beginning of March, I'm fed up with hearing about it. At first, I scoured every Korean entertainment blog on the Internet and read all I could about the rumors swirling around the band—with the help of my browser's translator tool. A lot of sources claim Jason's the instigator, but others say Yoon Jae wanted to go solo. I don't know what to believe, and Jason isn't forthcoming with information, so I'm left wondering.

One thing is for sure, though—Jason and Yoon Jae haven't gotten along since they met. Unnamed sources from the record label came forward and talked about how the two boys would argue in the studio and refuse to spend time together except at publicity events and concerts. Most of the articles lay the blame on Jason, but one mentions that Yoon Jae didn't care about being in the band in the first place and he made that clear early on because he wanted to be in a different kind of band, where he could dance instead of play an instrument. I can see how the two would butt heads.

I'd have thought everybody at school would be super interested in the recently deceased band, but our classmates give the boys wide berths. I also suspected Yoon Jae and Tae Hwa would ditch school now that Jason's no longer keeping them here, but they stay. Sophie says it's because it's too late in the year to transfer without huge hassles, but I suspect it has more to do with their label wanting to maintain an image of civility between Jason and the other two.

Sophie still hasn't forgiven Jason. Every time I try to bring him up in conversation with her, she changes the subject or laughs away my questions. Tae Hwa moved to another dorm, and the only time I see Jason is in class. But, as the weeks pass by, I can see him withdrawing any interest in school. He comes into class just as the bell rings, his clothes and hair disheveled, and he never turns in homework.

When he skips three days of school, in good conscience I have to investigate. But when I ask Sophie about it, she responds, "How would I know what's going on with him? I'm not talking to him."

I bite back any criticism, though I wish she realized how petty she's being. He's her *brother*.

Before dinner, I text him. But he doesn't answer, and as I'm picking at my broccoli, all I can think about is him.

On my way to his dorm, I call, but he doesn't pick up. Muttering choice words under my breath, I climb the stairs to his floor. I beat on the door. If he's taking a nap or studying, he can deal. I'll be honest—I'm worried. I just need to make sure he's still breathing, still eating. And once I surmise that, I can go back to thinking he's a terrible person.

I wait a few seconds at the door before knocking again. No answer. I call him again. And then three more times. On the fourth try, he finally answers.

"Grace?" he says, but his voice is muffled by a static of insanely loud noises in the background.

"Where are you?" I press my hand over my other ear to hear him better, heading back down the stairs.

"Grace!" He sounds uncharacteristically excited to hear my voice.

"Umm . . . are you okay?"

"Of course I'm okay!" he cries. "Why wouldn't I be?"

I'm officially scared now. "Jason, where are you?"

He laughs, and the phone crackles like one of us is losing service. "I'm at the bar."

"Which one?"

"Umm . . . " His voice trails off, and he calls to someone in Korean.

"Jason!"

My heart pounds against the inside of my chest, my mind flipping back to another phone call. One with Nathan. Oh, God, please don't let this end up like it did with Nathan.

That old anxiety threatens to assert itself, and I struggle to get it back down. I can't freak out right now. I've got to find Jason. I've got to help him. Like I couldn't do with my brother.

"Grace?" he says, like he's forgotten he's on the phone with me.

I force my voice to stay level. "Jason, which bar are you at?"

"The Lotus? I think. In Incheon."

"Okay, well, stay there. I'm going to meet you."

I hang up before he can respond, then do a Google search for a Lotus bar in Incheon and I scroll through my phone contacts in search of the driver Jason's management company employs. Once I find both, I call the driver, and after a few minutes of mixed English and Korean, he agrees to pick me up.

I meet the driver out front, and as we head down the highway, I mentally scream at him to go faster. I'm probably overreacting, but my mind keeps going back to Nathan. Where I found him that night. He'd called me, and I brushed it off as a drunk dial. I had no idea it would end the way it did.

I toss up another quick prayer that Jason doesn't do anything stupid.

We finally reach Incheon, and I jump out of the car on the street the Google map said the bar is on, searching for anything that says "Lotus." I'll even content myself with a picture of a flower. I'm afraid the name will be written in *Hangul* so I won't ever find it, when I spot a familiar face in the crowd on the street.

He slouches against a crosswalk sign, his head hanging and shoulders slumped. His hair's hanging in his face, but I recognize the jacket I bought him. People do a double take when they pass him, like they're not sure if that's Jason Bae.

"Jason!" Relief floods my body.

He looks up when I rush over to him, and a slow smile brightens his face but doesn't reach his glazed, bloodshot eyes. When I get close, I can smell alcohol on him, and my heart sinks.

"Hi, Grace." He takes a step toward me and stumbles.

I catch him, and he chuckles against my shoulder. "You smell good," he says into the fabric of my shirt.

"Well, you don't." But my chest still tightens at the warmth from his body soaking through my clothes.

I make a quick scan of the people on the street around us, but no one has whipped out a camera or cell phone, so at least we don't have to worry about any embarrassing shots showing up online tomorrow.

"We should get you home," I say, steadying him.

"But I want to have fun." He tries to pull away from me but almost falls. "Everyone thinks I'm a loser, so I might as well act like one!" he shouts.

People turn around, whispering to each other. A few cameras are pulled out, and an excited hum travels through the crowd gathering around us.

Sucking in a sharp breath through my teeth, I throw my arm around his waist and hold him upright. "Let's get into the car."

But when I turn around, the driver—and the car—is gone. I call him, but he doesn't pick up. I'm stranded. With a drunk Jason. In the middle of a city of 2.5 million people who all know his face.

Swallowing my panic, I half carry, half shuffle him to the bus station, because that's the only solution I can think of. He laughs in my ear the entire way there.

I dump him on the bench and ignore the staring and pointing from passersby. Relief floods me as our bus pulls up.

"Okay, let's go," I say.

He doesn't stand.

"Don't make this difficult," I mutter. "I'm not carrying you."

But I hoist him up from the bench anyway. He leans against me as we struggle onto the bus and shuffle to the back row. I sink into a seat beside him, shooting death glares at any passengers who dare to glance our way.

Jason leans his head back and closes his eyes. "Grace?"

"What?" I snap.

"Why are you here?"

"Because I'm going to school here."

"No, not in Korea." He jerks a finger between us, motioning at himself, then me. "Here. You told me you didn't want anything to do with me."

That's a good point. Why do I even care? I steal a glance at him, at the uninhibited dependency, and my heart constricts. He needs someone. Everyone thinks he'll be fine with the band's breakup, but it seems like he's the one suffering. And if Sophie isn't going to make sure he doesn't self-destruct, someone needs to.

But, beneath that, there's something I can't explain. Some instinct to be close to him, no matter how. Something deeper than my appreciation for the way his V-necks show off his collarbones and how his rare smiles light up his face. Something I'm not sure I'm ready to investigate.

We make it to our stop and somehow we manage to get back to campus without a fan mob descending on us. I should get a medal for this good deed.

"Get your key out," I tell him when we're at his building.

"Huh?" He hiccups.

"Your key."

He stuffs a hand into his pocket, then tries the other three. His features twist into a puzzled expression. "I don't . . . I don't have it."

"What?"

"I guess I uhh . . . " He laughs. "I guess I left it in my room." He pats his pants like the key will miraculously appear in one of his empty pockets.

"I can't believe this," I mutter.

He deserves to sleep on the street tonight, but I can't leave him out here. Should I go ask his RA to unlock the door? But the RA could take a picture of Jason or tell some gossip magazine about it, despite the ban on communication with the press. Jason's reputation would just get worse.

After a minute's deliberation, I make a quick decision, fighting the blush creeping up my neck. "Okay, come on. You're coming to my room."

He doesn't respond, just follows me. Sophie's visiting one of her friends from her old school who came down from Seoul, and they're spending the night in a hotel. Convenient. Maybe God is smiling on me.

I glance at Jason as he stumbles over a crack in the pavement. Okay, maybe he isn't.

When I get us to my room, it's already past ten o'clock. Jason slumps into a chair and starts looking through the papers sitting on top of my desk, then digs through my drawers and picks up a photo I stuffed in there when I moved in.

"Who's this?" He points to Nathan, who has his arm slung across my shoulders.

Panic jolts through me, and I snatch the picture from his hand, shrieking, "What are you doing? You can't just look through people's stuff!"

His face falls, and he looks so contrite I almost forgive him. "Sorry," he says.

I blow out a slow breath. "It's fine. Just stop acting like a kid I need to babysit."

I search through my drawers for something modest but cute I can wear to sleep in. I am *not* putting on my dad's old ratty T-shirt that I stole. When I come out of the bathroom in yoga pants and a tank top, I find Jason curled up on his side on my bed, snoring lightly, his shoes still on.

"You've got to be kidding." I just stare at him, frustration mingling with the butterflies swirling in my stomach.

Muttering a few choice words, I yank off his sneakers and toss them onto the floor. I nudge him, but he's out. I consider rolling him onto the floor, where he can spend the rest of the night, but my hospitable Southern upbringing kicks in and I can't go through with it. Instead, I climb up onto Sophie's bed and crawl between the sheets.

We're alone in my room, and Jason is sleeping in my bed, and I may want to strangle him for getting wasted—but my pulse leaps every time I remember the way he leaned against me as we walked to the bus station, how his breath warmed my neck, and how I could still smell his cologne underneath the stink of stale alcohol.

I shut down those thoughts, refusing to let my mind linger on them, and instead fall asleep listening to Jason's breathing, worrying that he has alcohol poisoning. But I wake up only a few hours later to the sound of him banging the bathroom door open. I sit up, blinking back sleep, just in time to hear him puke his guts out. I sit there a second, not sure if I'm awake or still dreaming.

KPOP superstar Jason Bae is throwing up in my bathroom.

Talk about surreal.

A groan floats from the bathroom, and it shakes me out of my reverie. I climb down from the bed and venture to look in on him. Jason is bent over the toilet, his forehead pressed into his arm, which rests across the seat.

"Are you okay?" I ask.

He doesn't look up, just moans, and I can't help thinking of what he told me about his dad's alcoholism. And connecting it to Nathan's drug and alcohol addiction. My brother spent a lot of time on the bathroom floor when he was on tour—I got the full story from his drummer a few months before I left for Korea.

I sit down on the tiled floor next to Jason and rest my hand on his back. He flinches at my touch but doesn't pull away, then empties the rest of his stomach. I swallow a gag of my own, rubbing my hand up and down his back like Momma did when I was sick as a kid—one of the few memories I have of her being maternal.

He pushes away from the toilet and leans back against the wall. "I'm sorry," he says in a hoarse whisper.

"Don't worry. You can clean it up in the morning." Even I hear the strain in my forced levity.

He slumps onto the floor, his head resting on the mat. With a sigh, I scoot closer and put his head in my lap. He tenses, but I brush my fingers through his hair and his muscles relax.

"I'm totally using this as blackmail one day, just so you know," I say.

He chuckles softly, taking my other hand and threading our fingers together. My heartbeat sputters, but I keep the butterflies under control.

"Don't leave me, okay?" he mumbles.

"Okay," I say around the lump in my throat.

"Promise?"

"Promise."

A shiver ripples down my spine, and I can't deny it anymore. I'm in love with this boy.

I love his hair that swooshes across his forehead, the jeans and colorful sneakers, and the way he sometimes cynically responds to life, like it's something to be endured instead of enjoyed. But, more than that, I love *him*.

It's not a crush. It's not me just kind of liking him the way I liked Isaac.

It's the L-word.

And that scares me more than anything I can imagine.

I lean back against the wall and marvel at this situation. It seems ridiculous, but I know this is where I'm supposed to be. Maybe it's crazy. Maybe I'm attracted to him out of some twisted desire for a redo, to help him where I couldn't help Nathan.

But what if Jason just gets worse? What if I let myself get close to him, and he self-destructs? Could I handle losing someone like that again?

But despite the fear, there's no way I'm staying out of his life. I can't leave him. I have to help.

Because that's what you do for people you love.

"You may be trying to ruin your life, but I won't let you," I say, more to myself than to him. "I'm not going to let you turn into your dad." I think back to the picture he picked up earlier, and my voice falls to a whisper. "I'm not letting you become like my brother, either. I promise. You and me? We're pulling you out of this."

And maybe when all this drama with the band is over, when Sophie's forgiven him and life returns to the ordinary—when he's not broken—we can be together. Maybe we can be normal.

Chapter Twenty

The next morning, I wake up before Jason and throw on some clothes and brush my teeth before shaking him awake. I couldn't sleep last night, waking up every hour to peek down from Sophie's bed to check on him. But he slept under my pink sheets through the night.

"Hey, wake up." I nudge his shoulder.

He turns away from me, muttering something unintelligible under his breath. I try not to notice how adorable he looks hugging the pillow to his chest.

"Jason." I shake him. "Wake up."

He bolts upright and knocks his head against the top bunk. Crying out something in Korean—probably a curse—he rubs at his forehead, then notices me laughing at him. He startles and glances down at the bed.

"Did I sleep here last night?" he asks.

"Obviously."

The blood drains from his face.

"Get up." I slap his arm before we can veer into awkward

territory. "We're going out for coffee, because you're going to have a wicked hangover."

He crawls out of bed and looks down at his rumpled clothes.

"Go get your RA to let you into your room, then take a shower. Change your clothes. I'll meet you in front of your building in an hour." I toss his shoes to him.

Avoiding eye contact, he slips on his sneakers and exits. I stand in the middle of the room and stare at the door, an emptiness settling in my chest in his absence. But I shake off any dark thoughts and spend the rest of the time getting ready.

Before heading out, I strip my bed. I poke my nose into the sheets and recognize a familiar smell—Jason's cologne. My stomach somersaults.

My bed.

Smells.

Like Jason.

I have to wad up the blankets and stuff them into my laundry basket to curb my rambling thoughts.

I find Jason waiting for me, sitting on the steps of his building. He stands when I approach, and I smile at the anxious look on his face. I can't remember him ever being this embarrassed around me before.

"Are you ready?" I ask.

He nods, stuffing his hands into his pockets and falling into step beside me. We head straight for the coffee in the dining hall.

We choose a table in a quiet corner, and he sips his coffee in silence, though I can tell by the way he winces when people talk too loud that he's not feeling great. I slip a couple ibuprofens across the table, and he takes them with a weary smile.

"I'm sorry about last night," he says.

"Don't worry about it. No big deal."

He grimaces. "Yes, it is. It was incredibly irresponsible of me."

"Yeah, it was." I shrug. "But that's okay. Now you owe me."

He cocks an eyebrow. "I do?"

"Yup, and I'm cashing in now."

His face melts into a smile. "What do you want?"

"For you to get better," I say, ignoring the nervousness growing inside me.

"Get better? What's wrong with me?"

"I don't know. You tell me."

He stares at me in confusion. "I don't know what you're talking about."

I sigh. "Jason, let's be real here. You're depressed. I'm assuming it's because of what happened with the band, but if I had to guess, I would say it started before that. Am I right?"

He bristles, frowning. "This isn't—"

"Don't deny it. I know the signs. Trust me."

Though he doesn't argue, he scowls at me. But I take his silence as a sign to keep going. I'm not an expert, but I know enough to realize he needs help. Maybe not counselor-type help, but at least someone to show him they care. And, apparently, I'm the only one lining up.

"If you're having a hard time, you need to ask for help," I say. "Whatever's going on, you need to talk to somebody about it. And do other things that make you happy. You can't wallow in your problems."

"I'm not wallowing!" he cries, then winces and lowers his voice. "This is ridiculous."

"Is it? Then why are you going out and getting wasted? Why are you missing school? Why don't you ever hang out with your friends anymore?"

"Because my friends won't talk to me," he snaps.

"Obviously, one of them still talks to you."

He scoffs, but I can see the fight seeping out of him. He gazes out the big window that faces the street, a wistful look in his eyes.

"Sophie's never been mad at me," he says. "Not like this." His voice falls to a whisper. "I can't lose her, Grace."

I nod, my chest tightening. I would kill to hear Nathan say that about me.

"You're hurting," I say, fighting the urge to take Jason's hand, which rests on top of the table. "Whatever you're going through, I want to help. Just let me."

"Why do you care?" he asks, not a challenge—genuine curiosity. "I thought you were mad at me."

I bark a laugh. "I still am. But that doesn't mean I'm going to ignore a friend who's in trouble."

This silences him. His eyes soften, and it takes all my self-control not to tell him that I forgive everything and to beg him to tell me he likes me. That maybe I could deal with his issues if he would kiss me again.

I clear my throat to get rid of the words that threaten to spill from my mouth. "You may not be ready to talk to me about whatever's going on, and that's okay. Maybe you'll never be ready. But I'm not leaving you alone until I've decided that you're better, okay?"

He nods, forcing his face into a look of mock seriousness. "Yes, ma'am," he says with an egregious fake Southern accent.

I wrinkle my nose. "That offends not only me but also every Southerner who's ever lived."

He laughs, flashing me a grin that sends a jolt of longing through my chest.

I shoot out my hand. "Let's shake on it—from now on, you're on the happy road to recovery."

He takes my hand and holds it a second too long. He stares at me with an unreadable expression that brings a hot blush to my cheeks, which I attempt to hide behind my coffee mug. I chug down the rest while my face resumes its normal coloring.

I drop Jason off at his dorm a couple hours later, and I find

Sophie in our room. She's eerily quiet as I flip through my note-book looking for the page I wrote my homework on.

"You shouldn't be hanging out with him, you know," she says, breaking the tense silence.

"Who?"

"Jason. Obviously."

"Sophie." I search for the right words, to keep myself from sounding judgmental, but not letting her off the hook, either. "Give him a break. He's taking it a lot harder than you think."

She scoffs, but I can see the uneasiness in her eyes. "What-ever. But you're the one who's having to pay for being the Good Samaritan."

"What do you mean, I'm paying for it?"

She holds up her phone, which has a Web browser pulled up. "Have you not seen this?"

I take her phone and see my face splattered across the screen. In a Korean tabloid. I can't read the article, but I would guess it has something to do with paparazzi spotting me and Jason together last night. Thankfully, in the photo, you can't tell he's trashed. It just looks like we're canoodling on the bus.

I cringe. "It's not what it looks like."

"It doesn't matter what actually happened, just what every-one sees." She clears her throat uneasily. "Do you . . . do you *like* him?"

My eyes widen. "What? Sophie, I—"

She shakes her head, forcing a smile. "Forget it. Silly ques-tion. But, Grace." She shoots me a pitying look. "If you're going to hang around him right now, you're going to get pulled into the press. You need to decide whether or not he's worth it."

I look down at the picture again, wondering how long it will take for reporters to dig around enough to discover who I really am and who my family is. It wouldn't be hard to put it together, that Nathan's my brother.

My first instinct is to shy away from this type of exposure. But I stare at the image, at Jason, at the guy who's a lot more talented, a lot sweeter than he lets most people see. And I realize: He's worth it.

He's worth everything.

"When was the last time you actually wrote a song?" I ask.

Plucking at the strings on his guitar, Jason shrugs. "Probably not since we wrote the song for the drama."

"Well, no wonder you're depressed," I say, sarcasm thick in my voice. "Your creativity is all bottled up. You've got to let it out."

He chuckles, shifting on top of the bed closer to me. With both of our backs against the wall and our legs close enough to almost touch, I have to focus on our conversation and keeping my breathing level.

"So, my mother emailed me last night," I say, surprise shooting through me that I would bring up the topic.

"Yeah? What did she say?"

I pick at the lint on his comforter. "She asked about graduation. You know, since that's coming up."

"Right." He pauses in the middle of his song. "Are your parents coming for the ceremony?"

I shrug, suddenly desperate to change the topic. I reach for the first question that comes to mind, which, unfortunately, happens to be, "So, are you ever going to tell me what inspired your epic downward spiral?"

I cringe at my lack both of transition skills and sensitivity. Though I do sort of want to know.

I expect him to make a snide comeback, but he says, "I don't know. I guess . . . it felt like everybody was against me, when I didn't do anything wrong."

"You ruined Tae Hwa's and Yoon Jae's careers. I'm pretty sure that counts as wrong."

"But it wasn't just me. Yeah, I officially put an end to the band, but Yoon Jae suggested it first."

Okay, news flash. I guess the rumors about Yoon Jae hoping to go solo were true.

"Besides," he continues, "I'm pretty sure my career's ruined, too."

Jason plays a tune I recognize.

"Hey, that's 'Sweet Home Alabama,'" I cry.

"I thought you'd like to reconnect with your roots."

"I'm from Tennessee, not Alabama, you idiot." I slap his shoulder, and he flinches away with a laugh.

"Play something else," I order. "Play something new."

His eyebrows shoot up. "Are you trying to force my creativity?"

"Yes. Go."

He breathes out a dramatic sigh, takes a moment to think, then begins picking a few lazy chords. A few moments later, he sings a languid melody in soft tones. His voice wraps around me better than any hug and brings a smile I can't shake.

"Do I get a translation?" I ask, still caught up in the notes and how the foreign words spill from his lips.

He stops singing but repeats the song on the guitar. "No."

"Why not?"

"Because it's about you."

Heat rushes to my cheeks and I gape at him, but all he does is smile down at the instrument in his hands, watching his fingers move across the strings. He's singing a song about me.

Me.

Grace Wilde.

I've become a muse. Like Pattie Boyd, who inspired Eric Clapton's "Layla" and "Wonderful Tonight."

Though I'm sure my song isn't as cool as those. It's probably about how my feet smell or how I don't always chew with my mouth closed. But still. I have a song.

He picks the lyrics back up again, and I try to memorize the sounds of the words so I can repeat them to Sophie so we can figure out what they mean. But then I realize she probably wouldn't translate them for me anyway—another week has passed and she's still angry with Jason.

I pull out my phone and type out phonetically what I hear him sing. He pauses to look over my shoulder.

"What are you doing?" he asks.

"Trying to write down the words so I can translate them later."

He spits out a laugh, pointing to the phrase I just typed. "That's not even close to the right word. How did you ever pass your Korean midterm?"

"Then tell me what the right word is."

"Not a chance."

We spend the rest of the afternoon joking about his music and singing Backstreet Boys and Girls' Generation—the KPOP band I haven't been able to stop listening to since Sophie suggested them—at the top of our lungs until someone in the room next door bangs on the wall and yells for us to stop. And I wish we could share moments like this outside his room, outside school, and outside Ganghwa Island. I want them where everyone can see us so I can know that Jason doesn't want to hide me, that he's proud to have me beside him. Because I'm worth something.

My throat tightens, and my eyes sting with unshed tears. Annoyance flares at the knot of emotions growing inside my stomach, and I clear my throat, glancing down at my watch.

"It's already six o'clock," I say, forcing the dark feelings to the back of my brain. "Do you want to go grab dinner?"

Jason reaches around me to set the guitar in its stand, and his hair dusts against my face. I suck in a sharp breath but mask it with a cough, trying to hide my flaming cheeks from his view by pretending to be absorbed in my phone.

"I'm not really that hungry," he says.

"But it's Friday night. We should go do something fun."

"You said I'm not allowed to do anything fun anymore."

"When did I say that?"

"You said no more bar hopping."

I roll my eyes. "Just because you can't drink yourself into a stupor doesn't mean you can't have fun. I'm here, aren't I? I'm plenty fun."

He chuckles under his breath. "Yeah, I guess you are."

"I'm not a distraction anymore?" My breath stills as I wait for an answer that shouldn't mean as much as it does.

He cuts his eyes to me, a sly smile curling his lips. "Oh no, you're definitely still a distraction." When I frown, he adds, "But the best possible kind."

My palms moisten, and a tingly sensation stretches up from the pit of my stomach to the tips of my fingers. I try to look at his eyes and not let my gaze slip lower, but it does anyway. I glance at his mouth, visually tracing the lines, drawing them inside my head.

He must catch me staring, because his smile fades into a smirk. If heat wasn't licking up my neck, I would smack him.

"What if we go pick up something to eat and come back to watch a movie?" he asks.

But he doesn't wait for an answer. He hops down from the bed and grabs my wrist, pulling me with him. I groan, hanging back just to annoy him. He practically shoves me into my shoes and out the door, but I'm laughing the entire way.

We grab food from the dining hall because, after Jason's drunken escapades, the press discovered where he's going to school and are now camped out just off campus, waiting for their shot.

I'd have thought this would've upset him, but whenever I mention the loss of his secret, he just shrugs.

When we return to his room fifteen minutes later, with our take-out fried food in hand, Jason's happier than I've seen him in weeks. Maybe ever. There's no hesitancy in his smiles, no sadness in his eyes. When he looks at me, I see no trace of the Jason I walked home from the Lotus Bar or the Jason who still grieves for the broken family his father split up. Just Jason, the boy with the colorful sneakers and dark eyes, the one I wish loved me back.

I dig under his comforter for the remote, then switch on the TV. Flipping through the channels, I spot a familiar face.

I drop the French fry in my hand. "Oh my gosh. That's *you!*"

"What?" His face pales.

"You're on TV!" I squeal, turning up the volume.

It's the opening credits for a drama, and Jason's face flashes on the screen. It shows him playing the guitar, holding hands with Na Na while she lies in a hospital bed, and running away from what looks like a mobster hit man.

"We have to watch this," I say. "Why didn't you tell me it was already airing?"

As the show continues, I realize it's the first episode. I press buttons on the remote until English subtitles pop up on the bottom of the picture, and I can't take my eyes off the screen. The story mostly follows Na Na, but we get a few scenes with Jason, the starving artist who plays guitar on the street to raise money for food.

Jason groans as the camera cuts to him playing a mopey song in a dark room—very emo. "Turn it off," he says. "We don't need to watch this."

"What are you talking about? This is golden."

He narrows his eyes. "You just want to make fun of me."

"Of course I do!"

But that's a lie. I actually want to see him sing the song we wrote. Our song.

He stretches for the remote, but I hold it out of his reach. "Grace, seriously. I don't want to watch myself."

"Well, we're watching it, so get over it."

With a huff, he reaches over me, but I keep it away from his hands. He leans farther and steadies himself with a hand on my thigh. I cry out when all his weight presses down into my leg, and he lunges for the remote, only to fall on top of me. Laughing, we both fall back onto the mattress, his chest pressed against mine and my arm stretched above my head to keep the remote away from him.

But as we stare at each other, my laughter dies. I watch the smile fade from his face and his eyes darken. He glances down at my lips, and my chest tightens. My fingers relax, and the remote falls onto the floor with a clatter, but neither of us moves to snatch it up. His voice, playing through the TV's speakers, echoes in the background, but I can't take my eyes off the mouth so close to mine, all I would have to do is tilt my chin up to meet it.

"Grace . . . " He traces the line of my jaw with his index finger. "I told Na Na there was no way we were going to get together, and I only hung out with her to help publicize our drama."

My heart pounds against the inside of my ribs, partly in elation at his words, but mostly from the adrenaline spiking my veins. All I want is for him to close the gap between us. But fear kicks in, and warning flags shoot up inside my head. You can't trust a boy with a guitar. I may wish he loved me, but that's just a fantasy. *He* is a fantasy.

Chewing the inside of my cheek and recalling the anger I felt in Seoul when he acted so embarrassed by me, I turn my head away and press both palms against his chest. I only have to exert a little pressure before he backs off, sitting up and running a hand through his hair. He doesn't say anything, but his eyes throw a dozen questions at me, none of which I can answer.

I hop off the bed, clearing my throat in hopes of shattering the awkwardness. "I should probably go back. It's getting late. I'll call you tomorrow, and we can plan something to do. Sound good?" But I don't wait for him to answer, just search the room for my things. "We can exercise. It'll be good for you to do something active, get those endorphins pumping. Maybe I'll even cart *you* around on the back of a bicycle."

"Grace," he interrupts my monologue.

"Hmm?"

"I—I'm sorry." Regret swallows his eyes, which punches my gut like a fist.

"What are you talking about? I'll see you tomorrow."

I flee before he can say anything else. But when I escape into the hallway, I stop. Tears prick the backs of my eyes, and I lean my head back against the closed door. I can't deny how I feel about Jason—how his smile makes my stomach flip-flop, how I celebrate a victory every time he trusts me with a new bit of his past, and how his presence helps me forget about everything I left back in Nashville.

But we will never work.

This thing between us—whatever it is—can never go past friendship. Even if he *is* interested in me, I need a guy who's stable, who doesn't remind me of my brother. I need someone I don't always have to take care of, someone who can take care of me, too, and who is happy to have me beside him, even in the public eye. But when I try to picture the kind of boy I want, the kind I need, all I can envision is Jason.

Always Jason.

Chapter Twenty-one

I try spending less time with Jason, but my resolve lasts for maybe forty-eight hours before I realize hanging out with Sophie isn't enough. But I tell myself that just because I'm spending time with Jason doesn't mean I'm committing to any sort of relationship. We're friends, that's all.

After school one day, we wander out to the lawn behind the dining hall, where we sprawl underneath one of the trees.

"Shouldn't we be studying for finals?" Jason picks random chords on his guitar.

"Probably," I answer.

But neither of us gets up. No one pays attention to us, just two people amidst the throngs of students chatting with their friends or biking down the sidewalks. I think Jason likes the anonymity—because once he's back in Seoul, he'll have none of that.

"When are you going to actually start writing music again?" I ask.

"I don't know."

I close my eyes and listen to him play the beginning of Cat Stevens's "Peace Train."

"Are you going to keep playing the same type of music?" I ask. "When you start whatever your next project will be?"

"You mean *if*—*if* I start a new project."

I roll my eyes. "You'll keep playing. It's in your blood. You've just got to figure out how you want to do it."

He hesitates, then says, "I've already talked to my agent."

"Hah!" I cry. "I was right! I knew you couldn't just quit."

Jason chuckles, his fingers pausing over the strings. His smile fades. "I can't go back to that same type of music." His voice falls to a whisper. "I just got out of it with Eden's breakup. I'm not letting myself get pulled back into it again. It's soul-sucking. I like listening to pop music sometimes, but it's not what I want to play."

"So, do something different."

He tosses his hands into the air. "Like what? We were already playing a type of music you don't hear much in Korea in popular music. If I go any closer to rock, my label will drop me, because they don't have those kinds of artists."

Anxiety permeates his voice, and his expression clouds with uncertainty. He chews on his bottom lip.

"Have you ever thought about playing music in the States?"

He barks a brittle laugh. "No way."

"Why not?"

"Because I can't write songs in English."

"It's the same as writing in Korean."

"No, it's not."

I prop myself up on my elbows. "What's so different about it?"

"I can't, okay?" He huffs. "The words just don't come. I don't know."

"Have you ever really tried, and I mean seriously?"

He scowls. "It won't work."

I lie back again, hands behind my head. "Try."

He sighs, then strums a chord. "I'm so happy." Another chord. "Can't you see?" Same chord again. "I love you totally, with er . . . broccoli."

We catch each other's eye and both burst out laughing at the same time.

"Okay, maybe you really shouldn't sing in English," I say through giggles. "Then try to change the music industry in Korea. Be a trendsetter."

He cocks an eyebrow. "And how do you propose I do that?"

"Why not introduce them all to music you already love? Who are your favorite musicians?"

He takes a moment to think. "San Ul Lim. Jang Kina and the Faces. The Beatles. Bob Dylan. Eric Clapton. The Doors."

"Then give South Korea the Doors."

He shoots me a skeptical look. "The Doors?"

"Sure! Jim Morrison translates into any culture."

He returns to his guitar, plucking out what sounds suspiciously like the Doors' "Crawling King Snake." Listening to him reminds me of sitting with Nathan, who refused to go anywhere without his guitar when we were growing up. He liked to play the old country and Southern rock we heard Dad listening to— Willie Nelson, Johnny Cash, the Allman Brothers. It's nice to be surrounded by music again.

"I don't know how you could go from writing songs to just not," I say. "I would do anything to have that sort of creativity."

"Have you ever tried?" He throws my words back at me.

I laugh. "Unfortunately, yes. And I was terrible at it."

"But you're really good at helping with the songs, adding things, knowing how to edit. I think you have your dad's gift. I've never met anyone with so little training who could do what you do with music. You should be a producer."

I roll my eyes. "Okay, now that's just ridiculous."

"Why? You're obviously good at it. You just need some training. What are you planning on doing after graduation, anyway?"

I toss my hands into the air and let them fall back down. "No idea. Probably end up living off my trust fund for a while until I figure out what to do next. I could get an apartment in L.A., maybe. I like it there."

"Well, I think you should go to music college," he says innocently. "Just a thought."

I shoot him a pointed look. "If you introduce South Korea's pop music scene to the Doors, I will try to become a producer."

He laughs. "Agreed."

We spend the rest of the afternoon outside, but as the sun starts to dip below the horizon, we head back to our rooms. I can't shake the memories of him in Seoul, how he basically ignored me, then said he liked me. And *that* Jason doesn't match *this* Jason, the one walking beside me so close our hands almost brush. The Jason who tells me his secrets and jokes about Jim Morrison. I like this Jason. But which is the real one?

"What are your graduation plans?" Jason asks, cutting through my thoughts.

I stumble over a crack in the sidewalk, and Jason grabs my wrist to steady me. My pulse spikes, the memory of the email I received this morning flashing through my brain: *Pick up your graduation tickets at the front office . . . Parents are cordially invited to Parents' Day, the Thursday before graduation day.*

I grip the straps of my backpack tighter, staring at the pavement. "I'm not sure."

"Is your family coming to visit?"

It's impossible to miss the curiosity in his voice. Sophie's asked me a few things about my family, but when I shut down the conversation, she knew enough not to bring up the subject again. And Jason doesn't pry, waits instead for me to talk if I want to. But I'm sure the twins—and Yoon Jae—have wondered about the mysterious Wilde family.

"I don't know if my dad will have to work or not," I hedge.

"Of course." He pauses, then adds in a soft voice, "My dad won't be there, either."

We walk in silence until we reach the front of my building. I turn to face him, but he's staring down at his shoes, which are highlighter yellow today and totally don't match his purple T-shirt.

"Thanks for—for hanging out with me," he mumbles, scratching his bangs across his forehead but only succeeding in brushing them even more into his eyes.

I wave off his comment. "Please. We hang out all the time."

His cheeks color, and frustration slips into his voice. "No, I mean . . . thanks for not ditching me after . . . you know. It . . . means a lot."

My stomach flip-flops, but I manage to keep my voice light. "No worries. We're friends."

"Friends. Right." He finally looks up, his gaze meeting mine, and a faint smile curls his lips. "I'll see you later, Grace."

I watch him head down the sidewalk toward his dorm, my mind playing back through our conversation. Neither of us said anything all that monumental, but I can't help wondering if something's changed between us. If maybe we regained a little of the connection we had before we lost it in Seoul.

In the middle of Korean class, my phone buzzes. I glance up at my teacher, who rattles on in Korean so quickly I have no idea what he's saying, then at my phone. I've got another email from Momma. I swallow a groan as I open it.

Grace,
I booked our flights today. Jane and I will be arriving
on the Wednesday before graduation. Our plane

comes in at 6:30 in the evening. I'll have to cancel my
yoga classes and get Jane out of school that week. I'll
let you book the hotel room for us.
Mom

I roll my eyes. She *would* make me book the hotel reservations. Not like I'm in school or anything.

I scroll through hotel listings online for the rest of class, and when we get out of school for the day, Sophie helps me find the right hotel in Incheon—close enough to school that they can get to campus easily via taxi, but far enough away that it's sort of inconvenient. I'm not really keen on any impromptu visits.

Weeks blur together as everyone prepares for final exams. And maybe I should pay more attention to my teachers and homework—and the fact that I'm graduating from freaking high school—but all I can think about is seeing Momma again. She's sent me a few more emails, mostly filled with questions like: *How hot will it be? Can you hire us a translator? Do I need to bring my own bottled water?* I consider writing back and telling her that, yes, she should bring her own French mineral water and she'll need another suitcase to pack it all. But then I realize she might actually do it, and change my mind.

Jason helps me study for my Korean final, but I still panic and almost throw up all over my test the second Mr. Seo hands them out. The entire week of final exams goes much faster than I would have thought, and I study a lot less than I probably should. But when faced with either burying my nose in a physics book or watching hours of dramas with Sophie, curled up with ice cream on our bunk bed, I always choose the latter.

And as I melt my brain reading subtitles and watching melodramatic romances play out on the screen, I have to consciously package up all my emotions and throw them into the back storage rooms of my brain. All the fear of seeing Momma, all the pain she makes me remember—I can't handle it right now.

My phone buzzes, and Sophie hisses at the interruption. With a growl, she pauses the TV, and I answer a number I don't recognize.

"Is this Grace Wilde?" an American voice asks.

"Yes?" Could be the hotel where Momma and Jane are staying, calling to confirm their reservation.

"Hi, Grace, this is Kevin Nichols from *Album* magazine, and I'd really like to talk to you about—"

"Do *not* call me," I bark into the phone, interrupting Kevin's soon-to-be monologue. "I don't want to talk to any reporters, okay?"

"My apologies, Miss Wilde," he says smoothly. "But my editor is quite interested in your story. I'd love to talk to you, but if you'd rather not, perhaps I'll just see you around Ganghwa Island."

And he hangs up.

I stare down at my phone, mouth gaping. I thought Korea would be my escape, the place my past couldn't find me. But I was wrong.

I have no more places to run.

Chapter Twenty-two

The day Momma and Jane are supposed to arrive, I see an email Jane sent me a few hours ago, her choice of all capitals making me wonder if either the caps lock on her phone is broken or Momma let her drink Mountain Dew again.

GRACIE,
WE'RE AT THE AIRPORT IN TOKYO! WE'RE SO
CLOSE, AND I'M SO EXCITED! BRING THE HOT
KOREAN WITH YOU TO PICK US UP. I WANT TO
SEE HIM!

also, Mom's being annoying. as usual. she complained the entire flight about the food—apparently, they should be serving better stuff in first class—and about the baby a couple rows behind us, who only cried for like, thirty minutes.

i can't believe i'm about to see you! WE'RE
GOING TO BE IN ASIA TOGETHER!!! there will be

*chopsticks. and dumplings. And CUTE ASIAN
BOYS!*
   bring it.
   *from narita international airport, HUGS,
   jane*

I spend the entire day in a cleaning frenzy. Every time I think
of Momma arriving on that plane, walking across campus, and
coming into my dorm, a shock of terror jolts through me. I glance
at the package of half-eaten Oreos and the dust bunnies I haven't
swept since before Christmas. She's going to have a heart attack
if she sees this place.

Sophie's at a party the school's hosting for graduating
seniors—carnival games, giveaways, free food. So I plug my iPod
into a set of speakers and blast my latest KPOP obsession, Shinee,
while I throw dirty clothes into a hamper and make my bed,
straighten my desk, sweep the floor, and throw Sophie's gossip
magazines under her comforter.

I keep glancing at my phone, checking the time. If I focus
on making sure I'm at the airport on time, I can't think about who
I'm picking up.

After a quick shower, I stand in the middle of the room and
take deep breaths to calm my frenzied heart rate. I've spent more
than ten months trying to escape my family and all the memories their presence dredges up. All those fears, those regrets—and
the guilt—that I thought would cripple me, now they're resurfac-
ing, and I can't breathe.

My gaze flicks to my phone again, and I realize it's already
past five o'clock. Adrenaline pours into my veins, and I snatch
up my purse with trembling hands and head out. Jason is letting
me use his driver for the day, and thankfully, none of the photographers outside the school notice a Western girl leaving
campus.

I collapse into the backseat and shove earbuds into my ears, cranking up the Rolling Stones as loud as I can handle.

"Chlorine, argon, potassium, calcium," I whisper under my breath, hoping the periodic table will be enough to occupy my brain.

The car reaches the airport way too fast, and I hurry through the lobby. Momma will kill me if she has to wait. I maneuver past a family pushing their luggage on one of those carts, almost overturning it, as I make my way to international arrivals.

I check the monitor displaying arrival statuses and see their flight has landed early. Cursing under my breath, I make my way through the crowd assembled around the sliding doors and search for any familiar faces.

A shout cuts above the buzz of voices around me: "Gracie!"

I whip around to face the voice in time to be practically tackled by a girl nearly four inches taller than me with shoulder-length blond hair and the body of an athlete. Jane throws her arms around my neck and squeezes until I can't breathe.

"Oh my gosh, *I'm here!*" she squeals, shoving me to arm's length and staring at me. "South Korea's been good to you. You look hot, girlfriend!"

I can't hold back a laugh at my sister's enthusiasm. "A hot mess, maybe."

We hug again, and it finally hits me for real—Jane is with me, in Korea. Which means . . .

"Grace?" another familiar voice says.

All the blood drains from my head, and my hand shoots out, latching onto Jane's arm to steady myself. Standing there with a Louis Vuitton suitcase at her side is my mother. She looks the same as when I left: The perfectly sculpted auburn hair, designer dress that's only slightly rumpled from the flight, and sunglasses so big they look like they're eating her face. It's like she's been transported here from last August, but I don't even feel like the same person.

She pulls me into a loose hug. "Honey, you look run ragged. If it was that much of an inconvenience for you, we could have taken a taxi from the airport. You didn't need to pick us up."

I hold back a snort. As if she wouldn't have screamed at me if she wasn't coddled 24/7. But I take the high road and choose not to comment.

"Here, let me help you with your bags."

I take the suitcase handle out of Momma's hand and lead them out front, where the driver is mercifully waiting for us. He loads the bags into the trunk, and we're off.

"So tell me all about school," Jane says, excitement bubbling out of her, despite being squished between me and Momma in the backseat. "And Seoul. Oh my *gosh,* I can't believe you got to go there before me!"

"Yes, you never told us about your . . . trip," Momma says in a pinched voice. She flashes me a polite smile, but I've known her long enough to see the anger simmering underneath her flawless skin.

I force a laugh, praying it doesn't sound as anxious as I feel. "Y'all don't want me to bore you with all the details—you just flew halfway across the world. We'll talk once you've slept."

The ride to the hotel is painfully long, although Jane cuts through some of the tension with her prattling. I've never been more thankful for her inability to keep her mouth shut than I am now.

Once the driver's deposited us at the front door and I've instructed him to wait for me, we wheel the suitcases into the lobby. Momma gives it a once-over, her nose wrinkling, as if this isn't one of the most expensive hotels in Incheon.

I drop them off at their room with the promise to pick them

up in the morning. On my way back to school, my thoughts are too jumbled for me to make any sense of them.

My pulse races like I'm sprinting down a track, and sweat lingers on my back and beneath my arms. I search for the detached calm I've held on to for so many months, but it's lost somewhere in the swirl of emotions I wish I could make disappear.

With shaking fingers, I sort through the stuff in my purse until I pick out my phone. I scroll through my contacts until I pull up Jason's number. My thumb hovers above the screen, but I just stare at his name.

I could call him, and he would answer. He would come over if I asked him. We could watch a movie or talk about music. But then he'd know something's wrong, he'd know I'm not as strong as I like to pretend to be. And even though he's been open with me, even though I've seen him vulnerable, I can't let him see *me* that way. I can't let him know—I can't let anyone know—just how messed up I am inside.

"I can do this," I whisper to myself. "I can do this."

I have no idea what *this* is, but the mantra settles my nerves. Sighing, I rest my head against the window pane and watch the city lights pass.

But when the driver stops in front of the entrance to the school, I realize my eyes are filled with tears.

Chapter
Twenty-three

I wake the next morning with a stabbing pain behind my eyebrows and an ache just above the nape of my neck. It feels like someone hit my head with a sledgehammer, but I force my body out of bed, anyway.

Since Sophie's mother isn't arriving until tomorrow, she helps me babysit Momma and Jane for Parents' Day, even though Momma talks to Sophie like my roommate's a toddler.

"I don't want to confuse the poor dear with English words," she says—right in front of Sophie.

My roommate maintains her usual enthusiasm, however, and she and Jane bond over their mutual love of a KPOP band I've never heard of and the color purple, which leaves me to listen to Momma's condescending remarks about the school, the food, and the culture all day—oh my gosh, is this what *I* sounded like when I first arrived? By the time Sophie and I have dropped them back off at their hotel and returned to our dorm, my head feels like it's going to explode.

I drop onto my bed with a groan, throwing the comforter over my face.

"Are you okay?" Sophie asks.

I peek out from underneath my blanket-tent and watch Sophie plait her hair into pigtail braids. She peers at my reflection in the mirror, her eyes wide behind her glasses.

"I think I'm dying."

"What's wrong? Does your stomach hurt?" She takes a few steps back, like she's afraid whatever has me cowering under the covers will spread to her.

"Migraine."

Her face melts into a look of sympathy. "Oh, I'm sorry! Maybe you were outside in the sun too long."

"More like I was with my mother too long," I mutter.

Sophie frowns, turning to look at me. "It's possible to worry so much that you make yourself sick, and you've been worrying a lot about your mother coming."

"You think I stressed myself into getting a migraine?"

She shrugs. "It's possible."

Yeah, it is, but the admission freezes on my lips. "Well, you don't know the Wicked Witch of the South the way I do. You saw some of her evil today. Multiply that times a million. Maybe if she was *your* mom, you would literally worry yourself sick, too."

Sophie spritzes herself with perfume and slips on a pair of high-heeled sandals, and I ask, "Where are you going?"

"Tae Hwa and I are going shopping in Seoul—I need a dress to wear for the graduation ceremony."

"But you're going to be wearing a robe on top of it."

"Not all day! Besides, I'll know what I'm wearing underneath, and if it's not pretty, I won't *feel* pretty, no matter if anyone else can see it or not."

I roll my eyes as she heads out the door, but I freeze when my phone vibrates and I recognize my mother's number.

"Let's go out to dinner," Momma says before I can even say hello.

"Uhh . . . I don't think tonight is good."

There's a long pause, then, "And what do you expect us to do without you?"

"I already told you about some good restaurants—"

She scoffs. "We're in this country to see you. No point in going without you."

A sigh passes through my lips.

"Don't sigh at me, Grace Loretta Wilde," she snaps, but the harshness in her voice somehow soothes the anxiety twisting in my gut—at least she's being honest about her hatred for me, as opposed to hiding it underneath layers of politeness.

"So what's wrong with you?" she asks. "Are you going out with a boy or something else supposedly more important than spending time with your mother?"

"No!" I cry, and I'm instantly rewarded with a slash of pain through my temples. "I have a migraine," I say through gritted teeth.

"Well, let's put the entire world on hold because you need an aspirin," she huffs. "Call us when you get better."

And she hangs up.

I blow out a slow breath, closing my eyes. I've escaped the noose for now, but I'll have to face her again tomorrow.

My phone vibrates against my hand, and my stomach drops. Please don't let her be calling back. Or worse, don't let it be that reporter again. But when I check the number, a flash of surprise hits me. I pick up.

"Hey, where are you?" Jason says. "I thought we were meeting in front of the dining hall for dinner."

I suck in a quiet gasp. "Oh, I'm sorry! I forgot to call you. I don't think I can come out tonight."

"Is something wrong?" he asks.

My stomach flips at the concern in his voice, but I immediately scold myself for reading into it. "No, I'm just not feeling well. I've got a killer migraine."

Pause.

"Do you want me to bring you anything?"

Now my face heats, and no amount of self-reproach will dampen the flames underneath my skin. "No, that's okay."

"Are you sure?"

"Yeah, totally, but thanks anyway."

We hang up after a few more times of me assuring him, but the second after I disconnect the call, regret clenches my chest. Maybe I should have let him come, let him baby me a little. Lord knows he should take care of me, for once.

I fall into a light doze maybe twenty minutes later, and drift in and out of sleep for the next hour or so until a knock taps on my door. I linger in that hazy space of almost-dreaming for a few seconds until another knock.

With a moan, I shove off my blankets and shuffle to the door, muttering under my breath, "If that's Sophie knocking because she forgot her key again, I'm going to kill her."

But when I open the door, it's not Sophie staring back at me. It's Jason.

All the blood drains from my face and pools in my bare toes, and I'm temporarily struck dumb.

He holds up a pill bottle, glances at it, then looks back at me. And earns extra points for not staring at my disheveled hair or the polka-dot pajama pants.

"I wasn't sure if you had anything to take for your headache," he says, and a soft smile plays at the corners of his lips.

"Umm . . . well . . . I . . . " Have lost the ability to articulate, apparently. "Thank you," I manage, taking the bottle from his hand. "I'm uhh . . . sure this will help."

I expect him to duck out, maybe throw a jab about my bedhead, but he lingers, stays in my doorway. He stuffs his hands into his jeans pockets, tilting his chin down and looking up at me through dark bangs.

After a few silent moments, he asks, "How's your mother? You took her to Parents' Day, right?" He clears his throat. "How are things going? I know you don't enjoy spending time with her."

A mixture of surprise and wariness twists inside me. Has Sophie told him anything about my fights with Momma? Does he know about my family drama? Fear claws at my chest, threatening to freeze the breath in my lungs.

I study his eyes, searching for any recognition or knowledge, but there's nothing. Just curiosity. And . . . worry. The realization slams into me so hard, for a few seconds I forget about the pain in my head and the mother who brought my fears across the ocean with her. Jason is worried about me.

Heat ignites in my stomach, spreads through my chest, crawls its way up my neck and all the way to my hairline. Until I'm bathing in the warmth of his attention.

I consider dodging his question, but instead I find the truth slipping from my lips: "She's okay. She hasn't really been impressed with the school so far." I laugh, but it's like I've been hit by a baseball bat.

We fall into silence, and I'm still waiting for him to jump ship, to tell me he's got better things to do than hang out with me. But he stays, almost like he's waiting for me. It's my move.

"Do you—" I stop, watching him carefully. "I mean, do you want to come in?"

Half of me thinks he'll laugh, wave a hand, and head down the hallway. But he doesn't. He flashes me a smile.

And he says, "Sure."

Jason comes into my room, and I get into the bed, and he sits at my desk, and we talk. I don't know for how long. But as the minutes pass, I feel my migraine weakening until it disappears altogether and I'm sitting up and laughing and wishing I could spend every day with Jason Bae.

The next morning, I wake up to a new text from Jason, asking if I'd like to meet him for dinner tomorrow. We agree on a time, and as we send messages back and forth, I can't stop smiling.

At noon, I head out to Momma and Jane's hotel to show them around town, and an hour later, I'm standing at their door. Momma answers, looks me up and down, and purses her lips.

Her eyebrows pull up. "Feeling better?"

"Yes, ma'am," I mutter.

As we get into the elevator, Momma asks, "So, where are we going? We should do a little shopping—I'll buy you a new purse." She juts her chin toward the fringe-covered one hanging from my shoulder. "That one looks like a cat tried to eat it. You should be carrying something nicer."

I take them down to a Korean market, then to the waterfront to watch the boats. Jane loves everything, but I can't get more than a semi-interested *hmm* out of Momma.

For dinner, I decide to take them to a nice restaurant, because surely Momma can't complain about gourmet food. We step into the building's air-conditioned lobby, then ride the elevator to the top floor, past the law offices, banks, and other high-end businesses renting the other floors. When the doors open, we're let out into a packed foyer, where a hostess takes our names and shows us to our table by the gigantic windows that look out over the city and the ocean.

"Geez, Grace, what did you have to do to get us reservations here—pledge your firstborn child?" Jane asks, glancing around at the full dining room.

"Hello." Our waitress arrives at the table and bows her head. "May I bring you a beverage?"

Momma takes the menu from the server, tilting her head in the girl's direction. "I'm sorry, dear, can you bring us what?"

"A beverage," she repeats.

A light laugh falls from Momma's lips, and she shoots me and Jane an amused look across the table, which she doesn't even bother to hide from the waitress, who can't be more than a couple years older than me.

She offers the girl a pitying smile. "I'm terribly sorry, but I'm afraid I don't know what you're saying." Her gaze shifts to me. "Do you understand her accent?"

"Your drink," I growl. "She wants to know what you want to *drink*."

Momma's eyebrows shoot up, and she looks down at the menu. "No need to get testy. It's not my fault they didn't hire employees with good English."

The waitress's cheeks turn pink, and her gaze drops to the floor.

"Water," I blurt, before my mother can do any more damage. "We'll all have water. Thank you."

With a nod, the girl turns and practically sprints away from our table. I shoot Momma a glare.

"Relax, darling. The girl probably didn't even know what I said."

I open my mouth to respond, but Jane kicks me under the table and I snap my jaw closed. So we sit in silence until the waitress returns with our waters, then takes our order.

We manage to last about five minutes before Momma says, "So, we haven't heard much from you since you got here. Did you get my email in January about your Vanderbilt application?"

I chew on the inside of my cheek, drumming my fingers across the white tablecloth, and ignore the apprehension scratching the back of my mind. "I got it."

She waits for me to continue, but when I don't, prompts, "And?"

"I'm umm . . . " I peer out at the city beneath us, at the myriad of lights just flickering on, which seem to stretch forever, and I wish I could get lost in them—wish I could escape this moment. "I'm not sure I want to go to Vanderbilt."

"Excuse me?"

Momma's voice has chilled to the point of freezing, and I lift my gaze to meet hers. She stares back at me with narrowed eyes, her lips pressed tight. Beside me, Jane shrinks into her chair, pulls out her phone, and pretends she can't hear us.

I swallow the lump forming in my throat. "I don't think I want to go to Vanderbilt. I don't want to go back to Tennessee."

"And where *do* you want to go?"

"I was actually thinking about staying in Korea somewhere. Maybe Incheon."

Or maybe Seoul. But Momma doesn't need to know about my insane dreams of living with Sophie, being far from my family, and keeping close to Jason.

Momma rests her elbow on the table, holding up her head with two fingers against her temple. She lets out a sharp laugh. "You're not serious?"

My silence must confirm that I am, because her face twists in anger, her nostrils flaring, eyebrows slamming down, eyes sharpening to daggers. Her hands drop to her lap, and she leans across the table toward me, pitching her voice low.

"I won't allow it," she hisses. "You don't belong here."

I snort, because it's easier to show her flippancy than the fear twisting inside my stomach. "And I belong in Tennessee?"

"Yes!"

The waitress saves us from a shouting match by bringing our food. We're icily silent as we're served our steak and sushi. Jane immediately digs into her noodles, keeping her head low, staying clear of the blast radius like she always does.

A mixture of blood and butter oozes across Momma's plate as she cuts her meat into tiny pieces. "You're coming home after graduation," she says. "No arguments."

I set my chopsticks back down, no longer hungry. "You can't make me go back."

She places a bite in her mouth, takes her time chewing, and levels me with an unflinching look. "Grace, you are my daughter. If I say you're leaving, then you're leaving. You're underage."

"Only for another month."

Her fork pauses on its journey to her mouth.

"I'll be eighteen next month," I say. "Then I won't have to do anything you say. Legally."

She sits up taller in her chair so she's looking down at me, and her hands shake as she places her silverware across her plate. "Just because you'll be eighteen doesn't mean I stop being your mother. As long as I'm supporting you—"

"You won't need to support me. I have money."

Her eyes bug, and she leans back in her chair. But I think I'm more shocked than she is. It never occurred to me to outright defy her, to completely cut ties from her and Dad, to do my own thing. But I could. She might be able to keep me from my trust fund until I turn eighteen, but I used to work at Dad's studio every summer, and he paid me. I have enough to pay for college or an apartment in L.A. or whatever I want for at least a year, until I figure out a more permanent solution. That reality sends a surge of power racing through me. Enough to keep me talking.

"I have money to take care of myself," I continue. "So I don't really care what you think."

The clatter of dishes and hum of voices fill my ears, and my chest heaves, like I've just run from my dorm to the cafeteria. She stays frozen so long, just watching me, I'm afraid I've shocked her into having a heart attack.

Her voice is hardly above a whisper when she says, "I've already lost one child. I'm not losing another."

The words slap me in the face, and my lungs collapse. Pain flares inside my chest, and I struggle to suck in any air.

"How can you even bring that up right now?" I say, buried agony in every syllable.

She crosses her arms, a smugness settling into the curve of her lips, the tilt of her head. "If you can't handle talking about your brother, then perhaps you're not mature enough to handle living on your own."

Oxygen rushes into my starved lungs, and it keeps coming as I pull in sharp gasps. I rake trembling fingers through my hair as terror shrieks inside my brain, clawing at my thoughts until it's all I can think about—the call, the fear, the discovery, the guilt. Always the guilt.

Momma keeps talking, but I can't hear her. I can't hear anything. The scene replays through my head again and again. I grip the edge of the table with both hands like it'll steady me, keep me rooted in the present instead of the past I've tried so hard to escape.

Momma's voice finally cuts through my consciousness. "Your brother is *dead*, Grace," she says in a frustrated voice, like she's telling me to take out the trash for the third time. "It's time you accepted that and stop running from the truth."

Running. That's what I want to be doing. Running out of here, away from her, away from reality. Away from the panic trying to force its way through my body.

I push away from the table so abruptly, my chair crashes against the wood floor. I snatch up my purse and make to leave, but Momma's on her feet fast and grabs my wrist.

"Don't you dare walk away from me," she says, her nails cutting into my skin. "I am your *mother,* and you will respect me."

I shake off her hand, ice filling my veins. "You lost my respect the day you blamed me for Nathan's death."

Jane stands, like maybe she'll try to stop me, too, but I freeze her with a look. She nods. She understands.

My trip through the restaurant and back down the elevator to the sidewalk is a blur. I stand at the bus stop, and, thankfully, the bus arrives a few minutes later.

Once it drops me off at Ganghwa Island, I look at the next bus, which will take me up the mountain to the school. But I start down the sidewalk a few seconds later. I have to keep moving, to keep my mind on the simple actions of picking up my feet, pulling in heavy breaths through my nose, and not remembering. I don't want to remember anymore.

When I finally reach campus, my legs are trembling, but adrenaline's still pumping through me.

"Grace Wilde?"

I turn at the familiar voice, the back of my neck prickling.

"I'm Kevin Nichols."

He trots across the street and underneath the arch, so he's standing on school property, and suddenly my escape—my sanctuary—has been violated. When the press stayed outside the school, I could still retreat back to campus, but here's that reporter, all the way from America.

He laughs, the self-satisfied kind, and gives me a wink, like we're old pals. "You're a tough one to find, you know that? I've been all over this campus looking for you. I even talked to your roommate, but she said you were out."

"You—you went to my room?"

He gives a hearty nod. "Sure did. So, about that interview . . ."

Kevin lets his words hang there, and I recognize that reporters' habit to create awkward silence in hopes of the interviewee filling it with something they wouldn't normally say.

I might have stormed off. I might have told him he was violating my privacy and to get lost. But my emotions roil around inside me, flexing, itching to get out, and before I can stop them, tears pool in the corners of my eyes.

"Please," I whisper. "Please."

No other words come to my mind—or lips. I don't bother wiping the tears that now trail down my cheeks into the corners of my mouth.

Kevin's fingers twitch toward his shoulder bag, and I realize he probably has a camera in there. Looking for a shot of my grief. Wanting to capitalize on Nathan's death to pump up his own career.

And my anger explodes.

Everything I felt toward Momma—the way I wanted to shriek and throw things at her—I let it bubble to the surface.

"You want a quote?" I hiss. "I'll give you a quote."

Kevin perks.

"You're disgusting. All you reporters are. You're vultures, hovering over Nathan's corpse, looking for your big break. Well, guess what? He isn't your highway to fame. He was my *brother*, and he's *dead*. He died alone in his own vomit because his sister didn't help him. Because *I* didn't help him." My voice builds until I scream, "Put *that* in your article!"

I turn and sprint away from him, my chest shuddering with barely contained sobs. When I let myself into my building, I slow to a walk, exhaustion suddenly swallowing my legs so I can barely climb the stairs.

Halfway up the flight, my phone rings. I can't even think enough to turn it off, and I answer without looking at the number.

"Hi, are you free right now?" Jason's voice floats through the speaker and cuts straight through me.

I stop in the middle of the stairwell, soaking in the simple comfort his voice brings. My eyes sting, and my heart pounds so fast I wonder if this is what hyperventilating is.

"Grace, are you there?"

I want to tell him where I am, what's happened, how every demon I've ever hoped to run from has found me again. How I want to see him. How all I want is to feel a pair of arms wrapped around me.

But all I say is yes.

"Are you okay?" he asks instantly. "Where are you?"

I choke on a sob, covering my eyes with my palm and trying to calm the adrenaline shooting through me. I won't panic. I won't panic.

"Now isn't a good time," I croak. "I'll call you back."

Without waiting for him to answer, I hang up. And I hurry the rest of the way to my floor. I just need to get to my room. I need to be there. I need to be alone.

Sweat runs down my chest and beads on my forehead as I fumble with the key, dropping it once, cursing under my breath, until I manage to unlock and throw open the door. I dash inside, and silence surrounds me, like the eerie quiet after a train wreck or a car crash, when you survey the damage in horrified awe. The same word echoes in my head, a word I've avoided since Nathan's incident, a word I've hid from for months. *Dead.* Nathan's dead.

Nathan's dead.

A sob catches in my throat, and my knees buckle. I sink to the floor, tears already spilling down my cheeks. I grab onto the hem of my comforter, clinging to it like I can hold on to the last whisper of my control.

I let all the anxiety, all the grief, crash into me. Everything I've held back for months—the memories that haunt me even in dreams, the constant background of feelings that buzzes beneath the surface all the time. I've spent so long holding them back, facing them now feels like I'm experiencing Nathan's death all over again.

"Hydrogen, h-helium," I whisper, but my voice catches. The elements aren't going to help me this time.

I pull my knees to my chest and curl in on myself, wishing I could shrink into nothing. Pain lances through me as fresh as when I walked into Nathan's room and found him lying in the middle of the floor, eyes open and chest still. Dead.

Nathan's dead.

A knock sounds on my door, but I can't get up to answer it. My breath comes in quick gasps, intermingled with choking sobs. I can't seem to suck in enough oxygen. Why can't I get enough? Is this what a panic attack feels like?

The knock comes again. But I just press my face into my knees and wait for it to go away.

"It's my fault," I whisper. "It's my fault."

I denied that fact for so long, no matter what Momma said at the funeral. She probably doesn't even remember saying it. But I heard her, and I remember.

We were at the grave site, watching them put Nathan into the ground. Momma hadn't stopped crying since that morning, since she put on the black Versace dress that smelled like new money and lost dreams.

She turned to me while they poured dirt onto the casket's shiny mahogany, and she said, "Why didn't you do something? Why did you let this happen?"

And what lay beneath her words was: *This is your fault. You should have done something. You're the reason he's dead.*

I never *wanted* to believe it, but those words sank in all the same. Maybe she's right. Maybe I could have stopped it, could have stopped him from taking too many pills, ending his own life. It was his choice, but maybe it was my responsibility.

I'm so lost in my own thoughts that I don't notice the door

opening and someone approaching until a hand touches my shoulder. I jerk away from the contact, my head shooting up. And I see Jason peering back at me.

"The door was unlocked," he says, then, after noticing my tear-stained cheeks, he pushes damp hair out of my eyes, cupping his hand around my face. "Grace."

At the tenderness in his voice, pain rips through me afresh, and a whimper escapes my lips. In an instant, he pulls me into his arms and nestles my head beneath his chin, my face resting against his chest. His back against the bed, he sets me in his lap and holds me tight against him. My body shakes with sobs, but his steadiness holds me together.

"Shhh," he croons, then murmurs Korean words against my ear, smoothing my hair over and over, the repetition its own source of comfort.

We sit like that so long, I feel like we've melded together. I finally stop crying, but I can't let go of him. I breathe in the cool, watery smell of his cologne, the tip of my nose dusting the skin on his neck. He smells like rain.

His hand slips beneath my hair and trails lines across the nape of my neck, dipping below the collar of my shirt and sending chills down my spine. I should let go, tell him I'm fine. But the hollow ache inside me tells me I'm not fine. And while nothing can fill the void, he's the only thing that can make it a little smaller.

"Are you going to tell me what's wrong?" he asks, his warm breath tickling my ear. His fingers twist in my hair absently. "Did you argue with your mother?"

I nod.

"And that's why you're so upset?"

"No," I whisper.

He hesitates a moment. "Does this have anything to do with your brother?"

My breath freezes in my chest. I lift my head so I can look at him. "My what?"

His gaze falls. "Your brother. Your brother was Nathan Cross, wasn't he? I didn't want to mention it because you never talk about it."

Fresh tears well up in my eyes. "You knew?"

He gives me a soft smile. "Everybody knows Nathan Cross was Stephen Wilde's son. Even KPOP singers." His smile fades. "Why did you think you had to keep that from me?"

"I didn't want anyone to think less of me," I say, barely loud enough for even me to hear it.

"Why would anyone think less of you? If anything, people would sympathize with you."

Not if they knew. It was my fault. But I can't bring myself to say the words.

"The funeral was in June, right?" he says. "It was really brave of you to come here right after all that happened."

I don't feel brave.

"I don't know what's going on between you and your mother, but I'm here for you, okay?" He presses his cool hands against my cheeks. "You said you were going to help me, and I'm going to help you."

Fresh tears threaten to seep out of my eyes, and I want to tell him how much he's already done for me, how he's helped me forget about all my pain. But I can't spit out the words.

"I'm tired," I say instead.

Jason slips out from underneath me and gets to his feet, then helps me to mine. I crawl into bed, feeling like I ran a marathon. It's still early, but I think I could sleep for days.

Jason stands there a moment, then says, "I guess I'll go. Do you need anything?"

I bite my lip, wondering if I should say what I'm thinking.

What I want. But I take in the empathy in his eyes, and I know he'll understand.

"Don't leave," I say. "I don't want you to go."

He hesitates a second, the deliberation visible on his face. For that brief moment, I hold my breath. But then he kicks off his shoes, flips off the overhead light, and yanks the comforter and extra blankets off my bed. And we make a nest on the rug, because he knows I don't want to be on the bed—I want to be somewhere new, somewhere just for us.

He rolls onto his side to look at me, and I offer him a grateful smile. I turn away from him, curling up on my side and listening to him breathing, feeling the warmth that radiates from him.

I drift in and out of sleep, but I wake completely when I feel the weight of an arm wrap around my waist. Jason presses his face into my hair at the back of my neck, and my breath catches. I force myself to keep still so he thinks I'm still asleep, but my heartbeat pounds so loud he must be able to hear it.

"Grace," he murmurs into my hair, and I've never loved the sound of my name so much. "You were the only person who was there for me when I needed you. I want to be there for you."

Then he says it, and every nerve inside my body prickles at the same time.

"Trust me," he whispers.

And I only wish I could.

Chapter Twenty-four

The next morning, I wake up to my phone buzzing. Jason mumbles something in his sleep and rolls away from me.

Am I allowed to come back to my room now? Sophie texts.

My cheeks burn, and I fumble with the buttons on my phone. *YES!* I respond. *I'M SO SORRY!*

She replies a moment later, **rolls eyes* If you're shacking up with my brother, I'm going to vomit.*

Even more heat rolls through me, and I type back as quickly as possible, *I am NOT sleeping with him. Well, I did. But totally in a literal way. Long story.*

She doesn't respond, but I decide it would be best if Jason were gone by the time she arrives. I sit up, stretching my stiff muscles—maybe the floor was a bad idea—and nudge him. He opens his eyes and blinks back sleep, then smiles up at me.

"Good morning," he says, voice thick with drowsiness.

My insides are doing backflips as I peer down at him, with his head on *my* pillow, but I stomp on all these emotions. Must keep level head. Must not be overwhelmed. Must not be over-whelmed.

"I think Sophie came in last night," I say.

He scrubs his face with both hands. "Yeah, she did. Around eleven, I think."

"Why didn't you wake me up?"

"I didn't think it was necessary. She left again."

I groan. "This is her room, too."

"She could have stayed if she wanted to."

Not if she thought we were getting busy. But I choose to keep that to myself. Just another thing to add to Sophie's list of grievances she has against me, I guess.

"I—I think you should leave."

He sits up. "Are you . . . mad at me?"

"No!" I cringe. "I just think it would be better if you left now."

My gaze falls to the comforter. Jason stays quiet a long time, then slips his hand over mine and squeezes it.

"Are you going to tell me what happened last night?" he asks. "Why were you so upset?"

I hesitate, wondering if I should tell him everything. He told me about his dad, and I've pretty much seen him at his worst. So it's not like he can judge me, at this point. I take a deep breath to steady myself.

"I ran into a reporter. From America. Who followed me here." I swallow. "I kind of screamed at him."

He winces but says nothing.

"And . . . I sort of . . . had a fight. With my mother."

He waits a long while before saying, "You mentioned that last night. What was it about?"

My throat tightens, and grief threatens to dry me to a sobbing husk, empty except for the lingering heartache that never seems to go away.

"About my brother," I answer in a hoarse whisper. "I don't

know what you know about his death, but it wasn't how the papers reported it. He did overdose, but—" My voice cracks. "It was a suicide."

His arm wraps around my shoulders, the warmth seeping through my clothes and soaking into my skin. "You don't have to tell me about it if you don't want to," he says.

I shake my head. "No, it's okay. My family have all heard the story, and I think I need to talk about it, anyway."

He pulls me against him so it's no longer just our sides touching, and I'm practically sitting in his lap, both of his arms wrapped around me. And maybe I should be embarrassed, especially after Sophie's text, but all I know is that this feels good. *He* feels good. I just want to talk, and I want him to listen.

"Nathan drank," I say. "A lot. I saw him do it but only ever told my dad, who said not to worry about it, because he'd take care of everything. I think he was more worried about Nathan's career than his alcohol problem." I snort. "Then I saw Nathan taking pills once. I just thought they were for a cold or something. So I didn't tell anybody." My voice wavers. "Then he called me right before he . . . did it. I thought he was joking. Guess he wasn't."

Jason shakes his head. "Grace, that wasn't your fault. You weren't responsible for him."

I blink back the tears that prick my eyes. "Maybe I should have been."

He places his hands on my shoulders and holds my gaze with his. "You can't think like that. You weren't responsible, and it wasn't your fault."

I bite my bottom lip to keep it from trembling. Jason blows out a long breath, holds me closer.

"I spent a lot of years thinking I was the reason for my dad's drinking," Jason says, close to my ear. "And maybe I could have been an easier kid, been less angry with him for leaving my mom. But he was the one who drained those bottles, not me. He was responsible for his own life. Doesn't mean I'm not still pissed at him, though."

I pull back so I can look at him. And I see it in his eyes—he knows what I'm feeling. Because he's felt it, too. Maybe it's a little different because it's his father. But he understands. He understands it all.

"Sometimes I feel like God is punishing me," I whisper, "like I failed some kind of cosmic test."

He cups a hand around my face, leaning close to hold my attention. "God doesn't make you feel guilty. That's all you. You're beating yourself up over something you had no control over, and it's time to move on."

"Okay," I say, even though I'm not sure how to digest his words. What am I supposed to do? How do you "move on," anyway?

Jason stands, tries to smooth his hopelessly wrinkled T-shirt, then slips on his shoes. He pauses, lingering in the middle of the room, between the beds and the desks, and he just looks at me. And in that moment, I could swear everything inside me melts.

He's seen me—all of me. Figuratively speaking, anyway. He knows about my past, he's had my grief seep into his T-shirt with all my tears.

And he hasn't given up on me yet.

Jason scratches the top of his head, fingers mussing his hair even more than it already is. "Are we still on for dinner tonight?"

"I don't know. I need to call my sister."

He nods. "Okay. I'll call you later." The hint of a smile brightens his face. "And if you're busy, we'll meet up tomorrow. My mom wants to see you again. Apparently, you made quite the impression."

I return the smile. "Sure."

Jason stares at me a few seconds longer, then opens the door and disappears. I watch it swing closed. And my stomach turns into a battleground. My chest tightens. Jason was so sweet to me. But so was Isaac. So was Nathan.

Then he killed himself.

I can't want Jason. I can't want someone like him. I need stable, and he's the opposite.

My phone vibrates again, and my entire body freezes. What if it's Momma? I can't talk to her. I'm not ready. But when I check it, I see Jane's name.

ditched mom 4 the day—she's being pissy. show me around! she wrote.

I type back, *Where are you?*

We spend the next ten minutes working out logistics. I push down lingering nervousness as I get dressed. She didn't say anything about last night. Is Momma angry?

I groan. My mother is the last person I want to think about. Spending the day with Jane is exactly what I need right now to keep my thoughts occupied.

As I'm heading out of my dorm, a thought pops into my head and I grin. I pull out my phone and dial a number I haven't called in a while.

Jane is going to love me.

With Yoon Jae's back turned, Jane raises her eyebrows sky-high and mouths, *He's gorgeous!* She mimes swooning, and I stifle a giggle.

The subway lurches to a stop, and we shove our way out onto the platform. Yoon Jae turns to make sure we're with him, and he smiles at me. I smile back, then look to Jane, who dramatically fans herself.

We take Jane into Seoul, to Myeongdong, a gigantic shopping area famous for cosmetics stores. It's a popular date spot, too, Yoon Jae tells us, but there're also lots of businessmen and tourists. The crowds are thick, but the upbeat atmosphere and tasty street food are worth it. We spend a couple hours browsing, Yoon Jae keeping his head down and hat's bill pulled low, then grab lunch at a local place Jane picks. She excuses herself to go to the bathroom, leaving me and Yoon Jae at the table.

When I called him, I worried what Jason would say but quickly decided it didn't matter. Yoon Jae's still my friend. Which is what I told Jason when I informed him of my plans. He couldn't really argue after that.

"It's official," I say to Yoon Jae. "My sister's in love with you, just like I thought."

He lets out a self-conscious laugh. "She's a nice girl."

"She takes after me, obviously."

Despite my sarcasm, he nods. "Yes, she does."

Jane returns, and she grills Yoon Jae about everything—his life, music career, future plans. I bump her elbow with mine when she asks about his past girlfriends, but he doesn't seem to take offense.

"I've only had one girlfriend," he says. "It was two years ago, back when my label hadn't given me any rules against dating."

"They have rules against dating?" The disappointment is obvious in her voice.

"Yeah, most Korean singers aren't allowed to have girlfriends or boyfriends, but now that Eden is broken up, I guess it doesn't matter anymore."

She perks. "So you're in the market for a new one, then?" she asks.

I gasp. "Jane!"

"What?" She shrugs.

Yoon Jae laughs, but I spot the redness creeping up his neck.

We head back outside, and Jane gets caught up in perusing a skin-care shop that's really famous in Asia. She throws a grin over her shoulder at me, and I can't help smiling in response. She loves it here.

Yoon Jae stands with me as I hover outside the store. "I—I want you to know something." He falls silent a moment, then says hesitantly, "Jane is a sweet girl, but I don't want to make her think I am interested in her."

I catch him squirming. "What? Oh, Yoon Jae, I'm sorry! I wasn't ever serious. I was just joking. She's got a major crush on you, but she knows you're a year older than her. And you live in a different country."

It's strange, being here with him. After hearing Jason's side of the story, I vilified Yoon Jae in my mind. But now I think it was all just a big mistake on everyone's part. Jason and Yoon Jae never should have been put together in the first place.

"Your sister was right about something, however," Yoon Jae says, breaking through my thoughts.

"What about?"

He stares down at the foot he scuffs across the pavement. "I *am* looking for a girlfriend."

"Well, I won't be able to help you there, unfortunately. The only girl I know here is Sophie, and she is pining away for someone else."

"Actually, I meant a specific girl."

I perk. "Really? Who?"

His mouth melts into a sad smile. "You really don't know?"

A whisper of unease settles over me as my mind processes what he could mean. But he couldn't—that's not what he meant—surely.

Jane appears, saving me from having to respond.

She holds up a skin cream. "Got it!"

The entire way back to the subway station, I'm thinking about what Yoon Jae said. When we drop him off in Incheon so he can take a car back to school, he smiles at Jane and even gives her a hug, although I've never seen a guy in Korea hug a girl he just met. My estimation of him skyrockets.

"It was very nice to meet you," he says.

"Y-you, too," she sputters, starry-eyed.

He shoots me an unreadable look, like he's waiting for something. "Goodbye, Grace," he says, with such a final tone that I pause.

I wave. "I'll see you later. At graduation, right?"

He flashes me that sad smile again. "Right."

Jane gushes about Yoon Jae the second he leaves. "He's even cuter in person than he is in pictures! And I like what he's done with his hair. Super cute. And his outfit? Adorable." She elbows me in the side. "But why didn't you tell me he's practically in love with you?"

I freeze. "What?"

"Like you've never noticed. You could wipe the drool from his chin every time he looks at you."

"Jane, that's not funny. Yoon Jae doesn't like me that way."

But my thoughts return to what he said earlier. Is that really what he meant? He never said anything to me about it. Not that I've said anything to Jason about what I feel for him. But still. Why didn't he ever mention it?

My phone buzzes, and I check the screen to see Jason calling.

"Are you free for dinner or no?" he asks.

Butterflies soar inside my stomach. "I'm actually showing my sister around today."

"Oh. Okay."

"But we'd love to go to dinner with you," I hurry to say. "Right, Jane?"

I mouth, *Yes!* to her, and she shrugs.

"She said she really wants to meet you," I say into the phone, causing Jane to roll her eyes.

"Great." I can practically hear him smiling over the phone.

We agree on a Western restaurant that also offers Korean options, close to Momma and Jane's hotel, and she and I head there directly. Along the way, Jane is suspiciously quiet.

"What's got you tongue-tied?" I ask. "You're never this quiet unless you're sleeping."

She takes a long time to answer. "You like him a lot, don't you?"

I mask the nervousness flaring inside me with a laugh. "I don't know what you mean."

She raises an eyebrow. "Gracie, it's written all over your face. You've fallen for this guy. Hard."

I bite back the denial, knowing I won't ever be able to say it with a straight face.

"There's nothing wrong with liking him. Boys are awesome—obviously." She grabs my arm and leans close, nearly tripping me. "Do you *love* him?" she asks, drawing out the *o*.

I shake her off. "Jane!"

She cackles. "I can't wait to meet him. I'm sure he'll get a kick out of all your embarrassing baby stories."

I shoot her a nasty look. "You weren't even alive when I was a baby."

"Yeah, but I've seen all the pictures. And I'm pretty good at making things up."

By the time we reach the restaurant, I'm about to strangle her. Jason arrived first, and he waits for us just outside. He takes off his sunglasses, and his entire face brightens when he spots us. He waves as we approach.

"Gracie, he's *cute*," Jane whispers into my ear.

"Shut up," I hiss.

"You must be Jane." Jason shakes her hand with a wide smile. "It's great to meet you. I know Grace was happy you came."

"Was she?" Jane raises both eyebrows at me. "You never said that."

"Because you wouldn't stop yapping for me to get a word in," I say.

We head inside and get a table in the back. A few diners point at Jason and whisper behind their hands, but no one approaches him. They stare, though. Not that I can blame them. With his black V-neck and cherry red sneakers, I'm staring, too.

"So how are you missing school right now?" Jason asks.

Jane shrugs. "My dad got me out of it. He's cool like that."

I snort but don't comment. *Cool* isn't the word I would use for him. *Intense* maybe, but not *cool*. Then again, he's always been a lot easier on my little sis—the baby of the family.

Jane clasps her hands on top of the table and leans forward. "So, Jason, I hear you and my sister are good friends."

"I guess so." He smiles at me.

"What are your intentions toward her?"

I kick Jane under the table, but she doesn't break her intense stare.

"No intentions," he says, maintaining a pleasant exterior I didn't know he could have for strangers. "Just friends."

Okay, ouch. Never thought *just friends* would sound so depressing.

The server brings our food, and Jane is momentarily distracted by her *seolleongtang*—ox bone soup—from continuing with the awkward questions. After a few slurps, though, she resumes with, "Have you asked her out on a date yet?"

I nearly choke on my rice, and Jane slaps my back as I cough.

Jason keeps up his smile, however, looking nonplussed. "No, but I would if I thought she'd say yes."

I gape at him, my chopsticks falling out of my fingers.

"You must have misread the signs, then," Jane says, "because I'm pretty sure she would say yes to anything you asked."

"Okay, that's enough." I shove back my chair and stand. "Jane, outside. Now."

She takes one more slurp, then lets me lead her to the sidewalk in front of the restaurant.

"What are you *doing*?" I cry. "You can't just embarrass me like that!"

"You obviously need a little help. You've been crushing on that boy for months, and nothing has happened. You both need a shove in the right direction."

"No, we don't! You don't understand anything." I run both hands through my hair, drawing in slow, deep breaths through my nose to calm myself. "Jane. Please. Just stop. *Please.*"

She shrugs. "Fine."

And without letting me say anything else, she heads back into the restaurant. The rest of our dinner is spent with her and Jason chatting it up and laughing like they're old friends, and me sulking, huddled over my food.

It's weird, seeing them together. Much weirder than Jane and Sophie squealing about cute Korean singers. Maybe because this feels more like she's meeting my boyfriend.

After dinner, Jason walks with me when I drop Jane off at her hotel.

Jane takes my arm and pulls me close to her. "We need to talk tomorrow. After the ceremony. I'm going with Mom to get our nails done tonight." Her eyebrows pull together in concern, a look I'm not used to seeing her wear. "And don't worry about her. I'll take care of everything."

"Thanks," I mutter.

She hesitates a moment, then says, "You didn't do anything wrong. You know that, right?"

I manage to offer her a half smile, but it feels like my insides are being squeezed.

Jane hugs me goodbye, waves at Jason, then disappears into the hotel. Jason and I walk back to to where the car will pick us up, the sounds of the city in the air between us instead of conversation, as I grapple with Jane's parting words.

His company's driver returns us to the school campus, and when we reach my building, Jason stops me. "Don't be angry with Jane. She was just joking. And she meant well."

I shrug one shoulder. "I guess."

He chuckles. "Besides, she managed to get some things out in the open that we've been tiptoeing around for months."

My pulse leaps, all thoughts of Momma blown out of my head. "What things?"

He takes a step closer. "I know I really butchered saying it last time, but I like you a lot. That hasn't changed. And judging by the way you act around me, I would guess you like me, too."

He looks at me with such hope in his eyes that I nearly break down and scream, *Yes! Yes, I like you!* But I don't. I can't.

"Jason, I don't think this is a good idea."

"Why?"

Because you're even more screwed up than me, I want to say. *Because I'm terrified that you'll end up like your dad and my brother, and because you may have no intention of hurting me, but one day, you will. Because all that stuff you said about me being a distraction, because you're embarrassed by me—it's all because you have issues, and I can't handle them.*

But all I say is, "Because we would never work."

He stares at me in confusion. "Why not?"

I grasp for any sort of excuse, but what comes out is the truth: "I don't trust you."

"Seriously?" His face falls. "What have I done to make you think I'm untrustworthy?"

"Nothing." I wave him off. "It's nothing."

He shakes his head. "I'm serious. I want to know so we can work this out."

"We're never going to be able to 'work this out,' so there's no point. And I'm not going to waste my time talking about it."

His confusion morphs into frustration. "Why are you saying these things? I know we had a rocky start, but I thought we were friends now."

"We *are* friends."

"So why don't you trust me?"

"Oh, I don't know," I say, sarcasm dripping from my voice. "Maybe because you always act like you're embarrassed by me."

He rolls his eyes. "That was one time, and you totally misinterpreted the situation, anyway. I don't understand what you want me to do."

"Nothing! I don't want you to do anything." My eyes sting, and I suddenly feel like I swallowed a rock. "I think . . . we shouldn't be spending so much time together."

"Are you serious?" He pauses. "You can't be serious."

"I'm sorry, I—"

"No," he interrupts angrily. "You don't get to make this decision alone."

"Jason—"

"No!" He jabs a finger at me. "You're accusing me of doing things I never did and painting me as some kind of jerk. But you're wrong. I—"

"You what?" I lower my voice to a hiss. "You're the one who acted like you didn't know me when we were in Seoul, like you were ashamed of me. And that stunt at the nightclub didn't fix anything. And what? You've changed your mind now? I'm not embarrassing anymore? How do I know you won't change your mind again if we get together?"

He swallows hard. "I really hurt you when we were in Seoul, didn't I?"

I throw my hands into the air, fear tightening my chest, knowing that he's right—he *did* hurt me. "I don't want to talk about this anymore," I say.

With a huff, I turn and stomp toward the door to my building.

But I pause with my hand on the knob when Jason says, "You're scared. You want to be with me, but for whatever reason, you're too afraid to try. Maybe it has to do with your family or your past, but don't blame this on me. I'll admit I've said some stupid things, but I'm not the bad guy you're making me out to be." His voice drops so I can barely hear it. "I really do like you, and you can believe me when I say I'm not going to hurt you."

And even though I know I shouldn't want it, a part of me hopes he *is* a good guy and someone I can trust, that he'll prove that to me. Because I want to be worth something to somebody.

Chapter Twenty-five

Big Brother,

Sometimes I want to blame you. I want everything to be your fault because you're gone and don't have to deal with the consequences. I wasn't the one who put the pills in your hand. So why do I feel responsible?

At your funeral, everyone kept saying you "passed away," like it was something peaceful. But it wasn't. You didn't "pass away." You died. We dance around the word like it could catch, like it'll leave a stain on us. And in the process, we give it more power, like just saying it out loud will somehow summon it.

I still miss you, but I'm also still angry at you for leaving us, for making me have to face Momma, for forcing me to run away. You got to escape, but I'm left here dealing with the aftermath. Even in Korea, I can't get away. No matter how many planes I take or how many miles I travel.

It's not fair. I don't want to feel like this. But I don't know how to stop. I don't know how to make myself better.

I love you—I do. I just don't understand why you did it. Maybe I never will. I think I'll probably always wonder.

I don't even know why I write you these letters in a notebook full of paper I'll never mail or why I pray every night that I'll wake up to a missed call from your number. The same reason I still expect to see your picture in celebrity magazines and your name on unread emails in my inbox, I guess.

Maybe one day, thinking about you won't hurt as much. Or maybe it will. Either way, these letters are from me to you . . .

From Korea, with love,
Grace

The graduation ceremony takes a lot longer than I thought it would. There're only fifty kids graduating—the smallest senior class the school has ever had. But after the third speech, I'm beginning to think an American public school graduation, where there are five hundred seniors, would be faster.

I'm the last person to walk across the stage, and when I take the diploma from the principal, it's like he's handing me my future. My entire life stretches out before me, choices I face now and ones I won't know about for years. I can be the obedient child and go home like Momma wants. It would be the easy choice, to go back to Tennessee, attend Vanderbilt, maybe work at Dad's label after I graduate.

Or I could take a risk.

I came to Korea to escape. I ran here, and somehow, I ended up loving this country and its people. And I don't want to run anymore. Does that mean I have to go home to face my past? Or can I face it here? Can I be happy in Asia? Can I really start over?

I want to try.

•   •   •

"I know what you're feeling right now." Jane re-crosses her legs, shifts in her seat, picks up her soda cup and sets it back down again. "So don't pretend like there's nothing going on."

I swirl the dregs of my coffee, unable to take my eyes off the inside of my mug—safer than actually meeting Jane's gaze. "I honestly don't know what you're talking about."

She huffs. "Don't be ridiculous, Gracie."

But she doesn't continue. I've never seen her this agitated, this at a loss for words. After the postgraduation lunch with Momma, Jane said she wanted to go for coffee in Incheon, just us. Which means me drinking coffee and her sipping caffeine-free soda from a straw she's chewed into submission, because Jane on caffeine is a scary thing.

"Everything went wrong after Nathan died," she whispers suddenly, and her voice sends a chill rippling down my back.

Jane catches my gaze and holds it with her hazel eyes. Eyes that look so much like Nathan's, it's like my brother staring back at me again.

I jerk my head away and stare out the window at the busy street with its sidewalks full of people. But it feels like my heart is cracking, little pieces of it chipping away. I don't want to be here. I don't want to talk about this. I don't—

"Grace." Jane reaches across the table and grabs my hand.

Tears pool in my eyes.

"Why did you move here?"

I clear my throat, giving myself time to get a better hold on the emotions twisting up my insides. "I guess I just . . . needed to get away."

Her lips quiver. "Because of Nathan?"

I nod.

She sighs and lets go of my hand so she can sit back in her chair. "You're being dumb."

My eyes widen, and I'm momentarily shocked enough to forget the grief threatening to shatter me. *"What?"*

She shakes her head. "You've always taken things too hard. You think everything's your fault. News flash—it's not."

"What are—" My voice falters. "What are you saying?"

"I'm saying you need to stop blaming yourself for Nathan's death, because it wasn't your fault," she says almost flippantly, like she's telling me to stop whining about not getting the Christmas present I wanted. "I don't know how you got it into your head that you were somehow responsible for Nathan, but that's just insane."

Jane levels me with a hard stare, and I realize I've never seen her this serious. There's a new maturity to her that she's never shown me before.

"You didn't kill Nathan," she says. "He killed himself. And if you had some responsibility in his death, then so do the rest of us. Because we're a family, and we take care of each other. Obviously, we didn't—" Her voice catches, and she has to start again. "We didn't do a good job of taking care of him. But that's on *all* of us, not just you."

She swallows hard. Emotion builds in my own throat. She frowns, licks her lips. "It hurt my feelings when you left." She crosses her arms, shifting in her seat. "I mean, I know why you did. I get it—you wanted to get away from everybody. But you left us all jacked up. Do you know what that did to Mom and Dad? They'd just lost Nathan, and then you left, too." Her voice drops to little more than a murmur. "There were a few times I thought Mom was going to lose it. You have no idea."

"Jane, I'm sorry—"

"No." Her eyes harden. "Don't be sorry. You have nothing to be sorry for. I just want you to understand. You think we all blame you for Nathan's death, but that's not true. *You're* the one who blames yourself."

"But at the funeral, Momma said—"

"We all said things we didn't mean that day," she interrupts. "We were grieving."

I still am—grieving. But I can't say that. I can't tell her how much pain I've carried around with me for months. She doesn't understand. She didn't know Nathan the way I did. She was too young.

"He was my idol," I whisper. "Why did he do it? I still don't understand."

She shrugs. "Who knows? He was messed up, Grace. Do you not remember the mean things he said about Mom when he was drunk, the way he and Dad fought all the time? He wasn't a saint, you know."

Anger sparks. "He was our brother!"

"And you're my sister," she challenges. "And I'm not letting you feel bad about yourself the rest of your life. I don't care if you go to Vanderbilt or spend the rest of your life here, but whatever you choose, do it for you, not because you're trying to get away from Nathan's ghost."

The tears escape my eyes now, trickle down my cheeks. I swipe at them, but more keep coming until my nose is running and my shoulders are shaking and I'm a wet, snotty mess in the middle of the café.

Jane clears her throat, her nose wrinkling. "You look disgusting right now."

But her eyes are shiny, and I know what she doesn't say—that when she says we're a family, she means it; that she loves me and that she wants me to be happy.

I wipe my nose with a napkin, and we leave the restaurant. When we get out on the sidewalk, I throw my arms around Jane and pull her into a hug.

I squeeze her tight against me. "Thanks, little sis."

She pats my back awkwardly, then when I keep holding on, tries to push me away. "Okay, okay, enough hugging!"

I let go with a laugh, and we make our way toward the hotel. Nothing has really changed since before our conversation—Nathan's still dead, my mother is still impossible to get along with, and Dad still treats work like it's more important than his family, which is probably the reason he didn't come to graduation—but I don't feel the same.

"What are you going to tell Mom?" Jane asks as we ride the elevator up to their floor.

"I don't know yet. But I know I can't go back to Tennessee."

She stares hard at the floor. "Are you going to live with Sophie?"

"Maybe." I punch her shoulder. "But there's no way she'll be nearly as cool a housemate as my little sister."

Jane's lips curl into a smile as the elevator doors slide open. She pauses outside her room.

"I'm going to miss you," she says. "Keep sending me letters, okay?"

My eyes sting with tears again. "Always."

"And make sure you say good things about me to Yoon Jae. I could use a sexy Korean in my life." Her smile turns wry, but it's forced.

I swing my arm to hit her on the back of the head, but she dodges my hand and pushes open the door. She pops her head back out, and I think I see a tear running into her mouth.

"I love you, Gracie."

My chest tightens, but I can't stop smiling. "I love you, too."

I see Jane and Momma off to the airport a couple days later. Momma and I spent hours going around and around about whether I had to go back home. But all it took was a simple explanation to get her to listen.

"I'm not ready to go home yet," I said. "It reminds me too much of Nathan, and I can't be there right now. I'm sorry."

She stared at me a long time, but there was no criticism in her eyes this time. All she did was nod. No declaration of blessing or promises to support me no matter what I decided.

But it was enough.

She didn't even mention the article plastered all over the Internet about Nathan Cross's sister being to blame for his death, à la reporter Kevin. There's no way she didn't see it. She just exercised self-control for once.

And in that moment, I realized something: Relationships may be messy and I may not be able to calculate them like an algebra equation, but they're worth it. And what Momma and I have is worth trying to save, as fragile as it is. Maybe we can be friends one day, maybe not. But I want to try.

I wave at Jane as she follows Momma into the security line. She points to the tall boy in front of her, then throws me a thumbs-up and pretends to swoon. I chuckle, the sting of missing her already settling in.

But I'm not sad. I guess I should be. It's going to be a long time before I see my family again. But I'm not.

Jason and Jane were right—Nathan's death wasn't my fault, and I need to stop thinking it was. I did what I could, and I've been carrying around a lot of guilt for too long. It still hurts, this pain that lingers, but it's not the crippling sort of pain it once was, just a residual ache. And that I can handle.

A calm assurance fills me, and a smile forms on my lips. For the first time since Nathan's death, I feel a sliver of freedom. I'm done hiding who I am, where I come from. I'm ready to start again. To be me.

No more running.

Chapter Twenty-six

I get home from the airport and find Sophie packing up clothes in one of her suitcases. Panic jolts through me.

"Sophie, what are you doing?" I ask, fear lacing my voice. "They're not kicking us off campus until for another two weeks."

She glances at the wad of clothes in her hand, then at me, and laughs. "I'm not leaving right now. I just wanted to get a head start on packing up."

A gigantic wave of relief floods me, but it dissipates when I realize just how soon this will all be over. Two weeks. Then what am I going to do with my life?

My visa runs out in a month and it's renewable, but the school's going to kick me out in two weeks. I could ask Sophie if I could stay with her in Seoul, but we haven't talked as much since I started hanging out more with Jason.

I sit down on the edge of my bed, tucking my head so it doesn't hit the top bunk. "So how's Tae Hwa?" I ask, realizing we haven't talked much about her personal life in a while.

"Fine," she says.

But there's something off in her voice.

"Are you guys okay?"

Her eyes narrow at me. "He said we shouldn't date. Is that what you wanted to know?"

"Sophie—"

"It's not a big deal," she assures me, returning to her packing.

I wait a moment, letting the issue of her and Tae Hwa drop. I won't push it if she doesn't want to talk about it. But we need to clear the air.

"Sophie, can we talk for a second?"

She stops folding clothes and forces a smile. "Yeah, what's up?"

I bite the inside of my cheek, searching for the best way to start this conversation. "I just want to apologize. I feel like I sorta ditched you after I started hanging out with Jason more."

She shrugs, despite the tightness around her eyes. "It's not a big deal. You guys got close, that's all."

"But I feel like I have to explain what happened." My voice drops to an embarrassed murmur. "Especially after you walked in on us the other night."

She cracks a smile. "I know you guys didn't sleep together, like, in *that* way. Jason is way too conservative to do anything like that. I was just making a joke the next morning."

I get to my feet, no longer able to sit still. "I know, but I don't want you to be mad at me. It almost felt like we were choosing sides when the band broke up, like you were Team Tae Hwa and I was Team Jason or something, but I didn't want it to be that way. It almost felt like you didn't like me hanging out with your brother."

Sophie forces a humorless laugh. "Why would I not like that?"

"I don't know."

We just look at each other for a moment, then she sighs. "It's dumb."

"You can tell me, anyway."

She sits on top of her desk, beside a pile of T-shirts, and stares at her hands, which she holds in her lap. "Jason and I are twins, so we've been really close since we were little. We were all each other had when we lived in New York. But then we moved back to Seoul, and it seemed like Jason sort of outgrew me." Her bottom lip quivers. "So when he decided to come to Ganghwa Island to get away from the music business, I came, too. I was hoping that we could reconnect again. But then he met you."

My insides twist, half in remorse for helping pull Jason away from Sophie, but half in expectance of what she'll say next. She thinks Jason saw me as important enough to keep him from hanging out with his sister? I can't decide how I feel about that—honored or concerned.

"At first, it was okay," she continues. "Although it bothered me that he didn't seem to like you."

I chuckle, thinking back to when Jason and I barely knew each other. The dislike was mutual.

She catches my gaze, sadness filling hers, and I sober.

"Then you guys started hanging out a lot," she says, "and he didn't have time for me. That's normal, I guess. I mean, I hung out with Tae Hwa a lot. It was natural for Jason to find someone else to spend time with, and I'm glad it's you—I like you a lot, Grace." She pauses. "I guess I'm just not sure what to do now, facing losing him."

"But you're not losing him! Just because he and I are friends doesn't mean that he doesn't want to spend time with you anymore."

She shakes her head. "You don't understand. It's different now. I never had to compete with a girlfriend. It's weird."

Heat burns the tips of my ears. "I'm not his girlfriend."

"Yet. I've seen the way you guys look at each other."

We fall silent, and my mind struggles to wrap around that word—*yet.*

"I should have sided with him during the band's breakup. He needed someone to back him up, and I didn't." Tears pool in Sophie's eyes, and she laughs them off even as one slips down her cheek. "But I was too distracted by Tae Hwa to even consider my own brother, my *twin.*"

"Oh, Sophie." I wrap my arm around her shoulders and give her a tight squeeze. "Don't feel bad. Jason wasn't angry."

"I know, but I still should have stuck by him. We're family. That's what you do."

Her words bring a dull throb to my chest, but I force myself to ignore it. Everything with Nathan is over. I can't dwell on it anymore.

"You're not mad at *me,* are you?" she asks.

"Please. No way could I be mad." I give her shoulder a light shove. "You're my best girlfriend."

She brightens. "Really?"

"Really."

But if I'm being honest, Jason's my best friend, period. And I just pray that, one day, he can be more.

"You're going to kill us," Jason says from behind me, and his arms wrapped around my waist seem to burn through my thin T-shirt.

I focus all my energy on keeping the bike upright and not ramming us into any stationary objects, like trees—the moving objects can get out of our way. The bike wobbles beneath us, and Jason chuckles.

"Shut up," I snap.

Why did I insist on driving us across the island again? Oh yeah, because I wanted to prove to him that I could. Dumbest idea ever.

"Turn here." Jason points to the left.

I peer over my shoulder to make sure no one's coming, then cut across three lanes of traffic to make a sharp left turn, just missing the side of a BMW. I suck in a sharp breath and peddle faster, like if we can escape the spot, Jason won't notice I almost got us pulverized.

The palm of his hand presses into my stomach, and it flip-flops in response. I follow his directions for another ten minutes until I spot the pebbly beach. As I pull over to a sidewalk that flanks the ocean, Jason hops off the back of the bike. I screech to a halt and stumble off, my legs like jelly.

"Gah, you should consider losing some weight, Bae." I rub my thighs. "You're heavy."

He bends down to lock the bike to a light post. "Or maybe you should gain some muscle."

I scowl at his wry smile.

With the sun setting, lights flicker on around us. Boats chug past, on their way to Incheon harbors. In the distance, across the water, the city lights glow, but here on Ganghwa Island, a stillness lingers in the air.

Jason and I meander down the walkway, close enough to brush hands occasionally, but far enough that I long for the quiet comfort of his fingers threaded through mine. I sneak a glance at him. He called me this morning, asking if I wanted to hang out tonight. Like we don't do that every night. But, this time, his voice sounded different, unsure, almost nervous.

"So, do you feel any different now that you've graduated?" I ask, if only to break the silence between us.

He gives a noncommittal grunt.

"You?" he asks.

"Not really. It was strangely . . . uneventful." Probably because I have bigger things to think about—like the future.

We fall silent.

"I wanted to talk to you about something." Jason shoves his hands into his pockets. "I umm . . . wanted to let you know that I'm leaving for Seoul tomorrow."

"Oh." My mood tanks.

"I talked to some people from the record label, and they want me to do some interviews with the media, make some TV appearances, that sort of stuff. They said I need to get myself out there again."

"That makes sense," I say. And it does. So why do I suddenly feel like I got hit by a truck?

"Yoon Jae has already signed a contract with another label." Sarcasm laces his voice. "I guess I need to catch up."

"Yoon Jae signed another contract? Doing what?"

"He's going solo. Apparently, they offered him the deal the day after the band released the statement about our breakup. He signed it a week later. He left school about a week ago—it was sort of sudden, I think."

My brain flashes back to the conversation I had with him the day I introduced him to Jane. Did he know we wouldn't see each other again? My stomach clenches when I remember Jane talking about him liking me. Did he think he didn't have a chance, was that why he never said anything about it? Maybe he was going to. Maybe he just got nervous. I'd like to think he at least planned on telling me about his new solo career.

My heart sinks when I realize I won't see his adorable smile again except on a computer or TV screen. Why didn't he tell me he was leaving?

Why didn't he say goodbye?

Jason picks up on my disappointment. "Are you going to miss seeing him?"

"Of course. He was my friend."

His shoulders tense, but he doesn't say anything else.

"So what are you going to do now, musicwise?" I ask.

He steps up to the railing, resting his elbows on top of the stone, and looks out over the water. "I don't know yet. I'm sure my manager has a lot of ideas, though." He tacks on a hollow laugh at the end.

"But you're the one playing the music. You don't have to do anything you don't want to. You've got a lot of talent. Use it!"

He doesn't respond.

"Jason, seriously. Do what you want to do. If you want to keep playing music, then go for it. But if you want to go to college and become an engineer or a teacher, then do that. You can't let other people rule your life."

He sighs. "You know why I left Seoul to come here? I knew I didn't want to keep playing music, not as Eden's singer. I hated every second of it. And being with Mom just reminded me of all my dad did to hurt her. I thought maybe if I could escape the city, I'd be able to just get away from everything. But I didn't have the guts to actually end it."

"You did, though. The band's not together anymore."

"Yeah, I guess. Crazy that I came to Ganghwa Island, though. I didn't want to go back to America because I'd have to see my dad. This seemed like the best place to disappear."

I laugh, though there's no humor in it. "Tell me about it."

We both gaze out at the water, and my insides knot. This is the last time I'm going to see him. Potentially ever. No more crazy bike rides, late night study sessions in the library, or making up dumb songs about broccoli.

My chest tightens, and I gasp, the pain so visceral I can't breathe. We could write emails or maybe text occasionally. But it'll never be the same. We'll never be the same. The first boy I ever wanted to really let in, and we end like this.

"I'm . . . going to miss you," he murmurs, flashing me a sad smile. "I know you probably think I'm lying or something else ridiculous, but I really do like spending time with you. I hope you believe at least that." His voice drops to a whisper. "And I *never* would have hurt you. I saw what my dad did to my mom. I'm not that kind of guy."

I swallow the tightness in my throat and nod.

"Promise you won't forget me when you become a famous music producer?"

I laugh, despite the tears pricking my eyes. "You're the famous one."

He pins me with an earnest look, his face shrouded in shadow from the lamppost light above us. "I'm serious. Don't forget. Promise?"

The knot in my throat grows, but I manage to croak, "Promise."

We stare at each other a long moment, and I can't help wishing that everything had gone differently. That I had been brave enough to trust him, to trust that we could handle his problems and my problems—together. But, mostly, I just want him.

I remind myself that this is my last moment to finally tell him, well, everything—that when I look at him, my heart aches a little in a good way and that I have an unnatural fondness for his bright-colored shoes and the way his hair hangs just a little in his eyes. But when I pull in a long breath to spill my guts, I can't. The expectant gleam in his eyes silences any words.

So I stand on my tiptoes and kiss him, instead.

Just a little peck. Chaste enough even for one of those Korean dramas. But butterflies explode inside my stomach, and a flood of longing fills my chest.

He stares at me with wide eyes, and a laugh bubbles to my lips at his shocked expression.

"What—I—that—" he stutters.

"Just thought since this is goodbye, I should send you off right."

"Now I don't want to leave at all."

I laugh, but my heart constricts. This banter is just that—banter. He's leaving, and even if I did believe he loved me enough not to kill my heart, it wouldn't matter. So I muster as much cheerfulness as I can, link my arm through his, and pull him farther down the promenade.

Because I don't want this night to be over.

Because this is our end.

Chapter Twenty-seven

I set my cup down with more force than necessary. "Sophie, why do you keep checking your phone every ten seconds?"

"Huh?" She looks up from the electronic device that's been glued to her hand all afternoon.

"Your phone. You haven't put it away since we got here."

She tosses me an apologetic smile but doesn't put it back in her purse.

I breathe out a long sigh, ready for this day to be over. I've been researching online for hours, trying to find colleges with late acceptance or any internships that don't require a college degree. My current list for both is zero. And while I keep telling myself not to panic, my unease is growing by the hour. I broke down and emailed Momma last night, telling her I might have to come home, and she answered back with one of the most enthusiastic messages I've ever had from her. Too bad the thought of moving back into that house triggers my gag reflex.

My *gimbap* turns sour in my mouth, and I set my chopsticks

across the plate. The dining hall's mostly empty, students clearing out for summer vacation.

"We need to get back to the dorm," Sophie announces, standing.

"Why?"

"I want to watch something on TV."

"Can't you watch it online later?"

"No, this is important." She picks up both my tray and hers, and puts them away.

Sophie hurries me the entire ten-minute walk, throwing phrases over her shoulder like: "I can't miss this" and "Seriously, Grace, you can't walk any faster?"

By the time we reach the room, sweat rolls down my back and my flip-flops have rubbed a sore spot between my toes. I crank up my box fan and aim it directly at my bed, then fall down on top of the sheets.

Sophie switches on the television she bought last month, flipping through the channels.

I stare at the slats holding up Sophie's mattress and let myself wallow in some self-pity. Because if I actually take my problems seriously, I'm going to start hyperventilating. South Korea is going to kick me out in a month if I don't renew my visa, the school says I have to be gone in less than a week, and I have applied to zero colleges.

On second thought, maybe I *will* start hyperventilating.

"Found it!" Sophie squeals.

She grabs my arm and yanks me off the bed and onto my desk chair, which she's set in the middle of the floor beside hers. Grinning, she folds her legs up underneath herself in her seat and stares raptly at the TV.

"Sophie, are you really going to make me watch this?"

"Shh!"

Rolling my eyes, I shut up and focus my attention on the show

I can't understand. Because it's in Korean. Which Sophie would remember if she stopped to consider it.

A snappy pop song blares through the speakers, followed by applause, as credits fade into a pan of a live audience composed almost solely of teenage girls. Many of them hold up giant signs, and I'm reminded of MTV's TRL, which Nathan watched religiously growing up.

The camera cuts to a young guy with trendy glasses and supertight pants holding a microphone. The crowd nearly drowns out his voice as he begins the show. I start to tune out the monotonous stream of words I don't know when the camera switches to a familiar face. My heart stops.

Sophie cuts her eyes to me, a sly grin curling her lips.

"W-what is Jason doing on TV?" I gape at the screen, soaking in every detail from his unfortunate orange-colored sweater to the way he forces an awkward smile at the show's host.

Sophie shrugs, though she snickers. I've been set up.

Jason shifts on top of a metal stool, the tension in his shoulders and tightness in his expression betraying his discomfort. If I didn't know him, I would guess he's just an awkward guy. Everything about his posture, the halting way he answers the questions, all scream "socially challenged." But in that moment, he's the sexiest boy I've ever seen.

"What's he saying?" I ask.

Sophie pauses, listening. "The host is asking him about Eden and why they broke up."

Jason answers.

"He says it was because of artistic differences," she relays. "They're all still friends, but they wanted to do their own things creatively." She snorts but doesn't give her own commentary.

I realize I'm leaning forward in my chair, like it will bring me closer to Jason. With a blush, I settle against the backrest, though nervous energy zips through my body.

"Now they're talking about his future career. Jason says he's planning on doing some solo stuff. He'll be working on his album starting in July."

Disappointment seeps into my brain. Why didn't he tell me that? He's only been gone like two days, and he's already keeping me out of the loop?

"He says the music is going to be a little different than Eden's music," Sophie continues. "His taste is different."

Jason keeps talking, but Sophie falls silent.

"What did he say?" I ask, my voice shrill.

She waves her hand in dismissal. "Nothing important, just about that dumb drama he was in and denying rumors about him dating Na Na in real life."

I swallow a growl, now more than ever wishing I had studied harder in Korean class.

Jason picks up an acoustic guitar, and he and the host banter for a few lines. The camera pans to the audience, all the girls staring at Jason with dreamy eyes. I recognize that look. I've probably had it on my own face for six months.

"The host is asking Jason if he'll play a song." Sophie cuts into my thoughts. "Jason says he will, but he doesn't want to play an Eden song. He's going to play the one he wrote for the drama he was in."

My breath catches in my throat as the audience explodes in expectant cheers and Jason plucks the first chord progression of the song we wrote together. Without the drums and bass, it has a chilled, unplugged vibe, but he infuses the lyrics with more passion than I've heard him sing in anything else. He leans over the instrument, his mouth maybe an inch from the stand-up microphone, and my heart thumps against the inside of my chest so loud Sophie must hear it.

If this is the severing of my last connection to Jason, it was all worth it. If this is how I have to say goodbye, I'm still glad for the experience. I'm still glad I knew him.

He ends the song, and the crowd erupts in applause. He bows his head with a smile and says, "Thank you."

The crowd giggles at his English.

The host asks another series of questions and Sophie translates for me, but I can't focus. My brain rewinds back to the fall, sitting in the practice room with Jason, reviewing every facet of that song over and over again. I realize that that's the most fun I've ever had, working on his music. Working on music, period.

Music's in my blood. Why have I spent so many years denying that?

Sophie nudges me with her elbow. "You might want to listen to this part."

I tune back in and see Jason's still holding the guitar in his lap. His discomfort has faded, so he interacts with the host more naturally. He even laughs, and a real smile brightens his face. My heart twists.

"Jason says he wants to play one more song," Sophie says. "But he's asking if he can say something in English first."

The host's eyebrows shoot up behind his thick-framed glasses, and he addresses the crowd, which responds with more applause. Jason nods his head to acknowledge them, then looks straight into the camera.

"Hey, Grace," he says, and I stop breathing. "If you're watching, I just wanted to let you know this song is for you." His face melts into a grin. "I'm holding up my end of the deal. Now, it's your turn."

Then he strums the guitar and launches into an acoustic version of a song I never thought I'd hear on an Asian TV show— one written by the Doors.

"Hello, I love you. Won't you tell me your name?" he sings. "Hello, I love you. Let me jump in your game."

I laugh, tears pooling in my eyes. Jason adds a dramatic growl into his voice during the second chorus, and I choke on a giggle, a sob catching in my throat. I don't realize the tears are spilling onto my cheeks until Sophie takes my hand and gives it a quick squeeze.

At the end of the song, the audience screams and claps even louder than before, and even the host joins in the applause. He says something into the camera, and the screen cuts to another commercial. But my mind is reeling. Jason sang for me. He addressed me on a television show. He sang *to* me.

My phone buzzes, and I fumble to pull it out of my pocket.

I answer without even looking at the number. "Hello?"

"Grace."

The familiar voice fills me with warmth that seeps all the way down to the tips of my fingers and toes, and I can't suppress the idiotic grin from forming on my face.

"Hi."

"Did you hear it?" Jason asks.

"Yeah."

He's quiet a moment, then says, "I just won major points there, right?"

I laugh, my entire body tingling. "Yeah. Yeah, you did."

"Grace?"

"Hmm?"

"I miss you."

"I miss you, too," I whisper.

"You don't have to miss me anymore."

"What are you talking about?"

He chuckles, and I feel like I've melted. "I left something for you."

I glance at Sophie, who points out our window. I peek outside and see Young Jo, the Bae's private driver, standing beside the car. He holds one of those signs chauffeurs have when they pick up people from the airport. It says **GRACE** in big, bold letters.

I gasp.

"Hey, I need to go," he says, another noise in the background muffling his voice. "Hopefully, I'll see you soon."

And he hangs up.

I gape at the phone, like it'll answer all my questions.

Sophie peers out at Young Jo. "Pretty romantic, if you ask me."

I stare out the window, my brain racing. I already said good-bye. It was sweet of him to stick with our deal about me trying to become a music producer if he introduced South Korea to the Doors, but I can't handle saying goodbye to him again. No matter if he is my best friend and I have difficulty breathing without him here. Because if I go now, I know I'll get sucked into loving him for good. And I can't lose someone else I love.

"What are you going to wear?" Sophie asks. "Because I expect to see you in something hot."

I collapse into my chair, my elation fizzling. "I can't go."

"What do you mean you can't go?" she demands. "He just sang to you on TV! You have to go!"

"Sophie—"

"What? What possible excuse could you have?"

"I need to keep researching colleges."

"You can do that on the way there. That's why you pay for expensive Internet on your phone."

"I can't leave all my stuff here. I need to move out of the dorm. Are *you* going to pack it all for me?"

She barks a laugh. "No way, but it'll be here when you get back. The school doesn't require you to get out for a few more days. You can come back and get it."

I squirm, searching my brain for any other excuse. "I don't have any clean clothes."

She raises her eyebrows. "What do you think Febreze is for?"

When I still don't move, she sighs and gets up to place both of her hands on my shoulders. Leveling a hard gaze at me, she says, "Grace, you know I love you, but you're being an idiot right now. A boy just did probably the cutest thing I've ever seen in real life for you, and you're not going to go be with him?"

I stare back at her a second, the truth of her words seeping in. Then I break away from her grip, pull my biggest purse out of my wardrobe, and start throwing in any article of clothing I can find. Sophie hands me my toothbrush and other toiletries, and I toss in a few pairs of shoes for good measure. I have no idea how long I'll be gone.

Slamming open the door, I give the room one more sweep to make sure I haven't forgotten anything important.

"Why are you taking so long?" Sophie cries, waving me off. "Get out of here! Go!"

And I do.

Chapter Twenty-eight

For the entire drive, I can't focus on anything around me. I keep looking at my watch, thinking at least twenty minutes have passed, only to find that it's been five. When we reach the outskirts of the city, I shoot Jason a text: *I'm in Seoul!*

A second later, he responds, *Waiting for you outside.*

I have no idea what he means until Young Jo pulls up in front of a gigantic building in the middle of downtown. I crane my neck back and spot the posters, the big sign that says STAR ENTERTAIN-MENT in both *Hangul* and English—Jason's agency.

I jump out of the car onto the busy sidewalk, searching each face that passes for the one waiting on me. My heart sinks when I don't see him.

I press the phone to my ear to call him, still scanning the sidewalk, when I see a familiar smile on a guy with aviator sunglasses. Standing at the bottom of the building's steps, he waves.

Catching my breath, I break into a run down the sidewalk.

Dropping my bag at his feet, I throw myself into Jason's arms with an embarrassing squeal.

He staggers backwards, nearly losing his balance. With his palms pressed against my back and the tips of my toes just brushing the ground, a chuckle rumbles deep in the back of his throat.

People around us stare, and a few of them do a double take, like they wonder if that's really Jason Bae, and if it is, why he's hugging a white girl.

I pull back until I can see his face, and I push the sunglasses up so they rest on top of his head. "Hi," I say.

He grins. "Hi."

A camera flashes, and I jump back from Jason. A girl snaps another shot with her phone, and Jason slips his hand into mine and leads me inside the building.

I'm still trying not to melt into a puddle at the feel of his warm fingers laced through mine when we pass the security guard and ride the elevator down to the basement parking garage. He leads me to a car I've never seen, and I can't help feeling like I've stepped into an alternate reality. I wait for him to say something, maybe whip out his guitar and sing a few bars. Anything. I just rushed all the way here from Ganghwa Island, and he's not even going to kiss me?

He takes my bag and puts it in the trunk of the black sports car, and I sink into the leather passenger seat in a sort of daze. This is his car, I guess. I'm riding in Jason's car.

He pulls out of the parking space and reaches for my hand. My breathing accelerates, and he shoots me a smile, like he can feel the way my heart can't stop banging against the inside of my chest.

Maybe he turns on the radio. Maybe he talks to me. I don't know. I just watch Seoul pass by us out the window, my chest constricting more with each passing minute. I'm crazy. Certifiable. I just threw away all my plans. For a boy. And a musician with a bazillion problems at that. I'm probably going to regret this later, but all I can think about is how much I want him.

I steal a glance at Jason, who drives with one hand, the other holding deftly on to mine. Like it belongs there. I've waited so long for it to belong.

Jason pulls into a tiny parking lot at the top of a hill just as the sun's dipping below the horizon. He shifts into PARK and gets out. I hesitate, not sure if my legs are even capable of holding my weight at the moment.

Jason pokes his head back into the car. "Grace, are you coming?" Hesitancy lingers in his voice—the added push gets me out of my seat.

I peer up at a needlelike tower that stretches into the darkening sky, its lights brighter than any of the stars. I recognize it from the research I did before visiting Seoul in December. This is N Seoul Tower, a popular tourist spot.

"Come on. I want to show you something," Jason says.

He presses his hand into the small of my back and pulls me along with him into a sky bucket like the ones at amusement parks. We're the only ones inside, and he keeps smiling at me, then glancing out the window, more excited than a kid on his birthday.

We step out of the lift, climb up an endless number of stairs, and finally reach an observation area. Only a few other people mingle around the fences that overlook the city. Lamps illuminate giant treelike sculptures covered in ornaments. The warm wind whipping my hair into my face, I approach one of the sculptures, which looks like it's decked out in trash.

But, when I get close, I realize they're locks—locks of all shapes and sizes, with print scribbled in Sharpie or smeared with ink pen. They hang so close together, it looks like they're all connected, one giant clump of locks.

Jason steps up beside me, his elbow brushing against mine and raising goose bumps down my arm. "They're called the lover's locks. You're supposed to write your names on them, lock it to the railing or one of these, then throw the key off the edge."

Biting his lip, he reaches into his back pocket and pulls out a plain silver lock with a three-number combination, the kind you would use on a suitcase. I swallow hard, my mind whirling.

"I couldn't find one with a key," he says, looking down at his shoes. "But I figured this would work."

He slips out a Sharpie from the same pocket and writes some Korean symbols on the front of the lock's shiny face. Then he spells out my name in English, each stroke of the marker making my heart race faster. He pushes back a couple locks until he finds a free space, then hooks ours onto the metal and clicks it shut, spinning the numbers so it's secure.

I stare at our lock, which almost disappears among the myriad of others.

Jason clears his throat. "I just wanted to show you that I'm serious about this. About us."

I catch his eye, and he peers down at me expectantly. But I can't speak, my brain still unable to form coherent language. When did I become a mute?

His expression darkens, disappointment shrouding his face. He looks away. "I guess this was sort of dumb."

I grab his hand, and hope alights in his eyes.

"It's not dumb," I murmur.

His lips curl into a soft smile, and the weight pressing down on my chest loosens a little, and my brain clears.

"I listened to what you said about the music thing, and you're right," he says. "I already talked to my manager and some of the record execs. They agreed to let me branch into rock music instead of pop. My album is going to be the music I like." His smile widens. "We can work on more songs that I actually want to play."

"*You* can work on the songs," I correct.

He shakes his head. "I want you to help me. Grace, you're a

great composer, a great producer. The song I wrote for the drama is the best I've ever done, and it's all because of you."

"I can't help you. You're going to be here in Seoul, and I'm . . . " I throw my hands into the air. "Well, I don't know where I'm going to be."

"You can stay with me. Live with Sophie." He steps closer. "Grace, you can't go back to America."

"Why? Because you need a collaborator for your songs?"

"No. Because—because I love you," he blurts.

My face flames, but I hold on to control of my voice. "It sounds even better than I thought it would."

His eyes soften. "So, does this mean you love me, too?"

Swallowing the sob that catches in my throat, I wrap my arms around his waist and nod my face against the soft fabric of his sweater. "I've basically been in love with you since that stupid music video shoot. But I guess I didn't admit it to myself until later. I didn't think I'd ever hear you say it to *me*, though."

A chuckle rumbles in his chest. "Well, I'm pretty sure my big gesture just blew your declaration out of the water. I mean, *hello,* I love you."

I join in his laughter, but my chest still tightens. My voice falls to a whisper. "I've had a lot of people in my life who've lied to me, who've manipulated me. Who left me. Please don't add your name to that list."

He smoothes my hair, resting his chin on top of my head. "I already told you—I wouldn't do anything to hurt you. I love you, Grace. Seriously."

I pull in a shaky breath, stepping back and swiping the tears from my eyes. "I know. But I just . . . " My voice breaks off.

He bends down so we're eye level. "You're worried I'm going to be like my dad."

"What? No, I—"

He shakes his head. "Don't lie to me, Grace. I know you, and

I know you're worried. You saw your brother on drugs, you saw him drunk, and when you found out that my dad drank, you assumed the worst of me. You let Sophie's fears become your own." His voice drops. "But that's *not* going to happen. I'm not my father. And I'm not your brother."

His words stab right through me, and I nearly lose my breath. He lets the truth sit between us a moment, lets it simmer, until I can internalize it.

My eyes slide closed. "I'm still scared."

He laughs, a throaty sound, deep and slow. "I'll be honest. I was basically terrified to sing that song to you. I was afraid it wouldn't convince you to come."

"But that was about our deal. With the music." My brain flips back to the conversation we had under the tree in the plaza, of the promise. "You said you would introduce South Korea to the Doors and I would become a producer. You even mentioned it on the show. You basically threw down the gauntlet."

"Yeah, but you could have rejected me and gone off to be some fancy producer in America." He stares down at his shoes, his voice getting soft. "I don't want you to leave. I want you with me."

I shake my head, awe filling my chest. "That's insane. You're insane to want to be with me. I'm screwed up, in case you haven't noticed."

He cups my face with his hand, leaning in close. "In case *you* haven't noticed, so am I."

No kidding.

I almost tell him that's one of the problems, but he beats me to it with, "But we're both fixable. Neither of us is perfect, but there's still hope for me. And for you. You stuck with me through everything, and now I want to be there for you." He chews on his bottom lip, a mixture of awe and nervousness mixing in his eyes. "Forever."

The intensity in his voice sends a shiver through me, tingling all the way down to my fingertips. "You love me," I whisper, clarifying for myself. "No one's ever loved me before. You know, like *that*. Hard to wrap my head around." I laugh, though my heart twists.

He wants me. And I want him. Even with his issues. I don't want anyone like him. I don't want anyone besides him. I just want Jason, despite the problems.

"Don't be so shocked," he says, brushing the hair off my shoulder and taking a step closer. "You're the first person to love *me* like that, too."

His forehead presses against mine, our noses just close enough to brush against each other, and he continues in a whisper, "I'm always excited to see you, more excited than I am to see anyone else. I get nervous if I think I said something stupid around you. I've never taken so long to get dressed in my life, trying to pick out something I think you would like."

I join in his laughter, our breaths mingling between us.

"Well, you've made good decisions thus far." I tug at his ugly orange sweater with a smile. "Before today, anyway. I like the way you dress."

He beams, his voice lowering to a murmur. "You're the only one that really sees me. Everyone else looks at me and sees Jason Bae the singer, the guitarist. But you look at me and just see Jason, the guy that doesn't know how to interact with fans and isn't good with words."

"You're doing a pretty good job with the words right now."

He grins. "Still, maybe I should try a different tactic."

And he closes the space between us. Our first kiss was like a collision, our anger and frustration crashing together in a swirl of emotion. The second was quick, my send-off when I thought we wouldn't see each other again. But this kiss is a beginning.

He cradles my face with both hands, his lips searing into mine with individual lingering kisses. His breath comes quickly, and I realize I've done that. I lean into him, and he takes a sharp breath, then pulls me even closer.

Everything he's said, everything he's done—it slams into me with such force it jars me into understanding. This is real. What I'm feeling, what *he's* feeling. This is for real. I let myself hold on to the guilt of Nathan for so long, I didn't realize how I had taken safety behind my fears. I didn't think Jason and I could ever work because he was so broken.

But everyone's broken, in their own way. And I'll never be happy holding on to the fear that someone will hurt me. I have to let it go. Like when Jane told me I had to keep living, to move on, to get past my grief. I need to keep living. Nathan would want that. *I* want that.

Jason's lips smile beneath mine, and I break away, laughing.

"Wait," I say, "does this mean I'm going to get accosted by enraged Jason Bae fangirls everywhere? Is your label even going to let us be together?"

"Yes and yes." He chuckles. "We're still negotiating my contract right now. I'll make it work. *We're* going to work. Maybe we're crazy, but you and me? I think we can handle anything."

"I don't know." I pause. "But I trust you."

His entire face lights up, and he reaches his arms around my back, locking me in his embrace. "That sounded suspiciously like the start of a long-term commitment to me."

I laugh. "Yeah, well, you're going to have to figure out my life for me—I have nowhere to go and nothing to do in Seoul."

He shrugs. "We'll work something out. I'm pretty sure any college would accept you." His smile turns wry. "Besides, wouldn't you rather be here than at Vanderbilt?"

He has a point. I already committed to leaving Nashville behind. I don't have to go home. I have options. And one of them is staring at me.

I reach a tentative hand out and brush my fingers across his collarbone. He glances down at them, then shoots me a questioning look.

"I'll stay, but you have to promise me one thing," I say.

"What?"

"You have to wear V-necks every day. Even when it's cold outside."

A smile stretches across his face. "Deal."

"And one more thing."

He groans dramatically, and I punch his shoulder.

"I want to hear you sing. All the time."

"What about right now?" he whispers near my ear.

I swallow hard, nodding.

"Oh yeah, I'll tell you something I think you'll understand," he sings in a whisper, repeating the words of his favorite band, the Beatles, and threading our fingers together. "Oh please say to me you'll let me be your man. And please say to me you'll let me hold your hand."

He cuts the lyrics short to press his lips against mine. And I let him kiss me, just because we're overlooking the lit-up Seoul skyline and he's a rock star and being with him makes me feel more confident, more comfortable than anything else. I breathe in his familiar scent—he still smells like rain. But now I notice he tastes like hope.

He tastes like a future.

Chapter Twenty-nine

Big Brother,

I think I found it—what I was looking for. And I found it in a boy who's kind of awkward and wears neon-colored shoes. I just wish you were here so I could tell you about it. I wish you could meet him and the other friends I made here.

I've decided not to run anymore. It's time to face life. It's time to face my future.

I'm ready for love.

I'm ready to trust.

I'm ready for my new beginning.

But I'll still give you this last letter,

From Seoul, with lots and lots of love,
Grace